TFS THESEUS

The Terran Fleet Command Saga – Book 2

*****

Tori L. Harris

ISBN: 978-0-9961796-4-5
TFS THESEUS
THE TERRAN FLEET COMMAND SAGA – BOOK 2
VERSION 1.1

Written and Published by Tori L. Harris
AuthorToriHarris.com

Edited by Monique Happy
www.moniquehappy.com

There are no great men, just great challenges which ordinary men, out of necessity, are forced by circumstances to meet.

Fleet Admiral William Frederick "Bull" Halsey, Jr.

Chapter 1

TFS Navajo, Earth Orbit
(Combat Information Center)

Vice Admiral Kevin Patterson, Chief of Naval Operations, stared intently at one of the large view screens lining one side of TFS *Navajo's* Combat Information Center. Rather than a simple live feed from a single source, the image represented the combined inputs from a dizzying array of sensor types, all focused on a single target and seamlessly presented in real-time by the flagship's AI.

"Bridge, Gun-shy," Patterson announced, using the call sign he had earned for himself years ago due to an unfortunate incident at the firing range.

"Gun-shy, *Navajo*-Actual. Go ahead, Admiral," came the immediate response from Flag Captain Ogima Davis, who had just hustled back to the bridge from his quarters after finally getting an opportunity for some much needed sleep.

"If the AI's projection is correct, our friend out there is coming straight at us. Go ahead and break orbit and attempt an intercept. I'm not sure how much difference it will make, but if we need to maneuver, I'd prefer to be out of Earth's gravity well."

"Understood, Admiral."

"Nice and slow, Captain Davis. I'd like to give the impression we are coming out to greet an old friend, not confront an intruder. Gun-shy out."

Within seconds, the ever-present background rumbling noise in the CIC increased slightly as *Navajo's* colossal sublight engines throttled up to begin pushing the mammoth, nine-hundred-fifty-meter-long heavy cruiser out of Earth orbit. Powerful Cannae thrusters mounted with varying orientations throughout the *Navajo's* hull allowed her to execute a gentle, banking turn in the direction of the approaching Pelaran ship with an easy grace that seemed to contradict her tremendous size. Watching an external video feed of the maneuver, Admiral Patterson couldn't help pausing to stare for a moment. Though she was nearly double the length of the largest ocean-going vessel ever built, *Navajo* executed the maneuver with much of the same nimble agility possessed by the much smaller *Ingenuity*-class frigates.

"I need an Emergency Action Message for immediate fleet-wide distribution," Patterson announced without turning to look in the direction of the nearest Communications console in the CIC. Hearing no response, he wheeled around to face the young ensign, who appeared to be transfixed by the drama playing out on the various screens as if it were a particularly interesting cable news feed. "Ensign!" he bellowed, uncharacteristically raising his voice.

Ensign Katy Fletcher jumped involuntarily, her normally fair complexion flushing bright red as she realized the admiral had actually been speaking to her. "Yes, Admiral Patterson, sorry sir."

The CNO raised a bushy eyebrow and regarded the young ensign momentarily. In spite of his irritation and the urgency of the current situation, a distant part of his mind quickly recalled a long list of similar transgressions committed by a young, particularly thickheaded ensign once known as simply "K.P." The old admiral stifled a chuckle and shook his head to let Fletcher know that she should consider herself duly chastised. "It's alright this time, Fletcher. If a sight like that doesn't make you want to stop and stare, I think TFC may not be the right line of work for you."

"Hooyah, sir!"

"Hooyah indeed. Now, let's get to work, shall we?"

With the enthusiastic help of a now fully alert Ensign Fletcher, Patterson took just over a minute to compose and transmit the following Emergency Action Message:

Z2129
TOP SECRET - MAGI PRIME
FM: CNO ABOARD TFC FLAGSHIP, TFS NAVAJO
TO: EAM — FOR IMMEDIATE TFC FLEET-WIDE DISTRIBUTION
INFO: PELARAN GUARDIAN SPACECRAFT APPROACHING EARTH

1. SPACECRAFT BELIEVED TO BE PELARAN GUARDIAN APPROACHING ON-ORBIT TFC FLEET ASSETS.
2. IMPERATIVE THAT SHIPS AND ORBITAL FACILITIES TAKE NO PROVOCATIVE ACTIONS WHATSOEVER.
3. SET STATUS OF ALL CIVILIAN SPACEFLIGHT OPERATIONS TO 'TERMINATE UNTIL FURTHER NOTICE.'
4. TFC ASSETS — HOLD ALL LAUNCHES AND ON-ORBIT FLIGHT OPERATIONS UNTIL DIRECTED BY FLAG.

5. ASSUME ALL TRANSMISSIONS MONITORED BY GUARDIAN SPACECRAFT. ADM PATTERSON SENDS.

TFS Ingenuity, Approaching Earth Orbit
(8.5×10^4 km from Earth)

Captain Tom Prescott trudged aft towards *Ingenuity's* Flight Deck for the short shuttle ride over to Admiral Patterson's flagship feeling like a man on the way to the gallows. Less than twenty-four hours earlier, he had taken his ship into battle despite explicit orders to avoid hostile forces altogether — orders issued by Duke Sexton, Commander in Chief, Terran Fleet Command, immediately before his ship's departure. Although his frigate's participation in the battle had not been entirely by choice, Prescott couldn't help but wonder if the admiral would view the situation in the same light.

The "Battle of Gliese 667," as everyone now seemed to be calling it, had been against two ships possessed of vastly superior firepower to his own that had been illegally commandeered from the Sajeth Collective — a seven-world alliance already teetering on open hostilities against Humanity. Although the Collective had officially initiated diplomatic relations with Earth via Ambassador Nenir Turlaka, she had been obliged to deliver potentially catastrophic news as one of her first duties upon arriving in the Sol system. Powerful political and military officials, in open defiance of the Sajeth Collective's Governing Council, had plotted to form a splinter group known as the Pelaran Resistance. Their stated goal was simple: Humankind could not be allowed to achieve military dominance in this region of the galaxy as a cultivated pawn of the powerful Pelaran Alliance.

Leaders of the Resistance movement had asserted for some time that the Pelaran Alliance had repeated a pattern of "conquest by proxy" countless times across a vast region of space stretching many thousands (if not tens of thousands) of light years. Through an apparently elaborate process, the Pelarans chose single civilizations — in this case the Humans — within a region of space to rapidly advance within a relatively short period of time. Once this process began, the Pelarans invariably continued to provide their proxies with technological and military assistance until such time that no other civilizations within a five-hundred-light-year cultivation radius could stand against them. All other worlds within this sphere of influence were then left with a simple choice of either subjugation or destruction. Given such a bleak outlook, it was easy to understand why so many within the Sajeth Collective sympathized with the Resistance. Unwilling to accept the will of either the Pelaran Alliance or their unwitting proxy, the Resistance offered another option — a preemptive military strike against the Earth in a last ditch effort to halt Humanity's progress before it was too late.

As if the current military and political situation wasn't bad enough, Captain Prescott's (albeit successful) battle with the Resistance ships had led to his allowing Admiral Rugali Naftur, a highly placed military commander from the Sajeth Collective, to come aboard his ship for the short trip back to the Sol system. At the time, Prescott had felt fully justified in doing so since

Naftur believed that he might be able to prevent the attack on Earth altogether if the Resistance forces could be located. Although he fully realized that it might be the height of naiveté, Prescott took the Wek officer at his word. It had, after all, been Admiral Naftur's ship, the *Gresav*, that had ultimately destroyed the more powerful of the two Resistance ships, almost certainly saving the lives of everyone aboard *Ingenuity*.

In any event, Admiral Naftur, his entire crew, and no doubt the *Gresav's* sophisticated AI systems, had witnessed *Ingenuity's* remarkable (and highly classified) capabilities in battle firsthand. At this point, Prescott doubted there had been much additional harm in allowing the Wek admiral to return to Earth as their guest.

What was it Commander Reynolds had said? Prescott mused. *"In for a penny, in for a pound?" I suppose it's too late to worry much about it at this point anyway. Patterson will either agree with my actions, or throw me in the brig for gross dereliction of duty. Too many more days like today and that may start sounding like a pretty good deal anyway.*

As Prescott reached the end of the corridor, he was surprised to hear the ship's synthetic voice make the all-too-familiar announcement, "Captain Prescott to the bridge!" He noted the urgency in the AI's announcement, which was designed to convey a tone appropriate for the situation. He found it a little difficult to believe that some new emergency had arisen in the sixty seconds since he had left the bridge, but if the past few weeks had taught him anything, it was to expect the unexpected aboard a starship. Still, rather than immediately heading back to the bridge and further delaying his inevitable unpleasant visit with the admiral, he elected to use the ship's comlink.

"Bridge, go for Prescott," he said aloud. Standing alone in the starboard command section corridor, he fought back the natural urge to stare at the ceiling for no apparent reason while speaking. It took the ship's AI only a fraction of a second to recognize the captain's desire to communicate with the bridge and route his call accordingly.

"Reynolds here, Captain. Sorry for the interruption," his XO responded, "but Admiral Patterson just terminated all flight ops. You're needed back up here immediately, sir."

"On my way. Prescott out." Spinning on his heels and heading back to the bridge of his ship, he couldn't help feeling a small sense of … What was it? ... Relief? That was probably overstating things a bit, but perhaps the delay would offer at least a temporary reprieve and some time for his actions to be overshadowed by the latest crisis of the day.

***

Inasmuch as such a thing was even possible for four heavily armed Remotely Piloted Space Vehicles, the flight of *Hunters* discontinued all active sensor transmissions and assumed a nonthreatening, defensive posture. The RPSVs, which were currently being controlled by the AI of the nearby cruiser, TFS *Shawnee,* established a loose escort formation well aft of the

Guardian spacecraft and made no attempt to obstruct its flightpath towards Earth.

The obvious question was what, if anything, Terran Fleet Command should do in response to the ship's arrival. It wasn't as if the question had never been considered before. In fact, Admiral Patterson's staff had recently prepared a number of command briefings — issuing them as mandatory reading for TFC personnel at all levels — covering precisely this topic. The briefings offered a set of general guidelines (very general, it turned out) describing how Fleet expected to handle the appearance of alien spacecraft (particularly Sajeth Collective vessels or the elusive Pelaran Guardian itself). While documentation of this type made perfect sense to staff officers sitting around their admiral's conference room table, in practice, there were far too many variables to consider. One could argue, for example, that it made perfect sense to intercept Sajeth Collective vessels as far from Earth as possible and regard them as hostile until proven otherwise. Did the same apply to the Guardian spacecraft, or should adopting such an aggressive stance in that case be regarded as unnecessary, futile, and potentially dangerous? The Pelarans, after all, had provided Humanity with a tremendous technological bounty — seemingly out of nothing more than a spirit of interstellar goodwill and cooperation (as the more idealistic members of the TFC Leadership Council were fond of pointing out). From a more practical standpoint, did we even have much of a choice in the matter? Based on all of the intelligence Fleet had managed to gather so far regarding the Guardian spacecraft's capabilities, and there was still precious little of it, Earth's nascent, space-based military forces could offer little if any resistance if it chose to attack. That being the case, was it reasonable to run the risk of a military confrontation just for the sake of enforcing what we considered our territorial boundaries? For the moment, Admiral Patterson thought not. Accordingly, all of TFC's warships in the vicinity — now nearly thirty in number — stood idly by and allowed the GCS to approach Humanity's homeworld as if it were an expected diplomatic vessel from our most trusted ally.

For its part, the Guardian proceeded in the general direction of the *Navajo* at a pace that did not give the impression of any hostile intent. Once it detected that the Terran vessels had discontinued their use of active sensors and targeting systems, it immediately reconfigured its own emissions, eliminating those that might appear threatening … at least those it believed the Humans were likely capable of detecting.

TFS Navajo
(Combat Information Center)

Aboard the flagship, Admiral Patterson had once again shifted his attention to the holographic table near the center of the CIC. "Any response, Ensign Fletcher?" he asked for the fourth time in the past ten minutes.

"Nothing yet, Admiral," she reported, working very hard to ensure that there was zero delay in her responses. "I just tried a laser comlink as well. I think we've tried just about everything short of breaking out the Aldis lamps, sir. It has to be ignoring us intentionally."

“I think that’s probably a valid assumption at this point. Thank you, Ensign.”

Patterson removed his glasses and rubbed his eyes momentarily, then stared once again at the holographic table display while wondering exactly what he was missing, just as commanders at all levels had wondered throughout history. *Well, there’s the situation laid out for me with a ridiculous level of detail,* he thought. *If Admiral Spruance would have had this kind of visibility before the Battle of Midway, I guess he wouldn’t have had much of an excuse if things had gone to hell on his watch.* He paused and noted the AI’s projected path of the Guardian spacecraft. *Then again, the Yamato and the rest of the Japanese ships didn’t have him outgunned a hundred to one.*

Resigning himself to the fact that there was nothing further for him to do at the moment, the admiral grabbed a tablet and took a seat at one of the Command consoles near the center of the CIC. He had noticed just before the Guardian’s arrival that TFS *Ingenuity’s* AI had transmitted its after action report, and this was as good a time as any to take a look.

Before the advent of ultra-sophisticated artificial intelligence systems aboard naval vessels, it had long been the duty of ships’ captains to complete a detailed report of their activities upon returning to port. While this was still the case to a degree, any report the captain chose to submit was now supplemented, and to a large degree replaced, by a standard mission log generated by the cold, unblinking eye of the vessel’s AI. On the plus side, the admiralty was provided with an unvarnished, objective account of everything that had transpired onboard. In addition, the captain was relieved of the administrative nightmare required to sufficiently describe the details of a starship's mission. On the other hand, there was no longer much of an opportunity for a captain to "spin" his way out of a tongue lashing (or worse) with a skilled turn of phrase in his written report. Privacy truly was a thing of the past in modern society, but this was particularly true aboard TFC vessels. The AI-produced report was arranged in a hierarchical style, allowing the reader to "drill down" to the minutest details, when required. Interested in comparing the number of times a specific weapon system was discharged with another? It's in the report. Reactor power output and efficiency? It's in the report. The meal choices made by an engineer's mate during dinner last Tuesday, including the … results of that dinner on his digestive system? It's in the report — and with a level of scatological detail that would have caused even the young man's personal physician to wrinkle his nose in disgust.

It took Admiral Patterson only a few moments of reading to realize that the already dangerously unpredictable situation had just gotten significantly more complex. He felt the hair on the back of his neck stand on end as he realized the implications of the Guardian gaining access to *Ingenuity's* mission report, particularly the details regarding Human interactions with members of the Sajeth Collective and the presence of Admiral Naftur aboard *Ingenuity* at this very moment. Patterson checked his progress momentarily and reread the previous section after noticing that Naftur was not only aboard, but currently sitting on the ship's bridge at a

Command console. *Really, Prescott?* Filing that tidbit away for later, he quickly checked the document's transmission time index and cross-referenced it with the GCS' arrival — or at least when the RPSV flight had *detected* its arrival. There were roughly ten minutes separating the two time stamps, so it was at least possible that the information had not been intercepted. In reality, Fleet had no way of knowing if their secure communications channels had been compromised by the Guardian spacecraft, but the Science and Engineering Directorate steadfastly insisted that their standard encryption algorithms were all but unbreakable. Being a student of history, however, Patterson knew better than to take such assertions at face value. Based on the data the Sajeth Collective had provided thus far, it seemed prudent to assume that anything transmitted in the presence of the Guardian was no longer private.

"Ensign, I need Captain Prescott from *Ingenuity* shuttled over here immediately. Please let Captain Davis know that we are going to risk the flight. Depending on how that goes, we may go ahead and allow *Ingenuity* to deorbit within the hour."

"Yes, Admiral, sending now."

TFS Ingenuity
(5 km astern of TFS *Navajo*)

"Captain," Lieutenant Dubashi reported from the Communications console, "*Navajo* is transmitting the 'captain repair aboard flag' signal again, sir."

"Thank you, Lieutenant. Please let Flight Ops know that I will be departing after all." Prescott turned to

Commander Reynolds and Admiral Naftur with a disconsolate look on his face. "I'm guessing that means he just got around to reading the AI's mission report."

Naftur studied him for a long moment before replying. Then leaned forward and spoke into his tablet in a low voice, pausing the translation before handing it to Prescott for a reply that only he could hear. "I would counsel you to avoid spending too much time worrying about the importance of your role in this story so far, for better or worse. The same can be said for all of your other officers, for me, and for Admiral Patterson as well. Nor does responsibility for the ultimate outcome rest on any one set of shoulders alone. I understand the anxiety you feel, and I share it. Keep in mind, however, that Admiral Patterson's view of the situation has a completely different frame of reference. You must not assume that his desire to speak with you in person as quickly as possible has anything to do with any impropriety on your part. I would be very surprised and indeed disappointed if that were truly the case. I can assure you that he has much more pressing matters to which he is attending. If it helps you feel any better, I believe I can objectively say that I can find no fault with any of your actions since our rendezvous at Gliese 667 C, and doubt that he will either. What you *do* have is critical, time-sensitive information. This, he *does* require immediately in order to make the best decisions possible. The ship's report will have provided some of the information he needs, but there is no substitute for a face-to-face conversation with his battlefield commander. Take heart, young Captain, you may yet survive to fight another day."

Prescott stared intently at the Wek's expressive, leonine face as the tablet played back the translation using a perfectly synthesized facsimile of the admiral's actual voice. *Well, then,* he chuckled to himself, *I think I may have just become the first Human being to receive an ass-chewing from an extra-terrestrial ... and the funny thing is that I absolutely had it coming! Let's see, summarizing in Human terms, he said, 'Suck it up and drive on, kid, because none of this is about you!'* Prescott looked around the bridge momentarily, letting out a long sigh before replying, "I apologize, Admiral. You are absolutely right and I greatly appreciate your candor. Even in the midst of momentous events, it's all too easy to start thinking in a selfish manner. I know better and will do better."

Naftur chuckled on hearing the playback of Prescott's reply and simply nodded in return — also aware that he had just issued a mild reprimand to a member of a different species. As a senior military commander in an alliance spanning seven star systems, however, managing subordinate commanders from multiple civilizations was just a routine part of the job.

TFS Navajo

Although the *Navajo*-class cruisers had been developed primarily as a massive weapons platform, the design still provided significant capabilities to handle flight operations. Just as with the much smaller destroyers and frigates, the stern was dominated by the ship's primary flight apron, used for launch and recovery of various types of smaller spacecraft. This included the ubiquitous *Sherpa* Autonomous Space Vehicle, often referred to by TFC personnel as simply the "shuttle." Although they tended to rack up more flight time than just about any other type of small spacecraft, due primarily to the wide range of missions they handled, they were widely considered one of the least attractive ships ever produced. In fact, their less official, and certainly less sophisticated moniker was simply the "turd." Anyone seeing their shape for the first time was immediately clear on where the nickname had originated, and the standard, brownish-gray color scheme widely used by TFC only served to further reinforce that impression. Despite her many detractors, the *Sherpa* had an ingenious, modular design, many features of which had been in use well before the introduction of Pelaran-based technologies. They were relatively fast for a utility/transport vessel, and could be quickly reconfigured to handle various types of missions from cargo delivery to personnel transport. In addition, a heavily armored (and similarly armed) version of the ASV with more powerful engines and gravitic systems, known as the *Gurkha,* was currently being deployed as TFC's first assault transport.

As Captain Prescott emerged from the cargo ramp at the rear of his shuttle, the *Navajo's* AI sounded the traditional boatswain's "Pipe the Side" call, followed by the announcement "*Ingenuity*, arriving," to signify the presence of a visiting ship's captain aboard.

Flag Captain Ogima Davis approached from the forward entrance to the hangar deck with an outstretched hand. "It's quite an honor to have a living legend aboard," he said with a mischievous grin.

"Uh huh, you clearly haven't read *Ingenuity's* mission report yet. The 'legend' part I humbly accept," Prescott mocked, bowing his head slightly, "but the 'living' part may only last until Admiral KP gets me alone somewhere. In fact, you might want to assign me a Marine security detail," he laughed.

"What did you do now, Prescott, fly off on another top secret mission in that super frigate of yours and start a war or something?"

"Something like that, yeah. Hey, maybe your 'babysitter' will let you read my report if you behave yourself," he said, raising his eyebrows. It was unusual for two senior officers to be afforded the opportunity for an open, friendly conversation aboard ship without being behind closed doors. In this case, however, the activity and background noise on the cruiser's massive flight deck provided the two captains a rare moment of privacy.

"Oh yeah, the old man's gonna have nothing but love for you."

"In that, I have no doubt, my friend. It's good to see you, Ogima. How's life as a 'flag captain?'" Prescott asked, referring to Davis' current assignment as the officer in nominal command of the admiral's flagship. Since the days of sailing vessels, the job had been considered somewhat of a dubious honor since the admiral's presence aboard tended to significantly diminish the captain's authority to exercise command of his own ship. For that reason, the role tended to be assigned to relatively junior captains even though the flagship itself, which was typically a major combatant, would normally warrant the presence of a senior captain nearing their own promotion to admiral.

"I can't complain, or at least I don't complain *much* ... especially since there's no one to complain *to* when you're the boss. In all seriousness, most days I feel guilty and selfish for enjoying my job so much. You know, with the world coming to an end and what not," Davis said, smiling broadly. "All the simulator training was great, and very accurate, but in no way did it prepare me for the reality of this ship. This thing is an absolute *beast*, Tom, and if we can get some downtime to incorporate all of the features the Science and Engineering guys are talking about ..."

"I know exactly what you mean," Prescott said, nodding his head. "Unfortunately, time is a commodity that's in precious short supply at the moment."

"True enough, and you know how much my 'sitter' loves to be kept waiting, so I had best get you up to the CIC. Right this way, my friend."

Guardian Spacecraft
(1500 km from TFS *Navajo*)

In spite of their occasional failure to apply history's lessons as a guide for their actions, the Makers were dedicated students of the past. In fact, documenting the cultural and technological effects of Pelaran intervention on cultivated species was an important aspect of the Guardian's mission. The period of time immediately following direct contact was of particular interest, since it tended to be a reliable indicator of how well the cultivation program had been applied to date, as well as the likelihood of its long-term success.

So far, the signs were gratifyingly positive. The Terrans were going out of their way to avoid any sort of aggressive posture, which had often not been the case for this species when they perceived an obvious threat. In addition to discontinuing their use of active sensor scans, there had been no spacecraft launches from the planet's surface since its arrival. Vessels already in orbit and in the immediate vicinity of Earth were holding their positions and very little activity between vessels had been noted. The single exception to this, which was clearly the Humans' command vessel based on its emissions, had approached slowly and taken up a position at a respectful distance.

While all of this activity was taking place in the space near the planet, Terra's nation states were busily attempting to be the first to make direct contact, saturating the frequency spectrum with requests to communicate as if they were ancients hoping to be the first to earn the favor of a newly discovered deity.

Supplication, the Guardian observed. *Excellent*.

Chapter 2

TFS Navajo

Prescott had followed Captain Davis on what seemed like an extended aerobic workout as they made their way from the cruiser's cavernous flight deck to the CIC. Like the bridge, the Combat Information Center was located on the ship's longitudinal axis, buried at the center of the most heavily armored section of the hull.

Trying his level best to apply the lessons of Admiral Naftur's earlier admonishment, Prescott still couldn't prevent his inner voice from working overtime — apparently in an effort to convince himself that everything would be fine. *Surely he wouldn't be receiving me in the CIC for a public berating*, he thought. *Then again, this is Patterson we're talking about. He probably never leaves the room, especially in a situation like this.*

"Man, I don't think I'd ever need to hit the cardio equipment if I had to take this hike several times a day," he observed, struggling to keep up with Captain Davis' rather aggressive pace.

"That's a fact. I'm telling you, the size and power of this ship still blows my mind. As far as walking yourself to death, though, the carriers are even worse. I was on the *Jutland* right before we launched and half those guys wheel around on electric scooters and such. It's damned undignified, if you ask me," Davis laughed, pausing at the top of the final stairway. "You know, it may just be that you're getting old, Prescott."

"I don't know about that, but I do feel like I've aged several years in the past month," he replied, drawing in a few deep breaths as they paused to authenticate their identities outside the heavily armored bulkhead door protecting the *Navajo's* CIC.

"Welcome, Captain Prescott and Captain Davis," the AI's synthetic voice announced. "All activity in the CIC is currently classified Top Secret, code word MAGI PRIME. You may now enter the CIC."

With the cruiser at General Quarters, the CIC's lighting was even more subdued than usual, and tinted with a red hue as a reminder of the ship's current status. Prescott paused momentarily just inside the entrance, both to allow his eyes to adjust and to give himself a moment to take in the room's daunting scale. Unlike her more general purpose bridge, the *Navajo's* CIC was dedicated to the task of employing the cruiser herself as well as various other military assets within her battlespace, as a single, coordinated weapon system. The fact that the ship was also acting as Admiral Patterson's flagship meant that the CIC tended to be standing room only — twenty-four hours per day. Even with well over fifty TFC personnel on duty, however, the room was eerily quiet.

Davis nodded towards the center of the room where Admiral Patterson stood gesturing at a gigantic holographic table while speaking into a headset. Even though he was obviously heavily engaged in conversation, the admiral noticed the two captains immediately. Without missing a beat, he motioned for the two of them to join him, then held up a finger to let them know he would be with them in a moment.

"The man's a machine," Davis said, leaning in close so that only Prescott could hear. "As far as I know, he hasn't slept in three days. He says he grabs naps in one of the attached conference rooms, but I'm not sure I buy it. Now that the aliens have finally arrived, we may have to take him down with a tranquilizer gun."

Prescott noticed that as the admiral spoke he was manipulating the holographic table display to get a better view of the space immediately surrounding the flagship. As he watched, the scale of the display changed so that only the *Navajo* and Guardian spacecraft were visible. Patterson then rotated the entire display so that he could see the *Navajo* with the Earth itself in the background from the Guardian's perspective. Seemingly satisfied with the result of his conversation, he removed the headset and approached the two captains.

"Welcome back, Tom," he said warmly, extending his hand.

"Thank you, Admiral," Prescott replied, still a bit apprehensive, but relieved that the CNO did not appear especially hostile.

"Pick up any other hitchhikers on your way back that I don't know about yet?" the admiral asked, deadpan, his face immediately shifting to a well-rehearsed scowl.

Prescott felt a chill run down his spine. This was clearly one of those ambiguous situations that could be read either way, but where choosing incorrectly could provide a particularly bad result. Rather than commit himself either way, he simply stared at the admiral for a moment, waiting to be either skewered or let off the hook entirely.

The admiral, for his part, simply raised his eyebrows and peered over his glasses as if waiting for a response, seeming to take pleasure in his subordinate's obvious discomfort.

Unable to endure the silence any longer, Prescott opened his mouth to respond. "Sir, I …"

"*Relax*, Prescott," Patterson interrupted, chuckling in spite of himself and finally starting to feel a tinge of guilt. "There actually *are* a few things I'm going to need you to explain to me, but I've looked over the highlights of your AI's log a couple of times already. So far, I haven't seen anything you did that I probably wouldn't have done myself. Besides, the truth of the matter is that you're now the only combat veteran captain we've got, so I'd probably be a little reluctant to take you out of the chair no matter what you did."

Captain Davis took a step back and stared in amazement. "Combat veteran? You *did* go out and start a war, didn't you, Prescott?"

"He didn't *start* anything, but he and our friend Admiral Naftur sure as hell finished something. Out at Gliese 667, they were attacked by a sister ship to Naftur's *Gresav* as well as one of the big cruisers we saw get wiped out by the Guardian last month. Since Prescott is standing here, you can draw your own conclusions as to how that went for the bad guys," he smiled, literally patting Prescott on the back. "Anyway, with the Guardian lurking around outside, I'm not going to have time to do a proper debrief, so I'd like the two of you to quickly document the lessons learned. I want what worked and what didn't work in the hands of every one of our captains within twenty-four hours. Questions on that part?"

"No, sir," they replied in unison, feeling a little like a pair of midshipmen who had just been handed an especially odious assignment for the following day.

"Next, I know that Naftur has some sort of bio-signature-scrambling gizmo that supposedly keeps the Guardian from detecting his presence. Frankly, I'm not sure if I'm comfortable with him remaining aboard one of our ships while we are sitting up here nose to nose with this thing. We have to assume it can read our encrypted comm, and we have absolutely no idea how it would react if it discovered we were collaborating with a Wek, particularly since that Wek happens to be a senior military commander. The picture that's emerging of this 'cultivation' program tells me that the Pelarans are looking for what you might call an … uh, rather *exclusive* relationship with us."

"So should we shuttle Admiral Naftur down to HQ to meet up with Admiral Sexton and Ambassador Turlaka?" Prescott asked.

"Yes, that's your first priority. It's critical that we get Naftur on the ground and see if we can get some additional information that might help us design a better defense against this potential 'Pelaran Resistance' attack. At the moment, we have very little notion of what to expect. I suppose we can hold out some hope that the loss of two of their vessels at Gliese 667 might persuade them to turn around and head home, but I doubt that's something we can count on."

"No, sir," Prescott agreed. "In fact, Admiral Naftur indicated that the Resistance expects there will be little to no resistance from Terran forces when their task force arrives at Sol. Their chief concern is the Guardian, and they believe they have developed some tactics that will allow them to keep it busy while they attack Earth from multiple directions with stand-off weapons. I suspect they will attribute the loss of their two ships to the *Gresav* since they believed *Ingenuity* to be unarmed."

"Well, that was an unfortunate mistake for them, but their intel was only off by a month or so."

"True enough, sir, and given our power deficiency at the time, we would have almost definitely been either destroyed or captured after they finished dealing with the *Gresav*."

"Precisely, and that's why I want *Ingenuity* on the ground at Yucca for repairs immediately. Commander Logan seems to have a good handle on what went wrong, and doesn't seem to think the fix will take long to accomplish — maybe a couple of weeks, tops."

Prescott took a deep breath before responding. The admiral appeared to have granted his career a stay of execution, so quibbling over his orders at this point seemed foolhardy at best. Still, he believed the best place for *Ingenuity's* crew was in space, working with Admiral Naftur to locate the Resistance forces before they could organize an attack.

Admiral Patterson paused, studying Captain Prescott's face with narrowed eyes and an expression that seemed to issue a direct challenge. "Did you have something to add, Captain?"

The old expression, "The better part of valor is discretion," echoed through Prescott's mind, and though Shakespeare intended it to illustrate cowardice, the words had an entirely different meaning at the moment. "No, sir," he answered evenly, realizing that he was by no means in a position to argue. "We'll get her ready to fly again in short order."

Patterson chuckled, "No, that's not what I have in mind, Tom. Your AI's report highlighted the fact that Naftur believes he might be able to dissuade the Resistance forces from attacking Earth if he can find their rally point. Honestly, that seems like a stretch to me, but at this point we need to pursue every available avenue that might prevent military action, because I can assure you that we are not prepared to counter a determined attack. We also can't count on the Guardian to pull our collective arses out of the fire. In fact, we are already working on our own strategy for taking that thing out in case it comes to that."

"Very well, sir, what are my orders, then?" Prescott asked, willingly taking the bait.

"I'm sure you recall that there were six *Theseus*-class destroyers nearing completion at Yucca while you were there. You may have also noticed that none of them are in space at the moment. Completion of the destroyers was always expected to run a bit behind the other warship classes … and that was by design. The idea was to field a credible defensive force with our frigates, cruisers, and carriers as quickly as possible and then integrate as many improvements as we could into the destroyers before they were launched. Obviously, I'm referring to fairly minor tweaks rather than any significant design changes, since we're only talking about a few months since *Ingenuity* was launched. Understand, though, that the destroyers also included a number of major improvements from day one. Using this approach, we hoped to minimize the risk to our overall deployment schedule while still managing to field at least one class with significantly upgraded capabilities. I think it's safe to say that *Ingenuity's* battle performance at Gliese 667 has served to validate that strategy to some extent. Unfortunately, final systems integration was taking a bit longer than expected, which prompted us to throw all available resources into getting the first destroyer from each of our three primary shipyards ready to fly as quickly as possible. If all goes well, the others will only be a week or so behind. In any event, at Yucca Mountain, the first out of the barn will be the *Theseus* herself."

"I'm assuming they have had their hyperdrives upgraded to include C-Drive capabilities then?" Prescott asked, taken aback by where it looked like the admiral was going with this line of thought and not certain that it made much sense from an operational standpoint.

"Yes, they have, although I suppose it's not technically an upgrade since the inclusion of a C-Drive was one of those high-risk design improvements I was referring to that was always part of the plan. Since, in many respects, the *Theseus*-class destroyer is an oversized version of the *Ingenuity*-class frigate, we'll need to ensure she won't suffer from the same power issues you experienced on your first run out to Gliese 667. I've already spoken with one of *Navajo's* engineers who has been intimately involved with the hyperdrive program. He took a look at Commander Logan's notes and does not believe the *Theseus* will have the same problem. Something about excess capacitor – energy density – something or other. In any event, I'll make him available to assist Commander Logan, as needed. Otherwise, *Theseus* represents the very latest and best of every system we have — C-Drive for the ship, C-Drive-equipped missiles, C-Drives for her twenty-four RPSVs, plus a number of other enhancements that I won't pretend I can adequately describe in any detail."

"Admiral, what are you asking me to do?"

"Jeez, Prescott, do I need to draw you a picture? You will proceed to the Yucca Mountain Shipyard where you will relinquish command of TFS *Ingenuity* so that she can begin undergoing repairs and a reactor refit under the supervision of Captain Oshiro. You will leave Commanders Reynolds and Logan in charge of assisting with getting that process underway, as well as transferring *Ingenuity's* crew to TFS *Theseus*. She's a much bigger ship, Tom, so we'll need to almost triple your crew complement. The good news there is that she already has a fully trained crew on standby. You can let your XO pick and choose whom she wants aboard. If I get my way, you'll also be taking on a full platoon of spec-ops Marines and their assault shuttles. After all, you never know when you might need to send some of *your* people out to meet some of *their* people … and then kill them," he smirked.

"You'll get no argument from me there," Prescott laughed. "Don't get me wrong, Admiral, I'm honored that you would place this kind of confidence in my crew and me, but we are just now coming up to speed on *Ingenuity's* systems. Is it wise for us to change to a completely different ship design at such a critical time?"

"Wise? Hell no, it's not wise, but we're pretty much up against it, in case you hadn't noticed, Captain," Patterson growled. He paused and took a deep breath, then softened his expression a bit before continuing. "Look, I understand your hesitation, Tom, but *Ingenuity* may be out of action for a couple of weeks or more. As I said earlier, you're my only crew that has seen combat, and that still counts for quite a bit in my book. You could say that *all* of our ships have green crews at this point, so I'm still better off putting your crew in an unfamiliar ship than having you cooling your heels at Yucca while we're being attacked by the Resistance, God forbid. Besides, a major design element of both the *Theseus* and *Ingenuity* classes was what the engineers referred to as 'mod/com,' which refers to modularity and commonality. The idea was that if you were trained up in one, you were essentially trained up in both. That interchangeability concept is also one of the main reasons we have been able to produce four separate ship designs so quickly — and build out all four designs at each of our three primary shipyards. Now I'm not going to stand here and tell you that *Ingenuity* and *Theseus* are exactly the same ship, but there should be enough in common between the two for your folks to feel at home pretty quickly. That's especially true since more than half of your crew will have already had quite a bit of time to prepare in the sim."

"Shut up and say 'Thank you Admiral,' before he changes his mind, Tom," Captain Davis laughed, struggling not to be jealous of his friend lucking into yet another plum, independent command.

"Thank you, Admiral," Prescott laughed. "We'll figure out a way to make it work."

"I suspect you will, Captain," Patterson chuckled. "As soon as you are on the ground at Yucca, there should be a shuttle waiting to transport Admiral Naftur to HQ for a quick debriefing with Admirals Sexton and White before the Guardian 'induction' call at 1000 Zulu. I want you to get Reynolds and Logan started on their tasks, then get yourself on a shuttle to HQ as well. The quicker you can get there, the better. I'm certain you can provide some additional insight that will be valuable to the Commander in Chief."

"Understood, sir. Anything else?"

"That's it for now. Don't forget I also want that 'lessons learned' document within twenty-four hours. I'm mainly just looking for you to provide our commanders with a high level assessment of the most important things they need to know if they find themselves in a scrap with a Resistance ship. Otherwise, just keep in mind that there isn't a moment to be lost. I need you and Admiral Naftur aboard the *Theseus* and back in space yesterday. Questions?"

"None, sir, thank you."

"Good luck, Tom."

Earth, Terran Fleet Command Headquarters
(0003 UTC — Leadership Council Meeting Chamber)

In the two and a half hours since the Guardian's arrival, Karoline Crull, Chairwoman of Terran Fleet Command's Leadership Council, had managed to assemble twelve of fifteen members for an emergency session. It was, in fact, unusual for such a large percentage of the membership to be available on such short notice for an on-site meeting. Since the Sajeth Collective incursion nearly a month prior, however, the Council had been in more or less continuous session. As was customary for important meetings such as this one, the representatives who could not attend in person participated via vidcon, their images displayed on large view screens situated on either side of the chamber. At the front of the room, Crull called the session to order from her perch behind an extravagantly carved, mahogany lectern situated atop a massive, two-level dais. Much to her annoyance, the largest view screen, situated in the center of the chamber immediately behind her lectern, currently displayed the careworn face of Admiral Duke Sexton, Commander in Chief, Terran Fleet Command.

"Before we can get started addressing the historic events that require our immediate and undivided attention, I agreed to allow Admiral Sexton a moment to register a concern," she began, speaking as if she was referring to an errant child who was interrupting a serious discussion between adults. "Admiral?"

"Thank you, ma'am," Sexton replied, ignoring her condescending tone. "I know that the Council is accustomed to utilizing secure vidcon so that off-site members have the opportunity to attend sessions remotely, but until further notice, I urge you to secure this meeting chamber and terminate all electronic emissions. That includes vidcon streams as well as both official and personal communications devices."

On the floor of the meeting chamber, there was a general murmur as some members discussed the Admiral's seemingly radical suggestion among themselves, while others consulted their respective corporate and governmental sponsors in an effort to determine how they were expected to respond. The Council chamber itself looked much more like a collection of fourteen miniature command centers than it did a traditional governmental meeting facility. Each representative was afforded a large workspace, complete with multiple computer monitors fronting state of the art computing resources designed to provide instantaneous communications with their various constituencies around the world. Like so many political representatives throughout Human history, members of the Leadership Council tended to serve many masters. Unfortunately, rather than striving to represent the will of the citizens they were sent here to represent, many had become nothing more than a mouthpiece for powerful special interests.

Crull waited for most of the conversations taking place in the room to die down before continuing. "Obviously, this would be a significant and disruptive departure from how we have always conducted business in the past, so I'm going to open the floor to questions for the admiral," she said, thinking that her fellow Council members would quickly dismiss his foolish suggestion out of hand without her ever needing to commit herself one way or another. "The Chair recognizes the representative from the European Union."

Lisbeth Kistler, the distinguished-looking fifty-year-old representative from Germany, was one of the few in the room who tended to make up her own mind rather than being issued an opinion by unseen functionaries thousands of kilometers away. She was also one of the only members who still strongly believed in adhering to traditional forms of etiquette during formal meetings. She stood and paused momentarily, allowing the room to go completely silent before speaking. “Thank you, Madame Chairwoman. Good morning, Admiral Sexton. As I’m sure you can appreciate, many of us rely heavily on secure communications during Council session for a variety of purposes. Would you please explain for us why this change is necessary?”

“Good morning, Councilwoman Kistler. Yes, ma’am, I would be happy to. Although we have no way of knowing for sure, the latest Fleet Intelligence Estimate provides compelling evidence that these Guardian spacecraft have demonstrated the ability to eavesdrop on encrypted communications. I am not able to go into much additional detail since doing so in this insecure setting could have unpredictable results where the Pelarans are concerned.”

“You are, of course, referring to intelligence obtained from our new quote, unquote ‘allies,’ the Sajeth Collective,” Crull interrupted in a voice dripping with sarcasm. “These are the same quote, unquote ‘allies,’ who appear to be on their way to attack the Earth at this very moment, are they not?”

Two years ago, Crull had been appointed as the Central and South American Union’s representative to finish out the final six weeks of her late husband’s term. The largely symbolic appointment had been intended as a statement of sympathy and support for a grieving widow as well as recognition of her husband's long and distinguished career. No one had expected Crull to ever actually attend a Leadership Council meeting, much less insist on taking over immediately as Chairwoman. Nor had anyone expected that her far-reaching connections would allow her to be elected for a follow-on five-year term in the powerful role.

"Madame Chairwoman, I think it prudent to avoid references to classified information until we resolve this matter," Councilwoman Kistler interjected in an effort to regain control of the floor. Crull scowled, waving her hand dismissively by way of reply, thus allowing the conversation to proceed.

"Again, I urge the Leadership Council to secure the meeting chamber and terminate all electronic emissions," Sexton continued, unfazed by the chairwoman's all too typical bullying tactics. "Our ships have likewise been ordered to cease all classified communications until further notice. I can largely guarantee the security of our network resources located here at TFC Headquarters, but there is simply no way I can do the same for external connections."

"Members of the Council," Kistler began again after a brief pause to consider the admiral's request, "I believe we would all prefer to have every one of our fifteen members available for these discussions, and we would also prefer to have access to our usual communications channels to our various constituencies. On the other hand, we do have a quorum present in the chamber and, as Chairwoman Crull mentioned, we are in the midst of historic, and potentially very dangerous events. To my knowledge, none of our esteemed members are experts on matters of secure communications. So, under the circumstances, I'd like to make a motion that we follow Admiral Sexton's counsel without further discussion."

"Second!" several other members responded immediately.

"Oh very well," Crull replied, pausing to take a deep breath in a vain attempt to hide her contempt. She made a quick mental note that Kistler's insolence would require an appropriate response at some point in the future before continuing, "Votes will be recorded by electronic device."

Within thirty seconds, ten of the fifteen members had voted in favor of securing the room. Not surprisingly, three of the five "no" votes were from the Council members who were not present in the meeting chamber — and all three happened to be political allies of the chairwoman.

"The motion passes," she sighed. "Before we continue, I'd like to apologize to our three esteemed colleagues who will now be prevented, unnecessarily in my view, from representing their member nations until they can physically return to Fleet Headquarters. I urge each of you to return as quickly as possible." Crull then glared around the meeting chamber, shaking her head as if it was necessary to further underscore her opinion on the matter. "The sergeant at arms will secure the room. Admiral Sexton, please have your people do whatever it is they propose to do."

On the giant view screen in the front of the room, Admiral Sexton nodded to a Fleet security specialist off-camera. In seconds, the three view screens displaying vidcons with remote members went blank as all external network connectivity was terminated. For the first time in the brief history of Terran Fleet Command, the Leadership Council would now be forced to make their own decisions rather than relying on the faceless bureaucrats and power brokers lurking behind the scenes.

Chapter 3

TFS Ingenuity, Earth Orbit

Knowing that both he and his crew were about to once again be under the pressure of an extremely aggressive, if not downright unreasonable, schedule, Prescott had signaled ahead for his XO and chief engineer to meet his returning shuttle on *Ingenuity's* flight deck. As the frigate's AI once again sounded the boatswain's call and announced "*Ingenuity*, arriving," the shuttle's rear cargo door slowly descended to reveal Commanders Reynolds and Logan anxiously awaiting his return. Both officers saluted smartly as their captain stood and headed for the *Sherpa's* exit.

"Have I got a surprise for the two of you," he chuckled, returning their salute before hopping off the still-descending cargo ramp.

"You seem to be in better spirits, sir," Reynolds smiled, shaking her head, "but I'm over surprises at this point."

"Don't pay any attention to her, Captain," Logan laughed, "she can't get enough of 'em, so go ahead and lay it on us."

"Alright, walk with me. We're in a hurry, as usual," Prescott said, taking off in the direction of the corridor leading to the command section at his usual brisk pace.

"Now *that's* not a surprise," Reynolds replied, following in his wake.

"Oh, before I forget to tell you both, Admiral Patterson has asked for a short background summary of lessons learned during our trip to Gliese 667, particularly items related to combat operations. He wants it ready to send out to the entire fleet by this time tomorrow. All three of us are going to be plenty busy, but I need some help getting it done."

"That should be pretty easy," Reynolds said. "I've got most of what we'll need in my notes, so I'll take the task if the two of you will just send me anything specific you want included."

"Great, thank you, Commander." After a few more steps, Prescott stopped in the middle of the corridor and faced his two most senior officers, having decided that the important part of what he needed to tell them was probably not appropriate to deliver over his shoulder while they walked. "OK, here's the deal," he began. "The repairs and additional work Fleet wants to complete on *Ingenuity* are expected to take at least two weeks, maybe longer."

"Seriously? Why do they think that?" Logan replied, incredulous. "I don't know of anything we can't get done within three or four days … maybe a week, tops."

"I understand, Commander, but apparently they have a number of follow-on changes they are planning to make and believe this is a reasonable time to do the work since she will already be at Yucca for repairs. You do, of course, also remember that we took quite a bit of weapons fire, including a glancing blow from a nuke at Gliese 667, right?"

"Right," Logan laughed, pausing as he realized that he had indeed forgotten that rather important bit of information for a moment. "There *is* that, but this still doesn't seem to be an appropriate time for a major refurb and overhaul — not considering everything that's going on."

"We're also combat-ready, Captain," Reynolds said, "and this ship is the logical choice for helping Admiral Naftur try to head off an attack from the Resistance."

"And the only large C-Drive-equipped ship … that I know of, at least," Logan added.

"I know, I know," Prescott replied, raising both hands in mock surrender to the logic of their points while also giving himself an opportunity to continue. "Both of you just relax and hear me out. Admiral Patterson agrees with you — at least in part — and that's why he has ordered us to take *Ingenuity* to Yucca Mountain, get the repairs underway, and then transfer our crew to TFS *Theseus*. I need the two of you to get her crewed, supplied, and ready to fly as quickly as possible. Unless something else changes, we will depart as soon as Admiral Naftur and I return from TFC Headquarters."

Both officers stared at their captain in silence as if he had truly and irrevocably lost his mind.

SCS Gunov, Pelaran Resistance Rally Point
(3.3 light years from Earth)

There was a brief distortion in the starfield followed by a flash of grayish-white light as SCS *Gunov*, nominal flagship of the Pelaran Resistance task force, arrived at the designated staging area for the first time. Wek captain and self-proclaimed commodore Naveen Sarafi was gratified to see that twenty-three other vessels had already arrived, including two additional destroyers of the same *Gresav*-class as his flagship. While most of the warships were older and less advanced in many ways, the remaining twenty-one vessels included seventeen *Shopak*-class heavy cruisers as well as four *Rusalov*-class battleships. The four battleships alone carried more than sufficient firepower to all but extinguish life on a world as small as Terra. This assumed, of course, that they could actually survive long enough — and fire their weapons long enough — to complete the type of attack for which they had been designed.

The Sajeth Collective relied almost exclusively on warships both designed and built on the Wek homeworld of Graca. Citing reliability problems as well as a desire to reduce the need for onboard munitions storage, they had all but eliminated kinetic energy weapons from their most recent designs — including the *Gresav* destroyer, *Keturah* BD cruiser, and *Baldev* battleship classes. This had been a grave mistake, in Captain Sarafi's opinion … and an ironic one, given that their own shields were still somewhat vulnerable to just such weapons. Even if they were no longer strictly necessary for ship to ship engagements, there were still situations where planetary bombardment was necessary, regardless of how "civilized" the other members of the Sajeth Collective might fancy themselves. While standoff nuclear missile attacks could certainly achieve the same result, the missiles themselves were relatively slow and easily intercepted by any species advanced enough to warrant an attack in the first place. Directed energy weapons, while still capable of doing a great deal of damage to specific targets from orbit, were not a practical choice as a strategic-level weapon of mass destruction. No, when a large-scale, planet-wide attack was the objective, there was simply no substitute for heavy bombardment with near relativistic kinetic energy weapons. Fortunately, the majority of the thirty-three-ship task force Sarafi hoped to ultimately have at his disposal were well-suited for precisely that mission.

Sarafi felt a chill run down the length of his spine as he briefly considered what it might be like to be on the receiving end of a large-scale orbital bombardment. In fact, under most other scenarios he could imagine, completely destroying a relatively advanced civilization would amount to the ultimate in immoral acts. Even putting all ethical considerations aside, such an attack was a tremendous waste of natural resources and habitable land mass, since the planet itself would likely be rendered uninhabitable for decades, perhaps even centuries, to come. In Sarafi's mind, however, just as with most other members of the Pelaran Resistance, this line of thought seemed to always end with a sense of hopeless inevitability — *they have left us no choice ... we have a right to defend ourselves ... this is our last chance ... at least the end will come quickly for the Humans.*

The stars on the main bridge view screen slewed to port as the *Gunov* oriented herself with respect to the other assembled ships in the Resistance task force. As the starfield stabilized on the screen, a bright yellowish-white star caught Sarafi's attention near the right side of the display. Using the touchscreen at his command chair, he selected the star, which was immediately surrounded by a red square and accompanied by a descriptive block of text on both screens. At the top of the text block appeared the star's rather simplistic name: "Sol."

TFS Ingenuity
(On approach to the Yucca Mountain Shipyard Facility)

Although it had been less than a month since *Ingenuity's* first landing at the Yucca Mountain Shipyard, the security situation had changed dramatically during the intervening weeks. Gone were the previous attempts to conceal the ship's ultimate destination using a clever approach profile coupled with low-level routing. Instead, the frigate executed a more traditional, low-powered descent from orbit that took her relatively close to the city of Los Angeles.

While Pelaran-derived technologies were now beginning to provide significant improvements in mass transportation on a global scale, the American love affair with the automobile continued unabated. Even with mandatory AI control of all vehicles traveling on interstate highways, today's evening rush hour on the 405 had transformed a thirty-kilometer stretch of the freeway from Los Alamitos to LAX into a twelve-lane-wide parking lot. Even though there had been no public announcement regarding a flyover, *Ingenuity's* relatively low altitude of ten kilometers coupled with the thunderous echoes of her double sonic booms made the ship difficult to miss. Along the freeway, and indeed throughout the South Bay area, people stopped what they were doing to catch a glimpse of the now familiar ship.

"Alright, everyone, we've done this once before, but it's certainly not something we want to treat as routine, right, Ensign Fisher?" Prescott said, working to keep his bridge crew engaged and highly alert as the ship made its final approach.

"Yes, sir," Fisher replied without taking his eyes off the Helm console, "but I'm actually hoping for something a little more routine than last time."

"Lieutenant Dubashi, have we received final clearance from Yucca?"

"Yes, Captain, we are cleared for landing. Course plotted and transferred to the Helm console. We are receiving autolanding cues from Yucca Mountain. I've transferred the profile to your Command console for approval."

"Very good, thank you," he replied, pulling up the detailed approach and landing profile on his touchscreen. Prescott took a moment to review the proposed routing as well as the landing sequence after reaching the shipyard itself. "Now *that* is certainly not what I expected," he said, quickly transferring the approach plate to Commander Reynolds' touchscreen. "They have us sequenced for a maximum performance approach and landing. It's the kind of thing they might do if the facility were about to be under attack and they needed to get the ship on the ground as quickly as possible."

"I remember one of the techs talking about the AI being able to handle 'combat landings,' but I haven't seen any of the details," she replied, scanning the details of the approach on her screen. "Wow, yeah that's pretty aggressive. Particularly when you consider what happened during our first attempt at an autolanding."

"Agreed. Dubashi, get us a vidcon with Yucca Mountain. Use priority one and request Yucca-Actual, if possible."

"Aye, Captain."

After a few seconds, Terran Fleet Command's official service seal appeared in a window on the starboard side of the bridge view screen, accompanied by an announcement from the ship's AI.

"Warning, Command Authority has deemed all external communications compromised. Fleet vessels and facilities should minimize all forms of wireless communication. No classified information may be transmitted until further notice."

"Well *that's* annoying," Reynolds grumbled.

"Yeah, I think everyone has the gist at this point. Everyone clear on the intent of that message?" Prescott asked, raising his voice to address the entire bridge crew and receiving an enthusiastic chorus of "yes, sirs" in response. "Excellent. Lieutenant Dubashi, you may acknowledge the AI's announcement so that it will not be repeated as long as this crew is present on the bridge."

"Will do, Captain. I now have a vidcon signal from Yucca Mountain."

"Great. On-screen, please."

The vidcon window on the bridge view screen was immediately filled by the smiling face of Captain Hiroto Oshiro, Facility Commander, Yucca Mountain Shipyard.

"Yucca-Actual here. Go ahead, *Ingenuity*."

"I take it you were expecting our call," Prescott chuckled.

"I had a hunch we might hear from you, but I was about to contact you anyway to give you a heads up," Oshiro replied. "Don't get me wrong, it would be interesting to watch the reactions of a crew experiencing an unexpected combat landing, but the results might end up being, uh, unpredictable."

"Right, and career-limiting for both of us. We're on final approach, so we don't have a lot of time here. Is this really something we want to do right now?"

"Want to, no. Need to, yes. It makes us a little nervous down here as well, especially for the larger ships, but Fleet wants all crews to experience at least one combat-landing sequence. Let me assure you that it's as safe as we can possibly make it at this point. If something goes wrong, both the facility and the ship's AIs will immediately terminate the approach."

"Anything in particular we need to do on our side?"

"Not really, no. Once you approve the approach, you're really just along for the ride. The goal is to get your ship inside the entrance cavern as quickly as possible so that the external blast doors can be secured behind you. You can expect an aggressive transition to hover right outside the entrance. Once inside, the approach should proceed normally, but without the dramatic ship unveiling you saw last time."

"That's good. I think Ensign Fisher may have gotten a little bored with all the drama last time. Thank you, Captain."

"I don't think that will be a problem today," Oshiro smiled. "See you on the ground momentarily, *Ingenuity*. Yucca out."

"Approach and landing profile approved," Prescott announced. "You all know your jobs, so let's get this done." With that, he settled back into his command chair, adjusted his shoulder straps for comfort, and lapsed into silence.

Like all good first officers throughout history, Reynolds fully understood that her primary role was ensuring the smooth and efficient operation of the ship and crew. She took great pride in her work and particularly appreciated those occasions when her commanding officer simply stepped aside and allowed things to run without his input. There was simply no greater compliment he could offer her than the assumption that he could trust his ship, his career, and indeed his life, to his executive officer's capable hands.

"All hands, this is the XO. The ship remains at General Quarters. We will be executing a combat landing with the potential for abrupt course changes and temporary excursions of up to 6 Gs. Crew restraints are mandatory. All personnel should be restrained at this time. Reynolds out." After her announcement, Reynolds shifted uncomfortably in her shoulder restraints for a moment before realizing the problem. "Lieutenant Lee, it's feeling a little 'thick' in here already, did you dial the grav system up a bit?"

"Yes, ma'am ... well ... the AI did anyway. The sensitivity increased almost immediately after Captain Prescott approved the approach. This should be about as bad as it will get. The good news is that it should also smooth out the ride quite a bit."

"Alright, but please keep an eye on it. That heavy feeling makes a lot of people even more uncomfortable than the rough ride would."

"Will do, ma'am."

"Lieutenant Dubashi, can you get us a better view of the entrance?" The bridge view screen had been displaying the general vicinity of Yucca Mountain for some time, but the direction of the ship's approach had thus far obscured their final destination.

"From our current position, we don't have much of a view, Commander, since the entrance tunnel is on the opposite side of the ridge and points east southeast. The facility itself did provide a video stream of the entrance at one time, though. That's assuming it hasn't been discontinued because of all the security concerns," Dubashi replied, zooming the center portion of the bridge view screen to display the southwestern side of the Yucca Mountain ridge line.

"Great, bring it up if you can. I think we can safely assume that it's okay for us to access the feed if it's still available."

With a few quick keystrokes at her console, Dubashi reconfigured the bridge view screen to display the ship's perspective on the left, accompanied by a live video stream of the entrance itself on the right. "There it is, Commander."

"That's perfect, thank you. It still amazes me that they've managed to make something that huge nearly invisible. You really can't even see the outline of the doors unless you know exactly what you're looking for."

"Commander, we are approaching the initial point specified on the approach plate for our final descent to the shipyard entrance," Ensign Fisher reported from the Helm console. "Gravitic fields now set at thirty percent mass. All systems in the green."

"Thank you, Ensign. Everyone stay sharp, it's about to get interesting," Reynolds said.

Ingenuity had maintained a shallow descent since crossing the California coastline just five minutes earlier.

Now, having reached the final segment of the approach, the ship still had a ground speed of nearly twenty-five-hundred kilometers per hour at an altitude of only fifteen-hundred meters. Late afternoon visitors to the Area 51 Travel Center, less than six kilometers away, were treated to a tremendous sonic boom as the ship headed north over the floor of the Amargosa Valley.

"Initial point reached. Ship will clear facility blast doors in three zero seconds," *Ingenuity's* AI announced, automatically displaying a graphical depiction of the approach with a countdown timer on the view screen beneath the video feed of the still-closed shipyards doors.

"Commander, this is making me a little nervous," Fisher said from the Helm console. "We're only fifteen kilometers away and still at Mach two, but the doors haven't even started opening yet. Does that seem right to you?"

"I think we're fine so far," Prescott soothed. "The idea is to minimize the ship's exposure and the amount of time the blast doors are open. The AI will handle the timing."

"Warning, prepare for a maximum performance turn accompanied by rapid deceleration in zero five seconds," the AI announced.

On the right side of the view screen, nearly forty acres of mountainside sank several meters below the surface as the blast doors began their opening cycle.

"It takes over thirty seconds for those doors to open," Dubashi noted from the Comm console.

"Good thing we won't need them to be all the way open," Fisher replied with a nervous laugh.

“Warning, initiate Anti-G Straining Maneuver to prevent G-induced loss of consciousness,” the AI announced.

With the onset of heavy G-forces now imminent, each member of the crew tightened the skeletal muscles in their arms, legs, and abdomens, then increased pressure in their respiratory tracts by saying the word “hick,” while bearing down for a few seconds before sucking in a quick breath and repeating the process. The Anti-G Straining Maneuver (AGSM) served to prevent blood from being forced away from the brain into the extremities, which otherwise resulted in symptoms that progressed rapidly from greyout and tunnel vision to a complete blackout and loss of consciousness, or G-LOC. As entertaining as it was to watching an entire bridge crew performing the AGSM on video after safely returning to the ground, the technique was highly effective at preventing G-LOC and the potentially dangerous convulsions and incapacitation that often followed. Seasoned fighter pilots routinely pulled 9 Gs or more, but Fleet starships generally limited their AIs to 6 Gs, except during emergency situations. Without the AGSM, however, even three to five Gs was sufficient to cause loss of consciousness, particularly when there was an unexpected, rapid onset. For this reason, the ship’s AI provided a warning to the crew whenever possible.

As the countdown timer on the view screen reached fifteen seconds, *Ingenuity* banked hard to port, lining the ship up on an extended centerline to the shipyard’s entrance cavern. The ship itself was capable of handling incredible G loads without sustaining damage, but keeping its Human passengers from being crushed in the process was a significant challenge. Accordingly, the ship's AI monitored a mind-boggling array of parameters, continuously adjusting control inputs and thrust from its sublight engines in concert with inertial dampening to ensure that its occupants never experienced more than 6 Gs. Now aligned both horizontally and vertically with the shipyard's entrance, the AI reversed the ship's sublight engines and executed a maximum performance deceleration.

Directly ahead, a small sliver of darkness was now visible between the shipyard's massive blast doors as the countdown timer on the view screen reached eleven seconds.

"Dubashi, let me know the second that opening is wide enough for us to pass through," Reynolds gasped, still straining against the force of the ship's rapid deceleration.

"Aye, Commander. So far just ten meters," she grunted. "We need eighty-eight meters."

Ensign Fisher leaned forward at the Helm console, struggling to keep his hands poised above the manual control joystick and throttle, but realizing that it would likely be too late to avoid slamming into the face of the mountain if the doors didn't open in time.

On the right hand side of the *Ingenuity's* bridge view screen, the video feed from Yucca Mountain's entrance displayed the impressive site of the massive, two-hundred-meter-long ship visibly slowing, but still rapidly approaching the slowly opening blast doors.

As the countdown timer reached six seconds, the window on the left side of the bridge view screen was completely filled with an unsettling, close-up view of the slowly parting blast doors' camouflaged surface. The space between the doors seemed impossibly small — their parting, maddeningly slow.

Time seemed to grind to a halt on *Ingenuity's* bridge as two more seconds ticked by on the view screen timer.

"Ninety meters!" Lieutenant Dubashi yelled. "Oh my God, we may yet live!" she laughed aloud, unconcerned about her military bearing at the moment.

With that, the frigate's bow passed through the still-opening doors — ultimately reaching a gap of one hundred thirty-two meters to provide a small factor of safety. Before the ship had even cleared the entrance, the doors had reversed direction to begin their close cycle.

Once clear, the AI quickly decelerated as she continued along the gradually downward-sloping entrance cavern. "Ship has cleared facility blast doors," *Ingenuity's* AI announced. "Proceeding to Berth Nine. Expected arrival in zero two minutes."

Less than ten seconds later, the massive blast doors were once again closed, plunging the ship momentarily into darkness before the entire entrance cavern was flooded with artificial light. The AI continued their trip into the heart of the facility at a steady pace, slowing only after reaching the "roundhouse" area at the center of the ten-kilometer-long shipyard itself.

"Gravitic fields have reached zero mass," Ensign Fisher reported. "I've also got six green indicators on the landing struts. Looks like they aren't taking any chances for a gear-up landing this time."

"Glad to hear it," Prescott replied, gratified to see that his young helmsman appeared to have relaxed a bit and was no longer poised over the manual controls. "Keep an eye on things, Ensign, but I think we'll be fine from here."

"Always, sir."

Prescott got his XO's attention and quietly said "*Theseus*," nodding his head towards Berth Ten, immediately to starboard of their destination.

Once again the namesake vessel of her class, *Theseus* had been moved as closely as possible to *Ingenuity's* berth so that the transition could proceed as rapidly as possible. The destroyer was similar to the smaller, *Ingenuity*-class frigates in many respects, but there was some quality about the lines of her hull that provided a much more aggressive — even menacing appearance. While a glance at *Ingenuity* left little doubt that she was a ship of war, the same design teams had somehow managed to imbue *Theseus* with an almost intimidating air — as if her very presence were intended to convey an implied threat.

"Wow. She looks a lot more …" Reynolds began.

"Badass," Fisher interjected, unable to resist the temptation to provide his input.

"Yeah, I guess that's pretty much what I was thinking," Reynolds chuckled. "Eyes on the road, please, Ensign," she chided.

"Aye, Commander. Sorry."

"Captain, incoming vidcon from Captain Oshiro," Dubashi announced.

"Thank you, Dubashi. On-screen, please."

After a brief pause, Captain Oshiro once again appeared in a window on the far right side of the bridge view screen.

“Congratulations on your first combat landing, *Ingenuities*. Everything still in one piece?”

“I’m not going to jinx us on that one until we’re on the ground, Captain. We’ve been here before, if you’ll recall,” Prescott replied under raised eyebrows.

“Ouch,” Oshiro sighed. “I guess I had that coming. Let me put it this way, I’m so confident that the rest of your landing will go smoothly that I’d be one-hundred-percent confident in standing on the concrete platform below your berth during the landing sequence. Well … if it weren’t for getting ripped apart by the grav field, that is.”

“I guess we’ll have to take your word for it at this point. We’ve pretty much been passengers since starting this approach, after all. Everything seemed to go fine during the landing, but I don’t think any of us expected how closely synchronized the timing of the whole thing would be. I’m pretty sure most of us thought we were about to make a big black mark on your front door,” Prescott chuckled.

“It really does feel that way from the ship’s perspective, I know. Frankly, I’m not looking forward to trying it with the carrier *Jutland*, but the truth is that there are safeguards on top of safeguards, and an abort is possible throughout the whole process. In any event, unless you end up doing one of those while we are actually under attack, Fleet only requires each ship to practice it one time. That brings me to the reason for my call. I will not be able to meet you at Berth Nine, but I understand that you and Admiral Naftur require transportation to Headquarters.”

"Yes, we do. Admiral Naftur is prepared to depart immediately. He will require a couple of Marine troopers in full combat gear as an escort. After I assist my XO and chief engineer with beginning the transition to *Theseus*, I'll be on my way as well." Prescott's mind registered the sound of several of his bridge crew shifting in their seats at his last statement.

"Twenty meters," Ensign Fisher reported in the background.

"I'll see to it. On a much more somber note, my sincerest condolences for the three members of your crew who were lost during the battle at Gliese 667. Fleet has a team standing by to make all of the arrangements for their services. They will coordinate with both you and Dr. Chen, but I believe the ceremony will occur sometime tomorrow."

The extreme level of activity since the battle took place had allowed Prescott to prevent the deaths of three very young members of his crew from completely dominating his every thought. Like every leader throughout history who had lost men and women serving under their command, however, he had already begun to struggle with the inevitable question of what he could have done differently that might have prevented their deaths. "Thank you," was all that he managed to say before quickly forcing his mind back to dealing with the multitude of tasks at hand.

"My XO will be at your disposal to assist your folks in making their transition and getting *Theseus* ready to depart. Welcome back to Yucca Mountain. Oshiro out."

"Five meters … touchdown," Fisher reported. The sound of the ship's six massive landing struts compressing under her weight could be heard as the frigate settled onto the landing platform.

"All hands, this is the XO," Reynolds announced over the comm system. "Secure from General Quarters. Power down non-essential systems and prep the ship for maintenance crews. All department heads are to meet on the flight deck at 0200 Zulu. Good job everyone. Reynolds out."

Chapter 4

Earth, Terran Fleet Command Headquarters
(0415 UTC — Leadership Council meeting chamber)

With just under six hours remaining before the expected contact from the Guardian spacecraft, Chairwoman Crull was busily laying the groundwork for how she expected the forthcoming "induction" process should proceed. "Surely, colleagues, we can agree from the outset of this discussion that the Pelarans have already earned our trust," she said from the meeting chamber lectern. "We now know that they have not only been sharing their knowledge with us for fifty years, but their Guardian spacecraft has actually been here protecting us from the likes of the Sajeth Collective and God knows what else for centuries. During all that time, they have asked for nothing from us in return other than following some simple, common sense rules designed to keep us from destroying ourselves with all of this new technology. I, for one, would like to see us put together a resolution, preferably a *unanimous* resolution, that officially welcomes the Guardian spacecraft and expresses our gratitude to the Pelaran Alliance for all they have done for us. Let me remind each of you that most of this work has already been completed. Our predecessors who were selected to serve on the very first Leadership Council drafted just such a resolution as one of its earliest official acts, and I would be honored to sponsor it again now as your Chair."

There was a momentary silence in the room as each member temporarily withheld comment while waiting to see how the others would react. “Will the Chair yield for questions?” asked the delegate from the United States.

“Of course, although what I have said so far seems beyond question to me,” Crull replied, forcing a smile. The Chair recognizes the Councilman from the U.S.”

It took a moment for Samuel Christenson to free his over-two-meter-tall frame from behind his work center desk. As was his habit, he walked to the center of the meeting chamber immediately forward of the other members while keeping his distance from the lofty dais in the front of the room. The current chairwoman had personally ordered construction of the elaborate rostrum, which was something her husband would never have tolerated.

The whole concept of the Council was supposed to be one of open cooperation among equal peers — a working group with an eminently practical mission, rather than a hierarchical, bureaucratic throwback from centuries past. The idea that the chairmanship was being purposely transformed into some sort of dictatorial overseer was, in Christenson’s view, not only offensive, but also potentially dangerous. Although the group had no authority as an international governing body, per se, it did make decisions regarding the dissemination of Pelaran technological data … implying that it wielded tremendous influence over governmental and corporate interests worldwide. In fact, one could argue that Terran Fleet Command’s Leadership Council was the first truly effective global, quasi-governmental organization. The United Nations, which had never been truly global and certainly never accused of being effective, had finally dissolved during the worldwide debt crisis of the mid twenty-first century. Fortunately, breakthroughs in fusion power had shortly thereafter marked the beginning of a long period of global economic growth and prosperity, during which there was little motivation to create yet another monolithic, governmental assembly. This attitude had changed rapidly with the first receipt of ETSI data in 2229, however, as the nations of the world realized that there was simply no way to fully benefit from the Pelaran data unless they were willing to cooperate — on an unprecedented, global scale.

Christenson always faced the Chair when speaking directly to her, but then turned his back on her to address the other thirteen members on the floor of the chamber. He was never sure whether this bit of subtle theater was lost on the other Council members, but he was absolutely certain that it infuriated the esteemed chairwoman, who expected all debate be directed to her as if she were a queen at court. "Madame Chairwoman, I'll be the first to acknowledge that we have all benefited greatly from the technological bounty that the Pelarans have literally rained down upon us like manna from Heaven," he began with a disarming smile before turning to face the other ten representatives currently present on the chamber floor, "but surely any declarations that give the appearance of committing our planet one way or another are premature, to say the least."

Even with only ten other members on the floor of the chamber, there was a general commotion in the room, including a few rather raucous exclamations of both support and disapproval. "Quiet please, everyone!" Crull said, pounding the gavel and raising her voice to the shrill monotone that had become something of a trademark of hers when speaking publicly. “I will not allow this Council to degenerate into some sort of political free-for-all. Now, Councilman, I know you still have the floor, but surely you’re not asking us to rehash this particular debate. Our predecessors decided nearly fifty years ago how we would respond when the Pelarans made first contact. Don’t you think it’s a little arrogant to imply that our current membership is somehow more qualified than they were to craft Earth’s response?”

“Councilwoman Crull …”

“That’s Chairwoman Crull,” she interrupted.

“My apologies, Madame Chairwoman,” he continued, gratified that he had once again goaded her into showing her true colors. “I don’t think it’s a matter of second-guessing our honorable predecessors. We do, however, have the benefit of fifty years of history to inform our decisions — particularly everything that has happened over the past month. There is no way they could have anticipated the situation we find ourselves in today. Also, since I appear to have placed myself in the position of once again bringing controversial items back to the table, there is still the unresolved issue of whether this body even has the authority to make such decisions or speak on behalf of the entire planet.”

“Oh, please,” she scoffed over the uproar that had once again erupted from the chamber floor, “that’s not bringing up a controversial issue, Sam, that’s beating the deadest of dead horses.”

“That’s Councilman Christenson,” he smirked, turning momentarily so that only she could see his face.

“Of course, Councilman, and I suppose you propose that the mighty United States of America should be the sole arbiter of who communicates with the Guardian spacecraft and what will be said when they do."

"I would never propose such a thing, Madame Chair, as you know very well. I do believe very strongly, however, that the presumption that this body has the authority to act almost in the capacity of a world government falls well outside the bounds of our charter."

"Oh, here we go. I wondered how long it would take for you to toss some red meat to the 'one world government' conspiracy theorists."

"Point of Order, Chairwoman Crull, but you yielded the floor."

"For a question, Councilman, not a political speech."

"Fair enough," he smiled, trying to maintain a positive air in spite of Crull's typically derisive tone, "but this is by no means a settled issue. And now that we find ourselves only a few hours from being forced by events into communicating with the Pelarans, or at least their spacecraft, I hope we can all agree that acting with an abundance of caution is in our world's best interest. Committing ourselves one way or another at this point seems both unnecessary and reckless, in my opinion."

Crull pounded the gavel against its sounding block as the room once again dissolved into chaotic debate.

Earth, Terran Fleet Command Headquarters
(Office of the CINCTFC)

"Welcome, Admiral Naftur, I'm Tonya White — Admiral Sexton's Chief of Naval Intelligence," the CNI greeted warmly with an outstretched hand. "I am so sorry that we were delayed and could not meet your shuttle to receive you properly. I assure you that such lapses in protocol are not the norm at TFC Headquarters."

Although there actually had been a hastily prepared honor guard present, along with a pair of captains thrown in for good measure, Terran Fleet Command's Admiralty staff had been conspicuously absent when Admiral Rugali Naftur's shuttle arrived from the Yucca Mountain Shipyard. After a brief ceremony, where the mostly unnecessary apologies had begun in earnest, the Wek admiral had been escorted into the main Headquarters building, then ushered into Admiral Sexton's outer office by his ever-present Marine guards.

Naftur paused, taking advantage of the translation delay to notice the striking appearance of the female Terran officer as he shook her hand. "Not at all, Admiral White," he smiled. "Indeed, my shuttle was met with a level of ceremony reserved for heads of state on my world. I am deeply honored and grateful for your courtesy, but I understand the gravity of the situation we now find ourselves in, so I beg that you will not trouble with additional formalities."

"You are too kind, sir. Just let me assure you that you are most welcome here, and if you can bear with us while we work our way through today's rather, uh, unusual events, I believe I can promise you the attention your visit deserves." Tonya shot the admiral her best smile, which he enthusiastically returned in kind, along with a deep rumble from within his massive chest that seemed to indicate that he was … *happy? — pleased? — maybe something that doesn't even translate. I'm not entirely sure which,* she thought, inwardly amused.

White had spent enough time in the company of their other Wek guest, Ambassador Nenir Turlaka, to understand that their species didn't just wear their emotions on their proverbial sleeves, they actually communicated them nonverbally in a variety of ways … the cat-like purrs and growls being White's personal favorite. Although she had found their openness a little unsettling at first, she now saw it as a refreshing change of pace compared to the thinly veiled emotions Humans pretended to conceal from each other. In any event, she couldn't help feeling slightly embarrassed and unsure what to say next, so she was relieved when Admiral Sexton entered the room.

"Admiral Naftur — Duke Sexton," he said, also offering his hand. "It's an honor to finally meet you, sir."

"Admiral Sexton, I am pleased to meet you as well, and the honor is entirely mine. Young Captain Prescott asked me to inform you that he will join us in a few hours. I have been impressed with him from our first meeting, but his performance in battle at Gliese 667 was nothing short of exceptional. If he is any indication of the quality of your officer corps, then Terran Fleet Command is a formidable force, indeed."

"That is quite a compliment. Thank you, sir. The situation here has been changing so rapidly that I have not had time to fully digest the details of the battle, but I look forward to having the opportunity to do so. I trust Admiral White apologized for our absence at your arrival? I regret the unfortunate timing on our part, but, as you can imagine, our Leadership Council has been in emergency session since immediately after the Guardian spacecraft arrived. They have kept our entire Admiralty staff fully engaged since then, and I suspect this trend will continue for some time. If you would like to step into my office, we will try to make up for our bad manners with some good food." Sexton beckoned Admiral Naftur towards the sitting area on one side of his inner office, dismissing the two Marine guards to the hallway with a nod.

"I suspect there will be precious little opportunity for sleep in your immediate future, let alone ceremony," Naftur said, taking his seat with a sympathetic smile, "so I will likewise dispense with formalities and proceed with the purpose of my visit. Please interrupt me at any time if something is unclear, or if you need additional explanation."

"Excellent," Sexton replied, nodding. "We are deeply grateful for your assistance. Please continue, sir."

"There are three primary areas where I believe I can provide some meaningful, and hopefully actionable, information," Naftur began. "The first thing I would like to do is provide you with some background information regarding the so-called 'Pelaran Resistance' task force. While there is a certain degree of supposition involved, I have a general idea of the makeup of their forces. Assuming my guesses are largely accurate, I believe I can offer you some idea of their military capabilities as well as their most likely strategy for conducting an attack on Terra."

"That information alone will leave us deeply in your debt, Admiral."

"Unfortunately, Admiral Sexton, the challenges your world faces at the moment are manifold," he replied in a mournful, guttural tone. "It is my hope, however, that we may yet be able to locate the Resistance warships while they are still in the process of assembling their forces. If we can do so, I believe I may have some hope of averting the attack altogether."

"I have no doubt of your sincerity, Admiral Naftur," White began, "but surely these vessels could be just about anywhere. How could you possibly hope to locate their staging area?"

"It would seem so, Admiral White, but this is one of the few circumstances that fall in our favor at the moment. The majority of ships the Resistance is likely to have at their disposal have been commandeered from regions of Sajeth Collective space where the threat of military action is minimal. In many cases, these are older ships nearing the end of their service lifespans, but still useful for missions such as regional patrol or what you might refer to as 'peacekeeping.' Please do not misunderstand the intent of my words here. What these ships lack where modern propulsion or shielding systems are concerned, they more than make up for in terms of raw firepower. In the hands of a competent task force commander, these vessels represent a serious threat, particularly when paired with the command and control systems available on the more modern vessels. Make no mistake, the combined resources of this task force are more than capable of mounting a truly devastating attack on Terra. Having said all of that, when most of these vessels were constructed, the state of the art in hyperspace navigation was much less advanced than it is today. At the time, Wek starships relied on standardized navigational pathways defined by a variety of stellar phenomena such as the X-ray emissions from pulsars.

This provided the accuracy they needed to avoid unfortunate events … transitioning from hyperspace within the interior of a star, for example."

Although never actually employed as a primary means of navigation on Terran spacecraft, the idea that the clock-like regularity of pulsar emissions could be used in such a way had occurred to Humans as well. During the late twentieth century, Pioneer 10 and 11 as well as both Voyager space probes included a pulsar-based "we are here" map. The drawing featured fifteen lines from a common origin, fourteen of which included binary representations of the unique emissions from specific pulsars. The length of each of the fourteen lines provided the relative distance from each pulsar to Sol, while the fifteenth line indicated Sol's distance to the center of the galaxy. A number of scientists had argued that providing a road map to our homeworld might eventually turn out to be a bad idea. Physicist Stephen Hawking was even quoted as saying that an alien visit to Earth would have likely resulted in an outcome similar to Christopher Columbus landing in America … which hadn't turned out very well for the Native Americans.

"So are you saying that these vessels are forced to follow somewhat predictable flight paths?" Sexton asked.

"With an understanding of how their navigation systems were designed as well as the stellar cartography of the region near the destination, yes. A few of these older vessels will likely be traveling to the rally point alone. Since the Sajeth Collective assumes that your world has at least some level of monitoring and early warning capabilities deployed within the boundaries of the system, it is unlikely they will gather their forces less than two light years from Sol. On the other hand, they will also seek to minimize the distance required for their final approach and attack."

"That being the case, how will the older vessels manage the final portion of their journey?" White asked. "Clearly, they will need to be much closer than two light years in order to make their attack run using sublight engines."

"Indeed. When attacking, they will endeavor to transition as close to Terra as they possibly can. This will be accomplished by coupling the navigation systems across multiple vessels. Although this still diminishes the tactical surprise capabilities of newer warships such as the *Gresav*-class, the task force should still be able to transition out of hyperspace within a few million kilometers of Terra. From there, they will approach as closely as possible from multiple directions, saturating whatever defensive systems you have in place with a barrage of missile and kinetic energy weapons fire. In order to achieve this level of navigational accuracy, their rally point will most likely be less than five light years distant."

"If I understand you correctly, we're still talking about the space between two concentric spheres with a radius of two and five light years, respectively, Admiral Naftur. That still sounds like an awfully large volume of space to search for potential staging areas," Sexton observed.

"Impossibly large, given the time we have available," Naftur agreed. "Before leaving the *Gresav*, however, I tasked our AI with simulating the area within five light years of Sol to look for the most likely staging areas. Although the analysis was incomplete when I departed, it was still able to narrow the list to three hundred thirty-six of the most likely locations."

"That still sounds like a pretty daunting challenge, Admiral," White sighed.

"It does, but we have Fleet assets that might be able to work through the list pretty quickly as long as they don't have to remain at each location very long," Sexton interjected, careful to avoid revealing additional classified information in spite of what he knew Admiral Naftur had already observed for himself firsthand. "Let's cover your remaining topics at a high level before I start issuing any orders, but time is of the essence where our search is concerned."

"Very well," Naftur continued. "The second item is one of long-term strategy. There are no doubt many within the Sajeth Collective Governing Council who would deem my actions and continued presence here as nothing short of open rebellion and treason. Fortunately for me," he grinned," the classified nature of my mission prevents my whereabouts from being generally known. In any event, I strongly believe that I am still acting within the bounds of the orders I was given when originally dispatched to the Sol System several months ago. One of the Council's objectives was to establish contact with your world, hopefully leading to formalized diplomatic relations. This was to be accomplished in spite of any interference the Pelaran spacecraft chose to employ. Accordingly, another significant part of my mission was to continue developing tactics to overcome some of its technological advantages. Ultimately, as you can well imagine, we hoped to discover a way to destroy the Guardian ship entirely, even with the knowledge that doing so might well undermine our relations with your world."

"It might at that, Admiral," Sexton chuckled. "Now that we are acquainted, I hope you will seek our counsel before you attempt such a thing. I also recommend that we keep that particular piece of information to ourselves, for now. There are members of our Leadership Council, notably the chairwoman herself, who seem to be in favor of Earth rushing headlong into membership in the Pelaran Alliance. Personally, I have a hard time understanding that position, since we don't yet have any idea what membership in such an alliance would entail."

"Humph," Naftur grunted. "I believe I might be able to shed some light on that question as well, in just a moment. And yes, if I have any say in the matter, Sajeth Collective forces will not attempt an attack on the Guardian without your prior knowledge. Returning now to the topic of charting a path forward, we must develop some sort of contingency plan for how we will proceed over the coming days and weeks. If, for example, I am either unable to locate the Resistance task force or unable to stop their attack on Earth even after locating their vessels, the manner in which we mount our defense of your world could have grave consequences for relations with the Sajeth Collective."

"Forgive me, Admiral Naftur, but I'm not sure I follow. Since we are the ones being attacked, why should the method of our defense be a concern for us?" Sexton asked under raised eyebrows.

“Your question is one of justice and fairness, Admiral Sexton, which is understandable. Unfortunately, such concepts have little bearing on the outcome of the current situation. Although the Resistance task force is not officially sanctioned by the Sajeth Collective, I fear the Governing Council has reached a tipping point — one that will determine their official stance towards relations with Terra going forward. I can assure you that both the Resistance and its sympathizers within the Sajeth Collective do not anticipate that their task force will encounter any Human military resistance during their attack on Earth. They believe the Guardian spacecraft itself represents the planet’s only significant defense, which they hope to decoy and/or avoid altogether during their attack. Furthermore, during the battle at Gliese 667, we did not detect the launch of any communications drones before the Resistance ships were destroyed. So I believe we can safely assume that they were unable to warn the task force of *Ingenuity’s* offensive capabilities.” Naftur paused, drawing in a deep breath and exhaling slowly before continuing. “Having witnessed *Ingenuity* in battle for myself, as well as some of the forces preparing to defend your world, I now believe that Terran Fleet Command might well be capable of destroying the Resistance forces outright. My fear is that such a victory will do little more than serve as a pretext for a wider war.”

“Surely you don’t mean to imply that we don’t have the right to defend ourselves against this unprovoked aggression,” Sexton asked, beginning to feel frustrated at where the conversation seemed to be heading.

"Not at all. Indeed, it is your duty to do so. What I believe we must consider, however, is how the complete destruction of Resistance forces might actually serve to strengthen their cause within the Sajeth Collective. Some within the Governing Council will see Earth's unexpected military capabilities, and their willingness to *use* those capabilities to destroy Sajeth Collective vessels," Naftur held up his hand, anticipating Sexton's objection, " — even though they were used in a defensive role — as proof that the Pelarans will soon begin their domination of this region of the galaxy."

"Using Earth as their proxy," Admiral White observed.

"Just so. Those members of the Governing Council who were previously unsure of their position might then be easily swayed to join those supporting the Resistance. The history of both your world and mine is replete with examples of criminals and traitors who were transformed by circumstance into heroes and martyrs."

"That depends on who is writing the history books, I suppose," Sexton replied, leaning back in his chair and staring at the ceiling as the implications of this latest complication raced through his mind.

"It is invariably the victors who do so," Naftur said gravely. "In any event, the outright destruction of the Resistance task force may well push the Sajeth Collective in the direction of an outright declaration of war against Terra."

"I hope you have some ideas regarding how we might go about overcoming that particular challenge, Admiral Naftur, because this sounds like what we commonly refer to as a 'no-win situation' to me."

"That concept is … unfamiliar to me," Naftur replied with a tilt of his head, "but the strategy I believe most likely to yield an outcome beneficial to both sides is to locate those ships and do what we must to prevent the attack altogether. Failing that, there may be few, if any, options available other than defending your world by whatever means necessary. If that occurs, we must then be prepared to move quickly to intervene with the more reasonable members of the Governing Council in hopes of avoiding an all-out war."

"Very well. Although I am reluctant to ask for more bad news at this point, please continue to your third topic."

Naftur looked at his Terran hosts in turn, as if to assess whether they possessed the mettle to deal effectively with the potentially world-altering decisions now facing them. "Unfortunately, my friends," he sighed, "the last piece of information I have for you also has potentially grave consequences, but it is unclear what, if anything, we can do to address it. As you know, the Sajeth Collective has amassed a significant amount of data regarding the Pelarans and their cultivation program. Although the process has some variation, depending on the species involved, it does appear to proceed along a somewhat predictable path. We have also been able to identify certain tools and tactics used consistently by the Pelarans. Our assumption, of course, is that the program has been implemented so many times that it has become routine to some extent. We have noted, for example, that the Guardian spacecraft will occasionally intervene when unexpected events threaten to derail the process. Otherwise, it tends to remain largely passive. One notable exception involves the communications devices that are used to disseminate highly sensitive information. I trust these devices are being used on Terra as well?"

Admiral White glanced at the Commander in Chief for confirmation that discussing such highly classified information, even in general terms, was something they were prepared to do with a high-ranking military officer from another world. Sexton furrowed his brow, then nodded his tacit approval, keenly aware that they were unlikely to reveal anything about the cultivation program that the Wek officer didn't already know. White smiled politely at Naftur before continuing, "The devices to which you refer are informally called 'talkies' on Earth. The Pelarans have used them as a means of compartmentalizing the most classified information. They are also used as a means of ensuring multinational cooperation, since key pieces of data are communicated only to specific individuals located in different countries."

"The devices are genetically coded to the intended recipient," Sexton added. "We don't really understand how the biometric scan works in any detail. Unlike most of the other technology shared by the Pelarans, the schematics for building these devices provided only enough information to complete their assembly. I can also tell you that they are damned effective at preventing anyone else from accessing them or eavesdropping on the data streams — and I can promise you it's not for lack of trying," he said, smiling wanly.

"Yes," Naftur nodded, "this is indeed consistent with what has been observed on other cultivated worlds. Are you aware that the devices are capable of two-way communication?"

"We considered that it might be possible. In fact, I believe the original plans included what our engineers thought to be a type of transmitter. We, of course, attempted to use it a number of times without success, and then omitted the transmitter from the final design, based on security concerns. No one was comfortable with the idea that individuals might somehow end up in unilateral discussions with the Pelarans."

"My guess is that the component your engineers removed was indeed a transmitter, Admiral Sexton," Naftur replied, "one that they were *intended* to find and remove. Unfortunately, there is another — one of such cunning design that it was clearly intended to be unwittingly included when the devices are manufactured."

There was silence in the room while both Terran admirals took a moment to process this latest revelation. "I don't like where I think this is going at all," White remarked. "So you are telling us that there have been recorded cases where the Pelarans initiated direct contact with the individuals who were in possession of one of these devices?"

"We have not been able to determine whether direct communications have ever taken place with an actual member of the Pelaran race, whatever that might be, or if the spacecraft itself was responsible for the contact. In fact, we have very little intelligence regarding the nature of whatever communication took place. We believe, however, that these Guardian spacecraft are so sophisticated that they have achieved some level of self-awareness. If you were to engage one in conversation, it would most likely be difficult to perceive that you were speaking to a thinking machine."

Human engineers had demonstrated something of an inherent talent for computer science since its advent on Earth in the early twentieth century, so the idea of a "sentient" machine wasn't particularly surprising to the TFC admirals. For well over three hundred years, Earth's processing power had continued to increase at the rate predicted by the so-called "Moore's Law," roughly doubling every two to three years. Although Gordon Moore himself predicted in 2015 that the pace would slow significantly within ten years, the exponential growth had continued unabated. The relentless progress was due in part to occasional quantum leaps in integrated circuit design inspired by the study of "Grey-enhanced" artifacts (which Moore, understandably, did not factor into his projections), but the primary driver had always been a natural Human aptitude for the field. As a result, Earth's computing power continued to grow at a rate more than double that of most post-industrial civilizations. Modern artificial intelligence systems represented the crowning achievement of over three centuries of such progress. As powerful as Human computing systems had become, however, none had reached a level that was considered "self-aware." The systems were capable of self-improvement on a number of levels and perhaps even what might be considered rudimentary consciousness. Self-awareness, on the other hand, implied not only an awareness of oneself as an individual, but also an introspective understanding of what was implied by that awareness. While seemingly a minor, even academic distinction, it still represented a thus far unbridgeable gap between man and machine.

"Let me make sure I understand. You have evidence that the Guardian spacecraft were somehow engaged in direct communications with these individuals, but you have not been able to determine the purpose of these conversations?" Sexton asked.

"Once again, what I can offer along those lines is based more on speculation than hard intelligence. We do know that the devices seem to be intended more for data acquisition than direct contact. Each device maintains a continuous data stream with the Guardian spacecraft. We really have no way of knowing how much information they are capable of gathering, but we can infer that they are incredibly effective. The biometric scans you mention, for example, do much more than simply identify the intended user. They seem to provide a sophisticated biological and psychological profile of every individual within its operating range. We believe it is this data that ultimately allows the Pelarans to exert the level of influence required to persuade a world into joining their alliance."

"The Pelaran equivalent of a Trojan horse," Sexton remarked. "In our defense, Admiral Naftur, I feel obligated to tell you that we have been extremely careful with these devices. Even though they are keyed to a single individual, they are only accessed in the company of others, and always within the confines of a highly secured facility."

"I have no doubt that you have taken the precautions you deemed appropriate, and I assure you that there is no implied criticism in my revealing this information to you. The Pelarans, of course, correctly assumed that such security measures would be undertaken, so the technology built into the devices is more than sophisticated enough to hide their intended purpose. Our chief concern is that they would not have gone to so much trouble unless they were attempting to conceal some sort of espionage. At the very least, their behavior seems to indicate the pursuit of an agenda they would prefer to shelter from the light of public scrutiny."

"Possibly," White replied. "Although our first contact protocols emphasize the idea that an alien race is likely to have very different notions of what they consider appropriate. The fact that the Pelarans went to such lengths to hide the true purpose of these devices is troubling, however. Most of the individuals the Guardian selected to receive them are members of the scientific and engineering community, in addition to a few military and government representatives. I believe we always made the assumption that their selection was based solely on their role in working with Pelaran technology, but clearly there was much more to it than that."

"We made similar assumptions on Graca concerning how we believed 'alien' races would behave during a first contact situation, Admiral White. Over time, we learned that most species intelligent enough to cross interstellar space and visit another world have remarkably similar ideas regarding what is and is not considered appropriate," Naftur smiled. "I do not believe, for example, that any species seeking a transparent, open dialog with another would hide their intentions in this manner. I will say, however, that we have seen no evidence that the Pelarans have engaged in any overt acts of espionage. The intent of the devices seems a bit more subtle. Apparently, the Pelarans seek to develop a level of influence sufficient to ensure their success before any formal communications ever take place. Accordingly, there are always a few individuals who become instrumental in assisting the Pelaran effort to induct their world into the Alliance."

"So let me see if I can sum up this final point," Sexton said. "The Guardian spacecraft has most likely developed highly detailed information that allows it to wield significant influence over individuals in positions of technological, governmental, and military leadership around the world. These individuals could very well be in some kind of contact with the spacecraft, but we do not know the nature of that contact, nor do we know exactly how this influence is being used to further the Pelaran agenda." Sexton paused, shaking his head while staring at the floor in thought. "I'm sorry, Admiral Naftur, I'm afraid I am at a loss as to what we are supposed to do with this information."

"I wish I had more to offer you. In fact, I seriously considered not revealing this information for that very reason. I recently read an old proverb of yours, however, that seemed to fit the situation. It said, 'praemonitus, praemunitus … forewarned is forearmed.' Perhaps you should consider publicly revealing this knowledge in the hope that it might mitigate the Pelaran influence somewhat."

"Perhaps, but this situation is already developing so fast that I'm afraid we may find ourselves committed to following a path not entirely of our choosing."

Chapter 5

TFS Jutland, Earth Orbit
(0605 UTC - Primary Flight Control)

"Attention on the hangar deck, this is the Air Boss. Stand by for a forty-eight-spacecraft launch event. This will be a rapid-turn, simultaneous launch utilizing all eight elevators — two *Hunter* RPSVs per elevator, sixteen ships per cycle, and three launch cycles. Spacecraft-handling officers report readiness and expect a green deck in zero four minutes."

Commander David Waffer scowled as he studied the bank of view screens lining the front wall of TFS *Jutland's* Primary Flight Control, or "Pri-Fly," while draining his fourth cup of coffee in the past two hours. The carrier had barely been in space for twelve hours, but, gratifyingly, she had still managed to maintain a fairly steady pace of flight operations during that time.

Within minutes of the ship's arrival in Earth orbit, Admiral Patterson had issued an order that at least two, four-ship formations of C-Drive-equipped *Hunter* RPSVs were to remain on patrol at all times. Waffer knew the admiral to be an extraordinarily detail-oriented officer, so he took it as a sign of just how overloaded everyone was at the moment that he had overlooked the fact that only the *Jutland* currently had any C-Drive-equipped *Hunters* aboard. Under normal circumstances, it would not have been particularly taxing for the ship to sustain heavy flight operations over an extended period of time, and keeping eight *Hunters* in continuous operation hardly constituted a challenging launch schedule in any event. The problem had more to do with the *Jutland* herself. At over a kilometer in length and with a displacement of six hundred and two thousand metric tons, she and her sister ships were easily the most complex vessels ever constructed. Now, without the benefit of a shakedown cruise, she was being asked to perform at an operational tempo traditionally required of planet-side carriers only after having been at sea for a year or more.

"Hey Nilla, any word on additional *Reaper* ops?" one of the F-373 pilots called from the bulkhead pressure door, his upper body leaning into the room from the corridor. The call sign "Nilla" had been an all too obvious choice for Waffer. A number of his fellow pilots had even commented over the years that the moniker was a perfect match for his personality, even without the added benefit of his last name. The same analogy did not apply to the Air Boss's flying, however, where his skills were likened to that of a true artist of the rapidly disappearing trade.

"Not for the moment, no. We'll continue to keep two sitting ready-five, but I doubt we'll put up a manned combat air patrol for a while. I suspect the admiral will continue the hold on nonessential flight ops until after the meeting at 1000 Zulu."

"Oh yeah, we heard about the conference call with our friend GORT out there. Sure hope that one doesn't go sideways on us," the pilot chuckled. The name "GORT" had recently gained popularity among the rank and file members of Terran Fleet Command, who had grown tired of constantly referring to the Pelaran vessel as "the Guardian spacecraft." GORT was a reference to the often remade classic science fiction movie "The Day the Earth Stood Still," in which a giant robot of that name was said to be powerful enough to destroy the Earth. As if that weren't enough, one of the movie's remakes even referenced the fact that GORT was actually an acronym for "Genetically Organized Robotic Technology." Appropriate or not, it seemed to be a name that was destined to stick.

"Well, if it does go sideways, I doubt we'll be around long enough to worry about it much anyway, so whatever. At least I'll get some rest," Waffer laughed. "Speaking of that, the CAG was in here a little while ago. Please let everyone know that he expects there will be quite a bit more activity within the next twenty-four to forty-eight hours, so they need to get some rack time while they can," he said, referring to the commander of the *Jutland's* air wing, still generally known as the "CAG."

"Will do, Commander. You might want to do that yourself, sir," he replied, allowing the bulkhead door to close as he headed back in the direction of his squadron's ready room.

"Right," Waffer muttered to himself. "I'll get right on that."

"Commander Waffer, three spacecraft handlers report a red status," his assistant, often referred to as the 'miniboss,' reported. "We're still having a pressurization problem on elevators four and eight, and one of the birds is showing a fault on one of its HB-7c missile racks."

Not for the first time this morning, Nilla drew in a deep breath and then exhaled slowly through pursed lips, commanding himself to relax and focus. "Tell them they have zero three minutes to sort it out and report back. Otherwise, let's reconfigure the launch event for six elevators and add another cycle. If they can't fix the missile fault, disarm that rack or replace the spacecraft. I really don't care which as long as we get this launch event underway soon. You can count on a call from the admiral otherwise."

"Aye, sir. They're on it."

As useful and truly versatile as the ubiquitous RPSVs were, less than twenty percent of the fleet were made up of the newest "Block 3A" version, which included a variety of improvements — most importantly the addition of a C-Drive as well as C-Drive-equipped HB-7c missiles. Out of the over four hundred RPSVs deployed across the various Fleet ships now on station in the vicinity of Earth, only one hundred and twenty were the latest model. So far, Admiral Patterson had ordered eight of these to be on continuous patrol and was now sending forty-eight more to search for the Resistance task force. These two relatively simple missions had already committed nearly half of their most capable RPSVs … not even taking into account the inevitable need for spares. It wasn't so much that the original *Hunters* weren't quite capable in their own right — and with over three hundred of them available, they still represented one of TFC's most important military assets. Without hyperdrive capabilities, however, earlier versions of the RPSV were limited to missions in the general vicinity of their mother ships. By comparison, the Block 3A upgrade provided a reconnaissance and strike capability with virtually unlimited range, rendering the previous models painfully obsolete less than a year after the first *Hunter* had rolled off the assembly line.

Outside, on the carrier's massive flight deck, four teams wearing EVA suits very similar to those used by TFC Marines struggled with the uppermost set of elevator bulkhead doors. Elevators four and eight were the largest of the ship's eight elevators. Each was designed to transport ships up to the size of *Ingenuity*-class frigates from the cavernous, pressurized hangar deck below to the flight deck during launch and recovery operations. Still largely based on technology that would not have seemed out of place centuries earlier, the mechanically-actuated doors were now providing a perfect example of the types of problems normally addressed during a ship's shakedown cruise. Thus far, in the brief but eventful history of Terran Fleet Command, however, there had been little time available for such luxuries.

"Air Boss, EVA1," came the call from the lieutenant in charge of the flight deck maintenance crews.

"EVA1, go for Air Boss."

"Commander, it's a no go for the top bulkhead doors on both of these lifts. We might be able to risk it in an emergency, but that would leave just one set of locking doors between the hangar deck and a hard vacuum. Seeing as how those doors are pretty much the same as the ones that are having problems, I don't think it's worth the risk. Elevators four and eight are inop until further notice."

"That's not good news, Lieutenant. How long do you expect it will take to fix them?"

"It's not a repair we really want to attempt in EVA gear, sir. I'd categorize it as more of an installation problem than a typical break/fix situation. In space, this will take a week or more if we work on it around the clock. At Yucca, both lifts can probably be fixed in a day."

Waffer paused to think through the implications of this latest problem. The main consequence would be losing the capability for larger ships to take advantage of the carrier's hangar deck as an in-space repair depot. As far as combat ops were concerned, however, there should be minimal impact — assuming the remaining six elevators remained operational, that is. "Alright, EVA1, seal the lift tunnels and get your people inside. We'll talk it over in staff and probably raise the question to Admiral Patterson, but I agree that it seems like an unnecessary risk at the moment."

"Sorry about that, sir. Will do. EVA1 out."

"Alright, there you have it," Waffer sighed. "Go ahead and reconfigure the launch event for six elevators and four cycles. We need those RPSVs away immediately."

"Aye sir, already done," his assistant replied. "Handlers now reporting a green status. They pulled two HB-7c missiles off the bird with the fault, so it's good to go with six missiles aboard."

"Very well. Green deck, get 'em out of here."

With the first cycle of the launch event now imminent, automated warning announcements from *Jutland's* AI echoed through the hangar deck: "*Attention, launch event commencing. Clear elevators one through three and elevators five through seven for immediate departure. Lift operation in six zero seconds."* On the floor of the hangar deck, six spacecraft directors, still commonly referred to as "bears," stood poised next to their respective elevator platforms with one arm in the air to indicate that their area was clear and safe for lift operation. Just a few meters away from each bear, one of the first six pairs of *Hunters* sat poised for takeoff near the center of their lift platform — reactors, engines, and flight systems fully online. Since each two-ship formation would be conducting reconnaissance at a distance of two to five light years from Earth, they were configured to operate in a completely autonomous manner after leaving the carrier. Each pair would be responsible for surveying fourteen individual regions of space. Even in a worst case scenario where their last recon target turned out to be the staging area for the Resistance task force, the operation was expected to take no more than six days to complete.

"Pri-Fly, bridge."

"Air Boss here. Go for Pri-Fly."

"Sorry to interrupt you, Commander Waffer," came the apologetic call from the on-duty bridge comm officer, "but we just got a message from the Flag asking what the holdup was on the *Hunter* recon flight op."

Well shit ... I guess I knew that was coming, Waffer thought cynically. "Understood. Please apologize for the delay and let Admiral Patterson know that the launch event is underway now. The first twelve *Hunters* will be away momentarily."

"Thank you, sir. Bridge out."

Waffer turned to look at his assistant, shaking his head. "Just so you know, I'm gonna say it was your fault," he chuckled.

"No problem, sir. That's what minibosses are for."

Simultaneous launch and recovery options were once somewhat rare aboard planet-side carriers. This was primarily due to the fact that such a large area of the flight deck was required for catapult-based launches and arresting-gear landings. Non-concurrent or "cyclic" launch and recovery operations also provided an added safety factor by building in additional separation between aircraft during the most critical (and dangerous) phases of flight. This had changed significantly as vertical takeoff and landing capabilities became the norm for carrier-based aircraft in the late twenty-first century. Much more recently, the advent of gravitic systems for "zero mass" approaches and landings, as well as advanced AI-based control of aircraft during approach and landing now provided the few remaining Earth-bound carriers the capability to rapidly launch and recover large numbers of aircraft. The result of this strange technological progression was a remarkable similarity between carrier-based flight operations, whether on the surface of the sea, or in the depths of space.

"Attention, launch event initiated. Lift operation in five … four … three … two … one …" the ship's AI announced. "Stand by for launch cycle two, commencing in three zero seconds."

All six of the *Jutland's* operational flight elevators rose simultaneously until each platform's surface was flush with the carrier's flight deck. Less than two seconds later, after a final confirmation of each of the RPSV's mission profiles, the carrier's AI granted autonomous control to each individual spacecraft. The *Hunters* then took an additional second to synchronize with the second spacecraft in their individual formations before running their own final set of pre-launch systems checks. In the silence of space, the departure had the look of a highly choreographed ballet routine as all twelve spacecraft slowly rose from the flight deck as one before each pair headed off in different directions, gradually increasing their speed to gain separation from the *Jutland.* A mere fifteen seconds after reaching the carrier's flight deck, the space around all twelve RPSV's distorted slightly as each spacecraft disappeared in a small flash of grayish-white light.

TFC Yucca Mountain Shipyard Facility

Having spent the past hour in the shipyard's command center with Captain Oshiro, Prescott made the long trek back to Berth Nine, where an ant-like line of technicians was already busily transferring equipment and supplies from *Ingenuity* to *Theseus*. He had not yet had the opportunity to complete a walk-around inspection of either ship, and was about to do so when he noticed Commander Reynolds standing alone at the end of one of the gangways connecting *Ingenuity* to the wharf. She was so engrossed in the information displayed on her tablet that she did not even notice her captain's approach.

"Where do you want all this stuff, lady?" he asked in his best, albeit poor, imitation of a gruff longshoreman.

Reynolds scowled without looking up at first, then glared at him over the top of her tablet. Expecting her captain to be well on his way to TFC Headquarters by now, it took a moment for his presence to fully register in her mind. Somewhat startled and embarrassed, she came to attention, tablet now at her side. "Oh, I'm sorry, sir," she replied, obviously flustered at this point. "I didn't expect you to be here and my mind is in about seven different places at the moment."

"That's quite alright, Commander," he laughed. "I'm impressed with how fast this transfer effort has gotten underway. There must be five hundred people working between these two ships."

"Over fifteen hundred total," she said proudly, "and that's just shipyard personnel. Captain Oshiro also let me have my pick from the six *Theseus*-class crews he has on standby. I probably didn't win us any friends there, but I didn't have a lot of time to waste."

"What did you do, Sally, strip every ship of their best people?"

"I wasn't quite that greedy, but I did end up grabbing five or six people from each ship with the highest overall eval scores for the specific roles we needed. I kept all of *Ingenuity's* original ninety-seven crewmembers, so we needed a total of one hundred and eighty-one more. All but twenty-seven of those came from the crew previously slated for the *Theseus*. The rest I shamelessly pilfered from the other five ships."

"Well, it's very rare that you get that kind of opportunity, so I guess it's fine. I might need to smooth out some ruffled tail feathers, though, so please send me the list of personnel you looted, as well as who you looted them from, so that I can start buying back some goodwill with favors of some sort. Any word on the Marine spec-ops unit?"

"They're coming straight from a big training exercise at Camp Lejeune, North Carolina tomorrow. Get this, they are specialists in boarding actions and tactics. I obviously knew that all TFC Marines were well-trained in EVA ops, but I had no idea that they still considered boarding and 'cutting out' actions to be likely scenarios for space-based units."

"Yeah, I've seen some footage from one of their demonstrations. It could end up being a pretty handy skill set under the right circumstances. I believe they still refer to those missions as VBSS, for visit, board, search, and seizure. A few months ago, I would have argued that we'd never run into a situation where that would come into play, but I guess I've already been proven wrong there. Master Sergeant Rios and his troops have had that training as well. On that subject, I asked Admiral Patterson that Rios and his assault section be integrated with our new platoon of Marines, but he couldn't make any promises. Did you see anything about him being reassigned?"

"No sir, he'll be staying on as the platoon sergeant. That's usually only a staff sergeant billet, by the way, which is probably one of the reasons they are sending us a first lieutenant as a platoon commander. I believe we will have a total of forty-three Marines, including the lieutenant and Rios."

"Outstanding. I'm really glad to hear that."

"I was too, sir, but you haven't even heard the best part yet. They're also bringing along four of their brand new *Gurkha* assault shuttles."

Prescott rubbed his chin thoughtfully. "That *is* good news. Those should provide our smallish Marine platoon something like the punch of a larger heavy weapons unit. I don't think we'd be getting this particular unit equipped with those new *Gurkhas* unless Admiral Patterson had something specific in mind, though. Please make sure their first lieutenant finds me as soon as he arrives. Hopefully, he'll be able to provide some additional insight."

"Aye, sir."

"You're just full of all kinds of good news. I keep waiting for you to get to the part where you start telling me everything that has gone wrong already."

"I'll get to that, just let me finish the positive stuff first," she smiled. "The *Gurkhas*, as well as all twenty-four of our *Hunters,* are C-Drive equipped. I can promise you that Captain Oshiro must have stripped those from other vessels. Those other destroyers down there, for example," she said, nodding towards the five additional *Theseus*-class destroyers in Berths Twelve through Sixteen, "are all scheduled to launch within the next week or so. They are getting no Marines, no *Gurkhas*, and only four C-Drive-equipped RPSVs each."

"Jeez, Sally, I'm afraid we're going to have a lot of senior captains with their noses out of joint."

"They'll get over it, sir. Besides, we're 'first and best,' remember?" Reynolds had come up with the "first and best" motto during *Ingenuity's* shakedown cruise. Although it seemed to have a different meaning at the time, the phrase now seemed destined to follow Captain Prescott and his crew, regardless of which ship they served aboard.

"Uh huh. I doubt they'll see things in quite the same way we do."

"By the way, why are you still here?" she asked with a suspicious, sideways look.

"Oh, right, I guess I didn't mentioned that yet, did I? The main reason is that I asked to be excused. The families of the crewmen we lost will be here later today, and I'm planning to spend some time with them." Prescott paused, looking down at the ground momentarily before staring directly into Reynolds' eyes. "I've reviewed the logs, Sally. We probably could have made another C-Jump and avoided the missile that killed those people."

"No, I really don't think …"

"Yeah, it's the truth," he interrupted. "What's really strange is that I'm okay with letting myself off the hook for that. It was in the heat of battle, we were low on power, we hadn't really trained for the scenario … whatever. What's bothering me is that I didn't know a single one of them," he said, tears now clearly visible in his eyes. "They were aboard my ship for almost two months — they died as a direct result of decisions I made — and I can't remember ever having a conversation with any of them."

Reynolds simply nodded, trying her best to offer a look not of sympathy, but of understanding. "Look, I'm not going to stand here and insult you by telling you that's okay. You and I both know it's not. What I *can* do is help you make sure it doesn't happen again. There are a number of things we can do along those lines. It's just going to take some time, particularly since we just tripled the size of our crew." She paused, watching to see what kind of impact her words were having. Once she was satisfied that Prescott was recovering a bit, she continued. "So I'll take responsibility for helping us to avoid this problem going forward. You good with that?" she asked, smiling and desperately hoping to change the subject.

"Yeah, I'm okay. Thanks … you're probably the only person I'd ever tell something like that." Prescott smiled, took in a deep breath, and made what seemed like a smooth transition back to their previous conversation. "Anyway … based on my request and what Admirals Sexton and White learned when they started debriefing Admiral Naftur, they flagged me off for the trip to HQ. They also reiterated in the strongest possible terms that our first priority is getting *Theseus* ready to depart as quickly as humanly possible … preferably quicker," he said. "So, at the risk of getting pushed over the side of this wharf, I am obligated to ask you …"

"How soon we can leave?" she interrupted, with an exaggerated roll of her eyes. "I *need* at least a week, but since I know that's not going to happen, I'd say a minimum of seventy-two hours, based on what I've seen so far."

"Commander, that sounds completely reasonable to me, but what I'm asking you to do right now is proceed as if you are expecting something completely unreasonable. Structure your thinking and then prioritize your tasks as if we're going to be forced to take her into battle on a moment's notice."

Reynolds took in a quick breath and opened her mouth to object.

"Relax," he interrupted in a firm, but soothing tone. "I'm not saying that's what's going to happen, but it just might. We're on a war footing right now, and we just happen to be the only crew available with combat experience. We may also be Fleet's best and only chance to avoid a shooting war with the Sajeth Collective. Admiral Naftur thinks that if we are unable to prevent the Resistance task force from attacking, and then we end up destroying their forces in detail, it may push the more moderate members of the Collective towards all-out war against Earth."

"Well it's not like we can just allow them to attack."

"Exactly. And if they do attack, I have no doubt in my mind that the old man will make damn sure we wipe them out completely. So our mission will be to do everything we can to prevent the attack from ever happening, if at all possible. The *Jutland* has *Hunter* recon flights out looking for the Resistance staging area right now. I suspect they will send us out with Naftur to meet them as soon as their forces are located."

Reynolds paused and stared in the direction of their new ship for a moment. "It's actually a little difficult to wrap your mind around the gravity of what we're doing. But all that aside, doesn't it bother you that we've never flown that ship before?" she asked, jutting her chin in the direction of the massive destroyer looming large on the far side of *Ingenuity*.

"How hard could it be?" Prescott laughed. "Captain Oshiro did give you the keys, right?"

"Oh, that's hilarious, sir. We're doing old pilot training humor again now, are we?" she smirked, referring to a practical joke that had been a favorite of military flight instructors since the mid-twentieth century. Before the student pilot's first flight, and usually after a long trip out to the waiting aircraft, the instructor would pretend to become irritated with the student for forgetting the keys. Typically, the hapless student was then given a tongue-lashing, along with explicit instructions to go and ask the unit's commanding officer for the non-existent keys which, of course, usually led to an even more comprehensive tongue-lashing.

"If you don't think *that's* funny, then you've obviously never seen it play out in real life," Prescott smiled nostalgically. "Okay, in all seriousness, that ship intimidates me a little as well. I mean, just *look* at her," he nodded. "Under the circumstances, though, we're going to have to take the Fleet Science and Engineering guys at their word that if you can fly the frigate, you can fly the destroyer. I do want you to schedule some time for our bridge crews to all be in the sim together, however, and that includes the two of us, if at all possible."

"Will do, sir," she sighed. "We'll just have to do the best we can in the time we have available."

"That's all we can do."

"One more thing I forgot to mention, I managed to cobble together some of my notes as well as the tactical assessments from our engagement at Gliese 667. The big things I thought our crews should know about regarding Sajeth Collective vessels were the limited field of fire on the big cruisers, their vulnerability to kinetic energy rounds, and the weaknesses their shields seem to have near the sublight engine nozzles. I also included all of our weapons' effectiveness data and some specific commentary on our use of the C-Drive-equipped missiles."

"Excellent. I'm sure that's exactly what Admiral Patterson was looking for. Go ahead and send it."

"Already done, sir. Believe it or not, he insisted on it being distributed via courier and designated 'FOR CAPTAIN'S EYES ONLY.'"

"That doesn't surprise me, given the sensitivity of the information. Thank you, Commander. I know I'm asking a lot of you, but I'm confident you're up to the challenge," he said. "Oh, one last thing. I need you to make sure our people are getting some rest too. Your hotshot, stolen crew won't do us much good if they're all asleep at their posts when we launch."

"Sounds great, Captain. In fact, I think I'll go grab a nap right now."

"Not you, XO. You can sleep when you're dead," he replied, already heading up the gangway towards one of *Ingenuity's* port-side entrances. "I'll check back with you later. I've got a couple of things to wrap up here, then I'm heading next door to find Logan and make sure he's not sleeping either."

Chapter 6

Hunter Formation "Nail 42," Interstellar Space
(2.3 light years from Earth)

The two-ship RPSV formation transitioned into normal space within just a few centimeters of their expected coordinates, their AIs' navigational accuracy having already benefited from data gathered during *Ingenuity's* trip to the Gliese 667 system. Within milliseconds of their arrival, both ships commenced an exhaustive search of the surrounding space, utilizing every active and passive sensor at their disposal. Rather than each ship searching the same, spherical volume of space, each was responsible for a hemispherical, dome-shaped region expanding outward from their current position at the speed of light. Although there was nothing that could be done to increase the speed of their search, coordinating their sensor coverage in this manner did at least offer the benefit of doubling the effective power transmitted as each ship scanned its own area of responsibility.

Unfortunately, not only were there three hundred and thirty-six potential rally points to search for the Resistance task force, but each individual location also came with its own degree of uncertainty. Having tasked the *Gresav's* AI with narrowing the search, based on the somewhat predictable navigation pathways favored by older Wek vessels, Admiral Naftur had also directed the system to determine the smallest effective search radius that could be used at all reconnaissance locations. Accomplishing this required the AI to account for a truly staggering number of variables including both the exotic: space-time distortions caused by Sol's bow shock wave as the star plowed through the interstellar medium, to the more mundane: the most likely deceptive tactics a Resistance commander might use to defeat exactly this type of search. With all known variables taken into account, the AI determined that the radius of each "recon bubble" should extend 11.33 billion kilometers. The AI further specified that passive scans should allow time for "new light" to be received from the entire search volume in order to provide the highest probability that any ships within the recon bubble would be detected. Once found, observing the enemy ships' movements over a period of time might also provide clues as to how their forces would eventually be deployed during an attack. In spite of these advantages, gathering "new light" was a slow process. Had a passive sensor snapshot been considered sufficient, the scan could have been executed almost instantaneously — much like a three-dimensional photograph of the area — which would have also allowed the *Hunters* to limit their potential exposure to enemy forces.

The use of active sensors presented an entirely different set of challenges for TFC mission planners. Although new techniques were under development that promised the capability of detecting distant targets in real-time using technology similar to Near Earth Real-Time Data Network (NRD) comm beacons, the active sensor suite aboard all current Fleet vessels relied on a much more traditional approach. A variety of signal types were transmitted across the search area and any return signals were then analyzed in an effort to detect the presence of ships or other anomalies. Since active sensor scans forced a vessel to wait for a return signal, the search radius was limited to only half that of a passive scan during a given period of time.

There had, in fact, been a spirited debate among the engineers at TFC Headquarters as to whether active sensors should be employed on this particular mission. Those opposed argued that the *Hunters'* passive sensors were more than adequate for the job, based on the size and number of warships expected to make up the Resistance task force. Active sensor emissions would only serve to alert the Resistance vessels that they had most likely been detected. As fighter pilots had been fond of saying for centuries, "Whoever lights up first, gets smoked." In the end, it was decided that using the *Hunters'* active sensor suites was worth the risk. There was a high probability that the enemy ships would be located near the center of one of the three hundred thirty-six recon bubbles. If that was indeed the case, an active scan would not only make their detection a virtual certainty, but would also provide a wealth of data that could then be used to plan for Earth's defense. Active scans were also capable of detecting the minute disturbances associated with vessels "parked" at a fixed location in hyperspace, although Admiral Naftur had indicated that this tactic was not one typically utilized by Sajeth Collective forces.

Now, for the next ten and a half hours, the two *Hunter* RPSVs would simply wait as the visible sphere of space surrounding their position expanded at just over one billion kilometers per hour.

TFC Yucca Mountain Shipyard Facility

On his way back to *Theseus*, Prescott finally took a few minutes to survey the damage to his ship. Since there was nothing in his (or any other Human being's) previous experience to use as a comparison, he had no idea what to expect. Nevertheless, the damage was much more extensive than he would have guessed. To put it mildly, the ship was a mess. The most visually striking aspect of the damage was that it seemed to cover the entire hull. In fact, it looked as if there wasn't a single square centimeter he could have walked up and touched that had been unaffected by thermal damage of some sort. As energy weapon bolts had struck the hull, those with sufficient power had melted, or even vaporized, layers of armor until their energy was consumed. Each time this had happened — and it had obviously happened many, many times — molten metal had splattered the surrounding area and then quickly re-solidified, resulting in a general disfigurement of the frigate's once proud appearance.

As Prescott made his way around the bow, he noticed a repair crew that appeared to be assessing the missile impact damage to *Ingenuity's* starboard hull. As he approached, what he saw above halted him dead in his tracks. He had in fact walked this same path immediately following *Ingenuity's* landing several hours earlier, but in his rush to get the process of transferring his command underway, he had been too distracted to notice the extent of the damage until now. The missile impact area was located nearly forty meters above the level of the wharf, where the uppermost section of the ship's hull smoothly transitioned into her dorsal surface. For several minutes, Prescott paced back and forth along the platform between *Ingenuity* and *Theseus*, craning his neck in an attempt to get the best possible view. He was simultaneously fascinated and shocked by what he saw. Although from an engineering perspective Prescott had a general idea of how nuclear-tipped missiles designed to detonate in the vacuum of space were configured, he had, of course, never had the opportunity to see the damage caused by such a weapon. By and large, the weapons were designed to generate what might be referred to as a massive, nuclear-powered plasma cutter. To create this effect, materials included inside the body of the missile and within the warhead itself flash-vaporized to produce a shaped-charge jet of ionized plasma traveling at over half the speed of light. In an ideal case, the missile would be situated so that the center of this superheated cone would come into contact with the target's hull at very close range. Luckily for *Ingenuity*, and most of her crew, the missile had been thrown off course at the last moment and forced into opting for a proximity detonation rather than missing its target altogether. The orientation of the warhead had channeled the blast along a path roughly parallel to the upper section of the ship's starboard hull, resulting in the majority of its destructive power streaming harmlessly away into space. Even a glancing blow from the atomic fury unleashed by the weapon had caused a level of damage that was truly frightening to behold, however. Although it seemed like a strange analogy, the area of impact reminded Prescott of the way a new box of ice cream looked after someone had taken a particularly generous first scoop. The damage began on the side of the ship with some scoring and a shallow scar, growing progressively deeper towards the top of the hull. At its deepest point, it appeared that nearly the entire two-and-a-half-meter-thick hull had been gouged away. An involuntary chill ran down the length of Prescott's spine as he considered the catastrophic structural failure that could have occurred if the angle of impact had been modified just slightly …

"We got awfully lucky, there, sir," Kip Logan said, unintentionally startling his captain as he approached from behind. He had noticed Prescott staring pensively at the damage and thought it appropriate to give him a few moments to be alone with his thoughts before starting a conversation. "Sorry about that. I thought you saw me."

"No, that's alright, Commander. I was about to come find you anyway. This is the first time I've had a chance to take a look at the damage. I guess I was in my own little world there for a few moments."

"Understandable, Captain. It's actually quite a bit worse than I thought at the time, and I should have known better. We have pretty much one hundred percent visibility of the hull when we're in space, but most of the optical sensors are collocated with the close-in weapon system turrets. We lost three of those to the impact, so the video feeds lacked the fidelity they usually have. It looked like we had lost a meter at the most, but still had several of the outer armor layers intact. See that deepest point up there at the top where it looks a little shiny in the middle? That's her inner hull, so there was only thirty centimeters or so between us and an explosive decompression."

"So we probably had no business straining her with a combat landing," Prescott said.

"I probably would have said no, just to be on the safe side, but we were still in pretty good shape structurally. It's just a good thing we didn't take another hit in that area, that's all," Logan chuckled, trying to lighten the rather dire tone of their conversation a bit. "I gotta tell you, though, *this* thing is a *beast*," he said, turning and gesturing with both hands towards TFS *Theseus* on the opposite side of the wharf.

"It's funny you would refer to her that way. Captain Ogima Davis on the *Navajo* said exactly the same thing about his ship earlier today."

"'*Navajo*-Actual' said that? You do know he's an actual Navajo, right?" Logan laughed. "If I were him, I'd call myself "actual Navajo" every time I got on the radio."

"You might not as a junior captain with a vice admiral who just happens to be the chief of naval operations looking over your shoulder."

"No, I guess not, but you have to admit it's a pretty cool coincidence. In all seriousness, Captain, the *Navajo*-class cruisers are incredibly powerful weapons platforms, but until they receive all of the upgrades *Theseus* here has, they couldn't touch us in a fight. One on one, we would absolutely tear her to pieces. In fact, I'm guessing we would be more than a match for several *Navajo*-class ships."

Prescott stared, incredulous, assuming that his chief engineer was either still joking around or indulging in a bit of false bravado on behalf of his new ship. "Well, I'm pleased that you are so enthusiastic about your new charge. I'm a little embarrassed to admit that I have barely had time to even begin digging into her systems, but surely she's not that much more potent than the *Ingenuity*-class."

"Don't worry too much about wading through the owner's manual, Captain, I've got you covered. I'll be briefing our bridge crews and senior staff on quite a few of the new systems tomorrow," Logan replied, smiling broadly. "But, no, I'm not exaggerating in the least. The reason Fleet delayed the destroyers out of the gate was to equip them with the newest and best of everything we have available tech-wise. If it wasn't for the situation with the Resistance, none of our ships would have launched until integration with the most critical of these new systems had been completed. Pulling together the data needed to do some final tweaks and calibration was one of the main drivers behind everything we were asked to do with *Ingenuity* over the past couple of months."

"Alright, you're forcing me to show my ignorance here, but you're mainly talking about the shield systems, correct?"

Logan paused and looked around furtively to ensure that no one was close enough to overhear their conversation.

"It's okay, Commander, the classification level of this entire facility has been raised to MAGI PRIME. With all of the new systems coming online, it had reached a point where it just wasn't possible to work aboard, or even in the vicinity of one of our ships without having the highest level of clearance. Otherwise, we'd have no business having this conversation out in the open like this, even if we didn't think anyone was within earshot."

"You're right, of course," Logan replied with a suspicious grin. "You were testing me with that question, weren't you?"

"Not really, no," Prescott laughed. "I'm way too tired for that, but it's always good to be reminded of how easy it is to create a breach of classified information. So, you were saying ..."

"Right, the shields are most definitely at the top of the list, and they will make up the lion's share of what I'll be covering tomorrow. It's not just the shields, though. Pretty much every system has been improved. Power-handling is dramatically better, for example. *Theseus* has six antimatter reactors, each of which generates about fifty percent more power than both of *Ingenuity's* combined. During combat ops, assuming all six reactors are online, we should be able to dedicate three of them to propulsion and the other three to weapons. So at any given time, there should be plenty of power available for firing all of our weapons more or less continuously while at the same time always having the option to C-Jump out of the area, if needed. I'll even go so far as to say that we should have an excess of power available, even if only four of the six reactors remain online."

"That's a major improvement alright. I'm assuming the reactors used for weapons will also feed the shields."

"Yes and no. I probably mischaracterized how things actually work when I mentioned dedicating reactors to certain systems. One of the biggest improvements is that the AI is now able to continuously vary how much power is being used by and routed to any given system.

It's set up with a number of default priorities that we can tweak over time, but with such an excess of generating capacity available, you'll probably never realize how big of a deal it is until we get in a situation where we only have one or two reactors online, God forbid. As far as the shields go, it's not far from the truth to say that the same power used for weapons is also used for the shields, since they don't technically operate at the same time … at least not in the same area, if that makes sense."

"It doesn't. So are you saying we still lose our shields when firing the weapons? I thought the Science and Engineering Directorate guys had found some sort of workaround for that."

"Alright, sir, you're starting to steal my thunder from tomorrow's briefing."

"Oh, right. Sorry about that, Cheng. I'm sure we'll both be better able to grasp the more technical aspects of this discussion after some much needed sleep."

"Well that's new, you hardly ever call me 'Cheng,'" Logan chuckled. The term originated from the abbreviation for Chief Engineer and was still sometimes used aboard naval vessels as a substitute for the officer's name and/or rank as well as an informal show of respect for the important position.

"I've called you much worse," Prescott replied with a wry grin.

"True enough. Just let me sum up by saying that under anything like what we might consider 'normal circumstances,' it could easily take a century or more of progress to go from the capabilities of *that* ship, to *this* ship," Logan said, pointing behind Prescott towards

Ingenuity and then gesturing in grand fashion towards *Theseus*. "I know that seems a little ridiculous, but it's all about where we are on the timeline of implementing all of the newest Pelaran and Grey-enhanced tech into each individual ship. Luckily, all four classes were designed to accommodate the systems that were already in the pipeline, so now it's just a matter of retrofitting each ship as quickly as possible. Before *Ingenuity* over there is ready to go back into space in a few weeks, she'll be a completely different animal than the ship we took into battle."

"Well that may be, but she served us pretty well, don't you think?"

"Yes indeed, sir. She did at that."

TFS Navajo
(0950 UTC)

"Admiral Patterson," Ensign Fletcher called from the opposite side of the *Navajo's* Combat Information Center, "I've got a secure laser comlink signal from the Guardian spacecraft — audio only. It's addressed to you personally, sir."

"Silence on deck!" Patterson bellowed.

The CIC typically had an air not unlike that of a library. The subdued lighting, as well as the ever-present threat of a lurking flag officer, had a tendency to suppress the sound of conversation in the room to the point where little more than the background rumble of the ship's engines punctuated by the hum and occasional chirp of electronic systems could be heard. As the time for the expected contact from the Guardian had approached, however, the room had become uncharacteristically noisy and chaotic.

"I'm about to open a channel with this thing and I need this room quiet and focused. If you don't have a good reason to be here, now would be a good time to excuse yourself," he announced in a tone that sent several officers quietly hastening for the exit. "Any changes that we can see, Lieutenant?" Patterson asked the young female officer at the holographic display in the center of the room.

"None, sir. The target has maintained its current position for over nine hours now. We have detected no emissions since immediately after we discontinued all of our active scans."

Patterson noted the tactical officer's use of the word "target" to describe the Guardian spacecraft with deep satisfaction. *You're damn right it's a target ... hostile until proven otherwise.* "Very good, Lieutenant. Ensign Fletcher, open the channel please."

"Aye, sir," she replied, followed immediately by a chime indicating an active comm channel had been established.

"This is Admiral Kevin Patterson aboard the Terran Fleet Command starship TFS *Navajo*." Patterson paused, having no idea what to expect.

"Good morning, Admiral Patterson," came the immediate reply. The voice was male, undeniably friendly in tone, and to the CNO's ear, seemed to have the rather bland, unaccented English of the American Midwest where he grew up. "The purpose of my call is merely to confirm that your ship is prepared to act as a relay for my conversation with your Leadership Council at 1000 Zulu. I also wanted to take the opportunity to reassure you that your forces are in no danger whatsoever. Well … no danger from me at least," it chuckled.

Patterson wasn't entirely sure what he was hearing. Did this thing just laugh at its own joke? Somewhat taken aback and unsure how to respond, he glanced at Ensign Fletcher, his narrowed eyes communicating what everyone within earshot was wondering … *what the hell?* The young ensign arched her eyebrows and shrugged noncommittally, happy that she wasn't the one who had to decide what to say next.

"I, uh … I'm happy to hear that. I, likewise, hope that we have not given the impression that we mean you any harm."

"Oh no," it laughed, as if such an assertion was humorous, based simply on how ridiculous it was. "Your considerable forces have kept a respectable distance and have obviously been working very hard to avoid doing anything provocative. I realize that's quite a challenge for a ship of war, so I appreciate the sentiment. Please feel free to carry on with whatever operations you have underway. It is my understanding that Terra is under threat of attack from forces belonging to the Sajeth Collective. I noted, with interest, the departure of a significant number of your scouting vessels a few hours ago. May I assume that their mission is to pinpoint the location of the enemy vessels?"

"As I'm sure you can understand, I am not at liberty to discuss military operations without specific instructions to do so from the TFC Leadership Council," Patterson replied. *Well, I guess that settles the question as to whether our secure communications are compromised,* he thought bitterly. *And it wanted to make sure I knew it too.*

"A wise and understandable precaution, Admiral. I hope we will have the opportunity to discuss this situation further after our meeting with the Council. I'm especially interested in learning how you managed to acquire the intelligence that appears to be guiding your search efforts. But no matter, please continue to deploy your forces as you see fit."

Uh huh, you know damn well how we know, Patterson thought. "Thank you," he answered in as pleasant a tone as he could manage. He was already annoyed at the prospect of needing to mince words with this alien machine, and even more irritated that it had just condescendingly granted "permission" for him to do his job. "To answer your first question, yes, we will be happy to provide secure comlinks between yourself and all of the other participants in the call."

"Oh, it is far more than a mere 'call,' Admiral Patterson. This will mark the beginning of your world's induction into the greatest alliance of civilizations in the history of our galaxy. Today will ultimately be recorded as the single most important day in the history of your world."

"Well then," Patterson replied, clearing his throat, "that being said, I am honored to assist you in any way I can. We will establish secure comm with all parties in just a few minutes."

"Thank you, Admiral Patterson. I look forward to working with you. Guardian out."

Chapter 7

Earth, Terran Fleet Command Headquarters
(1000 UTC - Leadership Council meeting chamber)

"Attention all Terran Fleet Command vessels and facilities, this is Ensign Katy Fletcher aboard Admiral Kevin Patterson's flagship, TFS *Navajo*. This vidcon is classified Top Secret, code word MAGI PRIME. All recipients of this data stream are responsible for ensuring that a secure environment, appropriate for this classification level, exists at your location. We have established a secure laser communications link with the Pelaran Guardian Spacecraft, which is standing by to join the call. Please note that the Guardian's feed will include audio only at this time. Control of the comlink will transfer to Karoline Crull, Chairwoman of Terran Fleet Command's Leadership Council in three … two … one."

There was a brief moment of silence as control of the vidcon signal passed from the *Navajo's* Combat Information Center to the lectern Command console in front of the Leadership Council's meeting chamber. Crull, who had been staring at her image on the small screen, allowed an additional moment of dead air before realizing she was now addressing the Leadership Council, the senior military leadership of Terran Fleet Command, and, for the first time, the Guardian Spacecraft itself. "Hello," she began hesitantly. "I am Chairwoman Karoline Crull. On behalf of Terran Fleet Command's Leadership Council, and all of Humanity, it is an honor to welcome you to our world."

Just a few meters away, Samuel Christenson felt the hair on the back of his neck stand on end as he contemplated the potential damage that Crull might do, intentionally or not, simply because she was arrogant and naive enough to believe herself entitled to speak on behalf of the entire planet.

"The honor is entirely mine, Chairwoman Crull," the Guardian began agreeably and without any hint of hesitation. "I bring you greetings on behalf of hundreds of worlds, many of which were fortunate enough to have been chosen for membership in the Pelaran Alliance in the same manner as Terra. Before we continue, please allow me to address a concern some of you might have regarding my status as a representative of the Alliance. I am what your people might still refer to as a synthetic or, God forbid, an 'artificial' life form," it said in a tone a parent might use when preparing to relieve a small child of an adorable, but potentially dangerous misconception. "On all of our member worlds, I am afforded the same level of recognition as a sentient being that any of you would be as a matter of course. I recognize that this idea takes some getting used to, and I bring it up now only to reassure you that I am fully empowered to speak on behalf of the Pelaran Alliance as an ambassador. Now," it continued, transitioning smoothly back to a tone of voice one might use when speaking comfortably to a close friend, "let us return to the business of welcoming your people into the fold, so to speak. This date will echo through time as the single most important day in the history of your species, and I am deeply honored to have been given the opportunity to take part in it with you. To say that we have much to discuss is a monumental understatement, so I am anxious and excited to get started."

"Thank you, uh," Crull stammered. "I'm sorry, what is the appropriate way to address you? Do you have a name … a title of some sort?"

"Humans, you may address me as 'Supreme and Mighty Celestial Emissary,'" it replied, deadpan. On the floor of the meeting chamber, as well as in the viewing gallery surrounding the room, there were murmurs of disapproval accompanied by the sound of people shifting uncomfortably in their chairs.

"I see. Thank you, Sup—"

"I'm kidding!" the Guardian interrupted, once again clearly amused by its own attempts at levity. "My God, and you were going to say it, too. I have to tell you that the historical records contain hundreds of variations of that joke coming up during induction proceedings. It's one of those classics that never gets old."

Just under five hundred officers and civilian officials from Terran Fleet Command were participating in the live vidcon. Most exchanged dumbfounded looks with their neighbors, none having expected anything resembling what they had heard so far.

"Well, I, uh, I'm happy to see that you have a sense of humor."

"Of course. If you think any sentient being, biological or otherwise, can spend hundreds of years alone in space without the benefit of a sense of humor, then we have much to teach you about behavioral psychology. In the interest of full disclosure, however, I can tell you that the use of humor has been part of what you might refer to as our 'first contact' protocols for a very long time. If you're interested in truly getting to know another species, one of the most revealing things you can do is to study what they find humorous."

"And what did you learn about us, based on our sense of humor?"

"Oh, a very great deal indeed, Madame Chairwoman. Understand that I've been out here observing for a very long time — just over five hundred revolutions around your sun, in fact. Over such an extended period, societal norms that tend to govern humor undergo significant change. What's interesting about your species, is that, to a large extent, you find humor in practically *everything*. And *that*, my friends, is a gift that is largely unique — even among very advanced and so-called enlightened civilizations. It should be celebrated … nurtured …"

"Cultivated?" Christenson interjected, already growing tired of the Guardian's rather smarmy tone, especially in light of the seriousness of the current situation. There were a few audible gasps, followed by a moment of dead silence in the meeting chamber. From behind her lectern, Crull shot him a look that could have melted steel, incensed that he would dare to speak without her explicit permission.

"Ah, Councilman Christenson, I presume," the Guardian began again, its voice taking on a decidedly darker tone. "The last thing I want to do is put a damper on such an auspicious occasion as this, but I find your use of that term particularly interesting. In fact, I have never once included that word in any of my communications with your species … other than referring to myself as a 'GCS,' which actually *does* refer to the Guardian Cultivation System in your parlance. I have specifically avoided the term because I believe it has a somewhat negative connotation, particularly in the rather ambiguous English language your world seems to prefer. I'm sure you will agree that, in a situation such as the one we find ourselves in at the moment, misunderstandings should be avoided as much as possible. Yet I can't help but wonder where you might have stumbled upon that term," the Guardian paused, allowing time for the implication to be fully realized by all those in attendance. "It is of no immediate concern, however," it said, resuming its bright, friendly tone. "As I said, this should be a day of celebration. There will be plenty of time to explore the details of matters such as this at a later date."

"I apologize for the interruption," Crull said, still furious and now also justifiably concerned that a major breach of information security had just occurred. "I believe you were about to tell us how we should address you."

"Yes, as to that, I am open to suggestions. I hope you will find me easy to communicate with, and not easily offended. In some cases, organizations such as yours suggest some sort of contest where the world's children vote on their preference, but, really, can anyone here think of anything more tedious?" it laughed. "Some of your military members have taken to calling me 'GORT.' Now, you see, *that's* a great example of the Human sense of humor. An apt reference, in my opinion … I love it."

"I am truly sorry. I'm sure they meant no offense. I will personally make sure that does not happen …"

“Nonsense,” the Guardian interrupted. “As I said, I am not easily offended, and that reference is not only fitting, but it’s all in good fun. In any event, if you are looking for a Human-sounding name to call me, how about ‘Griffin?’ I’ll admit to being a fan of Terran mythology, and the Griffin was a majestic beast said to be the king of all creatures — part lion, part eagle. Like dragons, they were said to be known for guarding hordes of treasure and priceless possessions, which, in a manner of speaking, is precisely why I was sent here in the first place. Besides,” he chuckled, “there’s one on our flag.”

“A griffin? On the flag of the Pelaran Alliance? But how is that even possible?”

“Ah, well, I expect that will be one of a great many topics that symbolic anthropologists will be poring over for the next several centuries,” he said. “Without getting too far off topic, I can tell you that there are common threads among the mythologies and their accompanying symbols of most intelligent species. That’s especially true when the species have quite a bit in common. When you consider that symbology tends to arise from how people interpret the world around them, it makes sense that similar species would come up with similar symbols.”

“So you’re saying that we are similar to the Pelarans, then?” Crull asked.

“That, Madame Chairwoman, would be an understatement, but let’s handle one earth-shattering revelation at a time, shall we?”

“Very well,” she replied after a moment. “Griffin the Guardian it is, then.”

“Perhaps we should just stick with ‘Griffin,’ but, yes, that should work nicely. Now, about this time, someone will typically ask the question, ‘What happens next?’ so, if you will permit me …”

“That was, in fact, my next question,” Crull interjected.

“Induction into the Pelaran Alliance can be a bit tricky from both a societal and political perspective. That’s particularly true for a world such as yours where there is no worldwide governmental body, per se. That’s because the more enlightened civilizations tend to follow a path of self-determination, which implies that most people are reasonably happy with their current form of government. Well, that is, happy enough that they will typically resist any significant change orchestrated by someone they perceive as an ‘outsider,’ which certainly applies in this case.”

Christenson arched an eyebrow at this, but reserved comment for the moment. He was keenly aware that his one-word contribution to the discussion, while justifiable, had probably been foolish and ill-timed on his part. The last thing he wanted to do was provide Crull with sufficient cause to mount some sort of campaign to have him ousted from the Leadership Council. He stared at her surreptitiously for a moment and noticed that she was sweating profusely. Odd. He could think of a great many adjectives to describe Crull, but nervous was certainly not one of them.

“So,” the newly dubbed “Griffin” continued, “that is one of the fundamental reasons we insist that our Regional Partners — and by that, I mean civilizations like yours that are invited to join the Alliance —

establish an organization such as your Terran Fleet Command once we begin the process of sharing our technological data."

"Is there some sort of formal invitation process?" Crull asked.

"There is indeed. After we have concluded here today, I will transmit a series of documents that, together, constitute our official offer of admission. Most of them are simply informational, but there are also copies of the actual legal documents we typically use when inducting new members. You are, unfortunately, already familiar with the Alliance's tendency to use rather legalistic documentation," he sighed. "I do apologize for that. Honestly, if there is any one thing I think we can and should improve within our organization, it's reducing the level of bureaucracy."

Christenson pressed a button at his console, providing an indication at Crull's lectern as well as on the floor of the meeting chamber that he wished to speak. She paused and stared at him for a moment as if toying with the idea of ignoring him completely. He was a popular representative, however, both publicly and among the other members of the Council. She also knew that, now that he had formally requested the floor, she ultimately did not have the authority to prevent him from speaking. Not yet, anyway.

"Griffin, I believe we have a question from the floor," she said pleasantly. She then stared momentarily at Christenson through narrowed eyes as an obvious warning that he was on very thin ice at this point.

"I expected we might," the Guardian replied. "I will do my best to answer questions for as long as you feel is necessary. I will tell you, however, that many of the questions you have now will probably be answered within the context of the documentation I'm about to provide. In any event, fire away … I'm guessing you'll get tired of asking before I get tired of answering."

"Thank you," Christenson said, coming to his feet. "Assuming that membership in the Pelaran Alliance is something we, as a planet, would like to pursue," he paused, taking the measure of his fellow Council members, "would you please take a moment to explain how we would go about the process of getting something like that approved? I'm sure you are aware that Terran Fleet Command has no authority along those lines, and, furthermore, Humanity has never even attempted to agree to something like that on a worldwide basis."

"That's an excellent question, Councilman Christenson, and does a great job of getting at the heart of the most common problem facing many prospective members. First off, yes, I do agree that Terran Fleet Command does not have sufficient authority to approve membership in the Alliance on behalf of Earth. You do, however, make decisions affecting the entire population of your world every single day, do you not?"

Christenson paused, not having expected such an immediate and direct challenge to the essence of his argument. "Within the context of our charter, yes, I suppose we do."

"You do indeed. I will further suggest that your charter implies a significant level of latitude in making those kinds of planetary decisions. Just as an example, the vast majority of Humans believe that Terran Fleet Command is largely a scientific organization, and that your ‘fleet’ consists of precisely one unarmed frigate. I assume that the long series of decisions that brought you to that state of affairs was made without the need for some kind of mass, planet-wide voting process. Am I correct?”

The corners of Crull’s mouth turned upwards in a barely concealed smirk.

“Although I have not agreed with all of the decisions that have brought us to this point, yes, that is correct,” Christenson replied. “Other than our being elected, or appointed in some cases, to our positions on the Leadership Council, we do not require the approval of our respective member nations in order to make decisions on their behalf.”

“Oh, I would not expect any duly elected representative to always agree with the decisions of their organization at large. Nor would I expect the people you represent to always agree with how you choose to represent them. Such, dear Councilman, is the nature of government by proxy. In any event,” the Guardian continued, satisfied that the momentum of the discussion was now in its favor, “a few minutes ago, I mentioned self-determination among individual nations. We believe strongly in this concept, be it at the local, state, nation, world, or Alliance level. Where membership in the Alliance is concerned, this can be accomplished in a variety of different ways, but the end result must be that the majority of Humanity as a whole must be in favor of membership, preferably by a two-thirds majority.”

“I doubt seriously you could get two-thirds of Humanity to agree that you even exist. So what do you propose?” Christenson asked, still holding the floor.

"Point well taken, Councilman," he said agreeably. "Although there are historical precedents for a global vote, most nations on Earth are accustomed to some form of representative government. In cases such as this, each nation's decision typically falls to the governmental body empowered to enact treaties on their behalf. In the case of your nation, for example, I believe the Senate will conduct the vote, hopefully based on the wishes of your people. Each nation's decision will then be weighted in direct proportion to their population. Since Terran Fleet Command is generally seen as trustworthy by the public, I recommend you take a lead role in disseminating information so that people can make an informed decision."

"I'm sure our membership would be happy to help distribute the information once we have had the opportunity to review it," Crull spoke up, anxious for Christenson to sit back down before he managed to cause his second "interstellar incident" of the day. "I'm afraid that I have to agree with my colleague, however. The Pelaran Alliance has shown a level of generosity towards our world that we can never hope to repay. Still, I don't have a great deal of confidence that the public at large will be particularly keen on the idea of membership. I believe many will see it as a threat to our world's sovereignty."

There was a discernable period of silence on the comlink as if the Guardian were considering how best to answer a particularly difficult question. "At the risk of concluding our first conversation on an ominous note, I feel it's important for you to understand that no civilization has ever declined an invitation to join the

Alliance. I suppose such a thing is possible, but would require us to examine a number of … shall we say … *legal* issues surrounding Humanity's use of Pelaran technology. In any case, let's not burden ourselves with such an unlikely outcome," the Guardian said dismissively. "After all, the only reason your population might be concerned about a threat to what they perceive as your world's 'sovereignty' is that they still labor under the illusion that Terra is an isolated island surrounded by an infinite, peaceful sea. For their own benefit, it is time they were permanently relieved of that rather childish notion. Leave that to me."

Chapter 8

Earth
(The following day — worldwide data stream broadcast)

Twenty-third-century communications being what they were, practically any news or entertainment of widespread, general interest was available to most of Humanity in real-time. The lines separating various forms of popular media had long since blurred, resulting in a single, global communications network, readily accessible on devices ranging from the ubiquitous tablet to the wall-sized displays present in most homes and businesses. Accordingly, it took only a single call from an "unnamed Terran Fleet Command source" to one of the leading commercial news corporations in order to alert the entire planet that the Guardian was about to make its first public announcement. In an unprecedented feat of modern, global communications, over seven billion of the planet's twelve billion Human beings (and two Wek) were watching live as the Guardian finally made "his" public debut.

The video feed began with an unassuming podium centered in the front of what appeared to be a tasteful, if somewhat plain, conference room — similar to those found in any corporate setting the world over. The only real decoration in evidence was the now familiar dark blue flag bearing Terran Fleet Command's seal to the speaker's left, and another, unfamiliar flag in the place of honor to the speaker's right. At precisely the top of the hour, a door on one side of the room opened and a young, athletic-looking Human male entered and strode confidently to the podium. His appearance was neat, but rather casual. His hair and skin tone made his ethnic origin difficult to guess. In fact, like the multicultural avatars used for centuries to represent popular commercial products, his computer-generated visage was carefully crafted to look like all Human beings, while at the same time looking like no one in particular.

"It's such an honor to finally have the opportunity to appear before you in person, so to speak, and communicate with each of you directly," he began, flashing a disarming smile. "We've actually been together for a great many years, you and I, and I'm pleased that the time has finally come for the next phase of our relationship. You see, I have been right here in your neighborhood doing the job for which I was created since long before any of you hearing my voice today were even born." As he spoke, the camera position and framing changed in a perfectly choreographed dance, highlighting his charismatic delivery and reinforcing the emotional impact of his words. "Nearly five hundred of your years have passed since I had the pleasure of seeing your beautiful world for the first time.

"Much more recently, over the past fifty years or so, my work here required me to make my presence known by sharing some of our technology with you. Since then, you have probably heard me referred to as simply 'The Guardian.' That's certainly fine, and it's an apt description of one of the primary reasons I was sent here. If you prefer something a little more personal, there are a few people who have started calling me 'Griffin.' This name is a reference to a creature from Human mythology that is remarkably similar to one used as a symbol for the

Pelaran Alliance. Yes, I know the idea of being on a first name basis with, uh, well, with some sort of 'thinking machine,' might seem a little strange at first. That's okay. I'm pretty easy to get along with and we'll get used to one other in no time.

"Now, I'm guessing if I could allow each of you to ask your top three questions, one of the most common ones would be precisely what I'm doing here in the first place. That's certainly a fair question. After all, this is your world and it's easy to understand how my presence here might be viewed as an unwelcome intrusion. If you will indulge me for a few minutes, I'd like to respond to that question by describing my mission in a broader sense.

"You could think of my work here as having three distinct objectives or phases. The first was to act, as my original title implied, as your world's guardian and protector. That part is fairly self-explanatory. Once your civilization was chosen as a candidate for membership in the Alliance, and I'll get to that in a moment, my first priority was to protect you until you reached the point where you were able to defend yourselves. That brings us to my second objective. When I judged that the time was right, I began acting as your guide and advocate. The most obvious way this was accomplished was by providing the information necessary to accelerate your technological growth. I hope it doesn't sound condescending for me to observe that your civilization has grown and matured in a wide variety of areas over the past fifty years … and not just where technology is concerned. You have worked together as a global society on a truly massive scale, and Terran Fleet Command is perhaps the most dramatic and visible evidence of your success.

"Finally, my address to you today is an example of my third role — acting as an emissary on behalf of the Pelaran Alliance. I will do my best to be transparent and honest with you in accomplishing this objective. For example, I can tell you without reservation that I hope to eventually convince you to become our newest member world. Simply stated, I think you're ready, and Terra's membership will reap tremendous benefits, both for you and for the Alliance as a whole.

"At this point, you might be thinking, 'You've told us what you're doing here, but not why you're doing it. Why here? Why now?' Well, as you can imagine, that's a complex topic with more detail than I can possibly share with you today, but I'll try to summarize as best I can. I've also started the process of making much more detailed information regarding the Pelaran Alliance available through Terran Fleet Command's Leadership Council. I encourage each of you to spend some time familiarizing yourself with some of our history and how the Alliance is organized.

"As to why Earth was selected, there are a great many reasons. The Alliance takes the process of inducting new members very seriously, and there is an exhaustive process used to identify candidate civilizations and then vet them over an extended period of time to ensure a good fit. In our long history, no member civilization has ever left the Pelaran Alliance, and that's largely due to our selection process. I won't bore you with a long list of criteria, but we look at everything from location, to natural resources, to the intelligence and temperament of candidate species.

"In Earth's case, one particular trait made your offer of membership much more likely. I have occasionally referred to you as 'Children of the Makers.' That title has a very specific and powerful meaning within the Pelaran Alliance. The Pelarans themselves are actually a single species that now reside on a great many worlds. When they first achieved faster-than-light travel and began exploring the galaxy, they chanced upon a world inhabited by a species with a genetic makeup that was nearly identical to their own. Even in an infinite universe, I think you will agree that such a coincidence is … unlikely, to say the least. Since then, many such species have been discovered. Sadly, even after millennia of study, the origin of these — what I believe you would refer to as Humanoid — species remains a mystery. Although a great many tantalizing clues have been discovered, the only certainty is that each of their homeworlds was seeded by some precursor civilization. The Pelarans refer to this parental species as the 'Makers,' and finding them remains one of our greatest aspirations.

"Incidentally, before I go any farther, I should explain that you might occasionally hear me also refer to the Pelarans as 'The Makers.' You'll have to forgive me, but this is something of a play on words. Sentient systems, like myself, who were created by the Pelarans, sometimes also refer to them as 'makers' as a show of respect and affection. Perhaps it would be more accurate for those like me to be called 'grandchildren of the makers,' but I suppose that would be even more confusing," he chuckled, clearly pleased with the turn of phrase.

"In any event, the fact that your species shares a common genetic heritage with the Pelarans places Terra in a position of special significance. The Alliance makes offers of membership at a variety of levels, or ranks, if you will. Most new members are inducted as what we refer to as 'Regional Partners.' Only after several centuries of productive membership can they petition for full membership. As 'Children of the Makers,' however, Humanity will be offered full membership from day one.

"And just what benefits does membership in the Pelaran Alliance provide? Again, I can't possibly give this subject the time that it deserves, but I will begin by telling you that a great many of our member civilizations credit their decision to join the Alliance with their very survival. In fact, I believe most of our members would tell you without hesitation that the first and foremost benefit of membership is security.

"To date, Terra has received only a small fraction of the technological data to which every member world is entitled. Once you do, I can assure you that Humanity will be more than capable of defending itself against any threat you are likely to encounter. In the event something unexpected occurs, your allies stand ready to come to your aid. Earth need not face a violent galaxy alone and, thanks to your status as a candidate member, has not done so for quite some time. There are many other benefits, of course — access to vast trade networks, the cultural riches of hundreds of worlds, and tremendous quality of life improvements, to name a few. For example, the average life expectancy for member species sharing your genetic heritage has now reached one hundred sixty-four years, well over fifty percent longer than yours is today. I realize that may sound like more of a curse than a blessing for a crowded homeworld, but Earth now stands ready to begin colonizing many worlds in this region of the galaxy. Although Humanity is already quite … uh … shall we say fruitful in terms of birth rates, adding significantly more productive, healthy years to your lifespan will prove a tremendous benefit.

"I could go on for hours, but it's now time for me to conclude our time together by addressing the 'Why now?' question I mentioned earlier. I realize that I will most likely anger a few of my friends in Terran Fleet Command by releasing some information that is not widely known outside their organization. Under the terms by which the Pelaran Alliance has granted technology to your world, however, it is within our prerogative to reveal certain details when we believe it is in either our, or your, best interests." With that, the video feed switched to footage of TFS *Ingenuity* inside her berth at the Yucca Mountain Shipyard. The picture was carefully cropped to ensure that no other vessels, nor the scale of the shipyard facility itself, were evident within the field of view.

"My friends, I wasn't exaggerating when I mentioned the need to ensure Earth's security — her need for a strong defense — her need for *allies* willing to come to her aid, when necessary. To illustrate, I believe by now that most of you are familiar with Terran Fleet Command's first operational starship, TFS *Ingenuity*." The camera started with a zoomed-out view of the frigate's starboard side, then slowly zoomed in and panned the worst of her battle damage in detail. “What most of you probably do *not* know is that, only a few short months after her launch, *Ingenuity* has already been heavily damaged in a brutal, unprovoked attack. Regrettably, the damage you see here resulted in the first Terran Fleet Command personnel being lost in the line of duty.” The image now switched to an overhead view as a procession of Marines slowly carried three coffins draped with flags bearing TFC’s official seal down one of *Ingenuity’s* port gangways.

There was a long pause, during which the haunting sounds of the Marine honor guard’s rhythmic steps, punctuated by an occasional command echoing across the vast shipyard, were all that could be heard. “On behalf of the Pelaran Alliance, I would like to express our deepest condolences for your losses. Those willing to put themselves in harm’s way to defend their fellow citizens deserve nothing less than our humble appreciation and sincere respect for their dedication and sacrifice. Truly, I wish I could tell you that your membership in the Alliance would mean the end of such sacrifice. Unfortunately, you need look no farther than your own history to know that such will never be the case. Indeed, the terrorists who attacked your vessel represent the most immediate threat, but they are only one of several potential enemies in this region of the galaxy. Terra’s somewhat remote location, in addition to my presence here, has provided a degree of protection for centuries. Unfortunately, as Earth’s neighbors have advanced, her relative isolation no longer provides the security your people deserve.” The video feed then returned to “Griffin’s” podium just in time to see him look off to the side for a moment — giving the impression that he was struggling to keep his emotions in check, or perhaps summoning the resolve to continue.

"The answer to 'Why now?' is that the external threat posed by neighboring hostile civilizations has reached a point where I alone can no longer provide adequate protection for your world. One month ago, I intercepted and destroyed an attack force from a group of planets known as the Sajeth Collective. At the time, they were just minutes away from reaching a position where they would have been able to execute a devastating attack on Earth … and by 'devastating' I am referring to nothing less than Humanity's extinction." Griffin paused again to allow the gravity of his words to weigh heavily on his audience before continuing. "Even though there are seven civilizations in the Sajeth Collective, their military is dominated by a hyper-aggressive race known as the Wek. Just a few weeks later, it was they who ambushed TFS *Ingenuity* during her very first mission beyond the bounds of the Sol system. It was they who caused the senseless deaths of the three brave crewmembers you just witnessed arriving home for the last time. Indeed, had it not been for the skill and resourcefulness of *Ingenuity's* captain and crew, they would surely have all been lost.

"The answer to 'Why now?' is that, at this very moment, Terra lies under threat of an imminent attack from the Sajeth Collective — an attack that I do not believe I am capable of stopping without your help. I am fully aware that my appearing before you today for the first time bearing such dire news might give you the impression that I am some sort of an alarmist. You might even assume that my goal is to use fear to persuade you into joining the Pelaran Alliance. My friends, if that were my goal, I could have easily done so long ago. Indeed, I wish the situation were truly that simple. Ironically, I believe the Sajeth Collective has chosen to target you because it is *they* who are afraid. For one thing, they fear the dissolution of their fragile alliance for lack of resources — resources most easily acquired by taking them by force from neighboring star systems. They have cast a greedy eye towards your beautiful, blue world, believing that they now have the capability to eliminate me, then easily enslave or exterminate all of you before claiming Terra for themselves. Their *greatest* fear, however, is of what you may soon become. They have some knowledge of the Pelaran Alliance and understand that your membership will ensure that they will never again have the opportunity to simply take your world, or to threaten other less powerful, neighboring civilizations with the same.

“The answer to “Why now?’ is that they, and indeed most of you, do not yet know what you have *already* become,” he said, increasing the power and confidence of his delivery with every word. “It has been nearly fifty years since your scientists first began detecting signals from space. I think most of you will agree that the data I have provided on behalf of the Pelaran Alliance has literally transformed life on your world. Now, don’t misunderstand me here. Your civilization had already reached levels of technology that very few manage to achieve on their own, well before you received the first streams of data from the sky. Once they begin receiving our data streams, many of the worlds offered membership in the Alliance make tremendous progress within a short period of time. Your achievements, however, have reached a level that is, in many ways, unparalleled in the history of the Regional Partnership program."

Once again, the video stream changed to display images skillfully selected to support the ongoing narrative. Short clips recalling various Pelaran-derived technologies with which most Humans were now familiar filled the screen. These ranged from the prosaic — day-to-day images of advanced food production techniques and medical diagnostics equipment — to the truly mind-boggling — automated spacecraft providing virtually limitless raw materials from the asteroid belt and gigantic transports hovering effortlessly before whisking several thousand people at a time to the opposite side of the globe in a fraction of the time previously required. As the video progressed, the images changed more and more rapidly to further emphasize the staggering pace of technological progress Earth had experienced over the last five decades.

"The answer to 'Why now?' my friends …" the Guardian said, pausing dramatically as the video feed returned to a view of TFS *Ingenuity's* port side. The camera started at the level of the wharf, rising steadily above the top of her hull and expanding to include a view of TFS *Theseus'* imposing side profile in the adjoining berth. "The *answer* is that your friends in the Pelaran Alliance have seen to it that you no longer have anything to fear from the Sajeth Collective, nor anyone else, for that matter." The camera again increased in altitude, the image now expanding to reveal the five additional *Theseus*-class destroyers preparing for launch along with the massive scale of the shipyard facility itself. The on-screen image faded briefly to black, only to be replaced by the awe-inspiring perspective of a location just above TFS *Navajo's* hull as her nearly kilometer-long bulk passed below, revealing the carrier *Jutland* in the background. Seconds later, twelve *Hunter* RPSV's launched simultaneously from six of her eight massive flight elevators. The camera remained fixed for several additional seconds until all twelve *Hunters* transitioned to hyperspace in unison.

"No, my friends. If we can continue to work together as trusted allies, it is *they* who have something to fear."

Chapter 9

Hunter Formation "Nail 42," Near the Neptunian Orbital Path
(4.2 light hours from Earth)

Had there been any Humans aboard either vessel in the two-ship RPSV formation, the tedium of C-Jumping from one target location to the next, then sitting motionless for over ten hours' worth of sensor scans, would long since have exceeded their attention spans. The two spacecraft — collectively known as "Nail 42" flight — each had their own, individual call signs of "Nail 42" and "Nail 43." Since the formation functioned as a single entity, however, it was referred to by the designation of the lead spacecraft.

Twenty-four identical formations of *Hunters,* launched from the carrier *Jutland,* were now well into the fifth full day of their reconnaissance missions. Thus far, there had been no sign of the Resistance task force — just a few false alarms caused by anomalous sensor readings that had turned out to be nothing more than naturally occurring phenomena.

With NRD-equipped surveillance drones and comm beacons now being deployed in ever-increasing numbers throughout the solar system, communications and reconnaissance coverage was steadily improving. At this point, practically any location inside the Kuiper belt, beginning just over four light hours from Sol, enjoyed something approaching real-time communications. Unfortunately, anything farther out was still plagued by the ever-present limitation imposed by the speed of light.

The Oort Cloud, for example, stretched from 139 light hours out to approximately 1.6 light years from Sol — well over a third of the distance to Proxima Centauri. Even though still very much in the local stellar neighborhood, there was currently no practical way to communicate with vessels at such distances … short of deploying more beacons or sending another ship out to act as a relay. So it was that the mission profiles of each *Hunter* formation called for a C-Jump back to the nearest NRD network node after visiting each reconnaissance location. This resulted in a progress report being sent back to the *Jutland* roughly once every ten and a half hours.

With its latest survey completed, "Nail 42" flight transitioned into normal space with two simultaneous flashes of light. Right on schedule, the two spacecraft established an NRD net connection using a nearby hyperspace comm beacon and immediately set about transmitting their latest reconnaissance data. It took the pair less than a minute to complete their data upload and then make the necessary preparations for the C-Jump to their next destination.

Although a remarkable feat of engineering, the current version of the *Hunter's* miniaturized C-Drive was based on the model used in Fleet's newest generation of anti-ship missiles. Intended to deliver a missile's deadly payload to the immediate vicinity of its target in a single, instantaneous bound, the capability to execute multiple, consecutive hyperspace transitions was not envisioned as a part of the drive's original design requirements. As was the case with the much larger version of the C-Drive recently tested aboard TFS

Ingenuity, the challenge was primarily one of power generation and handling. Accordingly, the *Hunter's* onboard reactor had been upgraded and a small capacitor bank added to allow for relatively short C-Jumps of up to twenty-five light years. Unfortunately, even for shorter range jumps, the miniaturized version of the drive still required a brief "dwell time" before executing its next transition … meaning that an instantaneous "emergency C-Jump" was simply not possible. The delay was primarily a function of how much power was consumed during the previous and subsequent jumps. In a worst case scenario, for example, when two, twenty-five-light-year jumps were executed one after the other, a delay of approximately thirty minutes was required between transitions.

Fortunately, the current reconnaissance mission in the immediate vicinity of the Sol system called for relatively short-range C-Jumps, each requiring only minimal dwell time before the *Hunters* were ready for their next transition. Now, with the data describing their thus far fruitless search transmitted back to the *Jutland*, the RPSVs banked gracefully in the direction of their next destination, accelerating rapidly before engaging their C-Drives and disappearing from normal space in two brief flashes of light.

SCS Gunov, Pelaran Resistance Rally Point
(3.3 light years from Earth)

The ships of the Pelaran Resistance task force were not expecting an engagement with hostile forces at the location of their rally point. In fact, Sajeth Collective scouting vessels had been visiting the general area for several years without interference from the Guardian spacecraft. It was these missions that had ultimately produced a model of the Pelaran vessel's data transmission activities, finally resolving its movements into something approaching a predictable pattern. So far at least, it did not appear that the Guardian considered the presence of vessels beyond the Sol system's outermost planets to be much of a threat, if indeed it was even capable of detecting them at all. Based on the recent destruction of Admiral Naftur's task force, however, it did now seem probable that the Pelarans had at least some capability of both detecting and tracking ships traveling extended distances in hyperspace.

Expectations aside, Commodore Sarafi had not survived nearly two hundred years of military service by ignoring the tenets of force protection. His squadron was now comprised of twenty-eight warships, and the recent addition of four *Keturah*-class battlespace defense (BD) cruisers had been welcome indeed. The cruisers' primary role was to rapidly detect and engage enemy ships, preferably before they had the opportunity to mount an effective attack. Accordingly, all four had begun the process of deploying the latest in perimeter surveillance drones immediately after their arrival.

Sarafi smiled at the irony implicit in this, the first operational deployment of a Sajeth Collective weapon system based in part on Pelaran technology. With other cultivated species engaged in open warfare across neighboring regions of the galaxy, Pelaran-derived technologies were beginning to make their appearance within the military forces of other civilizations. Even though cultivated species did tend to enjoy overwhelming military superiority over their rivals, their ships were still captured or destroyed on occasion … resulting in a slow but steady "leak" of Pelaran technology. In addition, cultivated civilizations were always prime targets for espionage, regardless of whether your particular world considered them friend or foe. Once obtained by another species, the tech was quickly reverse-engineered and then either sold or integrated into new weapon systems within a surprisingly short period of time.

"Defensive perimeter established, Commodore," Sarafi's communications officer reported. "We're still showing a few gaps, but should have full coverage within the hour."

"And we have established real-time detection capabilities within the perimeter?"

"Yes, sir. The detection zone extends just over one light hour in every direction. Once the screen is fully established, we can expect to receive a warning of any enemy activity inside the zone."

"With this configuration, how much warning will it provide?" Sarafi asked, arching his bushy eyebrows at the young comm officer.

"Worst case, we should get an alert in just under ten minutes. That number improves if the activity occurs closer to one of the drones, of course."

"Very good, thank you." It was certainly true that the new system provided a significant improvement over traditional defensive measures, such as the deployment of picket ships or RPSVs to create a defensive perimeter. The best a picket ship could do was transmit a warning back to the squadron at the speed of light, leaving a commander with the difficult choice of either a long comm delay or a small defensive perimeter. Instead, after arriving at their assigned surveillance location, the new drones deployed their own hyperspace communications beacon, enabling instantaneous, real-time data transfer with the distant BD cruisers.

If nothing else, Admiral Naftur's foolhardy incursion into the Sol system had at least provided some insight regarding the Guardian's preferred offensive tactics. Sarafi suspected that a reconnaissance probe had been used to obtain a passive "snapshot" of Naftur's forces shortly after they had arrived in system. With the squadron not expecting an immediate attack after an extended voyage in hyperspace, they would have all been following a predictable course with a predictable speed. This had, of course, made things incredibly easy for the Guardian, which was then able to anticipate each vessel's exact position in space and open fire before there was any possibility of detection. While not a pessimistic man by nature, Commodore Sarafi still doubted that his new perimeter surveillance drones would fare much better against the Guardian's tactics. He was also painfully aware that he had little defense against the Pelaran's vastly superior weapons. Based on all of the data gathered to date, however, he did believe that he could count on the Guardian spacecraft to behave in a manner at least somewhat consistent with their computer model. He, therefore, pinned his hopes on avoiding detection, if possible, and making things as difficult as possible for his adversary. Even the simple act of keeping his ships in continuous, random motion might be sufficient to delay their destruction long enough to allow most of them to escape — hopefully in sufficient numbers to execute a successful attack on Terra.

"Contact!" a young Wek Lieutenant called from the *Gunov's* Tactical station. "Two small ships — they're right on top of us, sir — only about ten light seconds out."

"Origin?" Sarafi snapped impatiently.

"I'm not sure where it came up with the data to make its identification, but the fire control AI has classified them as Terran scout vessels … stand by … the *Hadeon* is firing!"

At the time the Terran vessels transitioned from hyperspace, *Hadeon* was the closest of the four battlespace defense cruisers. Fortunately, protecting Sajeth Collective forces from a surprise attack was precisely the role for which she had been designed. Well before Commodore Sarafi had even been made aware of their presence, *Hadeon's* AI had already determined the enemy ships' origin and type. This led to their immediately being designated as hostile targets, which authorized the BD system to open fire without further authorization per the task force's standing rules of engagement. Although it would take the cruiser's active sensors over twenty seconds to begin processing detailed performance estimates for the two targets — an eternity in such an engagement — real-time remote surveillance drone data provided the AI with more than enough information to begin its attack. Shortly after the cruiser's first salvos began streaming downrange towards the two *Hunters*, drone data was supplemented with that provided by the "new light" gathered by the cruiser's passive sensors. The AI also had access to performance data obtained from a highly classified source. All of these data points were quickly consolidated to produce a probability-based model describing the targets as if their designers had handed over a set of detailed specifications. *Hadeon's* fire control AI now had everything it needed to begin placing its energy weapons fire at the most likely locations to intersect the flight paths of the Terran vessels.

"She's adjusting her fire, sir," the lieutenant reported, now using a much more disciplined tone.

Hadeon's position on the periphery of the assembled Resistance ships had provided the cruiser with a clear field of fire in the direction of her prey. Within seconds, the entire side of the ship was once again lit with energy weapons fire as she worked methodically to destroy the Terran intruders.

Hunter Formation "Nail 42," Near the Pelaran Resistance Rally Point
(3.3 light years from Earth)

The two *Hunter* RPSVs' onboard AIs concluded that they were in serious trouble immediately after completing their transition back into normal space at their latest reconnaissance location. In one of those chance occurrences that sometimes determined the fate of nations, or even entire worlds, the formation had arrived at a point so close to their quarry that they would most likely not be able to avoid detection and attack. The *Hunters'* passive sensors detected the presence of twenty-eight enemy ships, several of which were of a configuration similar to other Sajeth Collective vessels already contained in their onboard database. At an estimated range of just under three million kilometers, it would take only ten seconds for their light to reach the Resistance task force, thus alerting them to the RPSVs' presence. It was a virtual certainty that, perhaps as little as ten seconds later, enemy weapons fire would begin arriving at their current location. What the two *Hunters'* onboard AI did not yet know was that they had transitioned in the immediate vicinity of an enemy surveillance drone, which dutifully began relaying information regarding their configuration and exact position back to the Resistance task force in real-time.

The *Hunters* gave brief consideration to mounting an attack on the Resistance task force. Although two HB-7c missiles had been removed from the "Nail 43" spacecraft prior to launch, fourteen of the C-Drive-equipped missiles hung ready to fire beneath their fuselages and stubby wings. The chief difficulty in going on the offensive at this point was the distance to their targets. The enemy formation, as seen from the RPSVs' current position, appeared as they had been ten seconds earlier. The Resistance ships were already in motion when the two *Hunters* transitioned into the area, and looked as if they had been in the process of taking some sort of evasive action even before their arrival. This made for a poor firing solution for the RPSVs' missiles, which required precise targeting information in order to make their C-Jump and then emerge from hyperspace immediately before impact. Even in the unlikely event that all fourteen missiles managed to find their targets, the probability of inflicting any sort of meaningful damage was calculated to be less than ten percent. Based on the mission objectives they had been assigned before launch, the AIs from both ships concluded that their best option was to flee the area in hopes of delivering their critical reconnaissance information back to Terran Fleet Command.

Their course of action decided, the *Hunters* engaged their sublight engines at maximum power, accelerating away from the Resistance task force and also taking some random evasive action of their own. Each RPSV calculated that their C-Drives would need just under two minutes to reach a point where an escape transition would be possible, so their immediate goal was to confound the enemy ships' efforts to target them just long enough to make their C-Jump back to the nearest hyperspace comm beacon. After a few seconds, both of the *Hunters* broke formation simultaneously and began increasing the distance from its former "wingman" at varying rates in the hopes that at least one of them might survive.

Unexpectedly, from the AIs' point of view, energy weapons fire from the Resistance task force began arriving at their location just twelve seconds after their arrival. Both ships recorded the fact that the enemy must have access to real-time surveillance of the region surrounding their rally point in order to respond so quickly to their presence. Each also noted impassively that their chances of survival had decreased dramatically as a result.

Ten light seconds aft, well beyond the practical range of most warships' energy cannons, the battlespace defense cruiser *Hadeon* continued its massive barrage of energy weapons fire. Still relatively new to Sajeth Collective naval forces, the *Keturah*-class BD cruisers were equipped with heavy emitters capable of the increased power handling and beam coherence required for precisely this type of engagement. This, coupled with advanced fire control AI, placed the fleeing *Hunter* RPSVs still well within *Hadeon's* lethality zone, particularly given that they were lightly armored vessels with no shields.

For the first several seconds, it appeared that the RPSVs' evasive tactics might actually allow them to escape. Most of the incoming energy weapons fire passed well clear of their flight paths and initially gave the appearance of a randomized firing pattern sent in their general direction in the hope of scoring a chance hit. Over time, however, its accuracy steadily improved. Twenty seconds into the engagement, the fire control AI had gathered enough data to begin predicting how the *Hunters* would vary their flight paths in response to incoming fire. Just ten seconds later, *Hadeon* made her first kill. "Nail 43" took a glancing, off-axis hit that probably would not have been lethal under normal circumstances. Nevertheless, the energy bolt burned through the outer skin of one of the ship's HB-7c missiles, causing a malfunction that detonated its compact antimatter warhead. The resulting matter/antimatter annihilation event was marked by the creation of extremely high-energy gamma photons and a brief but spectacular flash of visible light as the RPSV was completely obliterated.

"Nail 42" fared slightly better at first, surviving for almost a full minute before the cruiser's ever-more-precise fire managed to coax the vessel into a predictable kill box. The beam that finally ended the *Hunter's* attempted retreat struck the small ship squarely astern, quickly overloading its small reactor's containment field and once again blotting it from space as if it had never existed.

As a matter of course, both *Hunters* had burst-transmitted their reconnaissance data in the direction of several of the nearest comm beacons, the last known positions of several TFC vessels, and towards Earth itself for good measure. Those signals, containing the crucial data needed for Earth's defense, now streamed away from the Resistance task force's rally point at the speed of light. It would take nearly eleven hours before Terran Fleet Command noted that *Hunter* formation "Nail 42" had failed to transmit an update via NRD net at the appointed time — and just under three years and four months before any of the RPSVs' signals arrived at their intended destinations.

Chapter 10

TFC Yucca Mountain Shipyard Facility
(Simulated Fleet Operations Training Center)

Terran Fleet Command operated the three most advanced full-motion simulation facilities ever constructed, each of which being collocated with one of their three largest spacecraft construction facilities. Here, the age-old military axiom of "train like you fight" was applied in the purest form allowed by the current state of the art. Every critical section of each Fleet vessel could be modeled with near perfect fidelity, including simulated weapons impacts with actual gravitic field manipulation that could be downright dangerous for any crewmember failing to follow real-world procedures to the letter. Although the cavernous rooms dedicated to reproducing the ships' engineering spaces were impressive in their own right, it was the arena-like bridge simulation facility that tended to garner the most attention. The "bridge sim" had already earned the reputation of delivering a terrifyingly realistic facsimile of combat operations aboard Fleet vessels — along with a humbling dose of reality for their sometimes-cocky crews.

For the past several weeks, the simulator had been dedicated exclusively to preparing *Theseus*-class destroyer crews for their first deployments. Since *Ingenuity's* arrival, however, her crew's urgent transition to *Theseus* had left little time for the other destroyer crews.

“Did you notice that our chairs on *Theseus’* bridge are much more comfortable than these are,” Reynolds asked, wearing a conspiratorial grin and leaning over so that only Prescott could hear.

This was the first time the entire first watch bridge crew had been present in the simulator at the same time. The frenzied pace of preparing the destroyer and her crew for departure had forced the XO into a “shotgun approach” to training where anyone not immediately required for duty onboard the ship was expected to be in the simulator. Although less than ideal, the entire crew had now successfully completed the minimal sequence required for designation as “mission ready” aboard the new destroyer.

“I was probably too distracted to notice. The rumor is that at least one person …” Prescott checked himself, looking around to make sure no one else was listening to their conversation, “soils themselves in here every day. Let’s just say that I was highly motivated to make sure that wasn’t going to be me,” he laughed.

“Seriously?” she grinned, suppressing what might have otherwise been uproarious laughter. “I never would have guessed something like *that* was happening, but thanks for giving me something else to worry about when I’m in here! Now that you mention it, though, I guess it shouldn’t be that big of a surprise, given how intense it can be. I think they finally got all the G-force stuff dialed in the way Fleet Training wants it, but I have to say I think they may have gone a little overboard. We’ve seen real combat once and also did a real-world simulation at the Live Fire Training Range, but I don’t remember it ever being anywhere near as strenuous as it is in here."

"I think that's all about adrenaline and distraction. In the heat of combat, a little G-induced discomfort from lagging inertial dampeners doesn't really register. We did briefly hit 6 Gs several times at Gliese 667, thanks to our wannabe fighter pilot helmsman over there." Prescott briefly raised his voice enough for Blake Fisher to hear the jab, prompting the young ensign to respond from the Helm console by raising his hand in a "thumbs up" gesture. "Kip says they updated all of their settings based on *Ingenuity's* battle data, so it should all be pretty accurate at this point. It's definitely not what I'd call pleasant, though," he said.

"No it isn't … and I had a slice of pizza for lunch while running between *Ingenuity* and *Theseus*, so I really hope they aren't planning on any of that kind of thing during today's briefing," Reynolds sighed, puffing out her cheeks.

"Hah, the old 'a pizza pie before you fly,' eh?" he laughed. "I think you'll be okay. As far as I know, it's just Kip doing the briefing, and I don't think he has any plans to demonstrate anything other than general system ops. By the way, I was pleased to see that you managed to get everyone through their initial qualification training sequence. That's quite an accomplishment, given the time crunch."

"Thank you, sir. I didn't think it would go over very well if Fleet gave us a launch order and we had to respond with a 'mission ineffective' status. Besides, it's amazing what you can accomplish if you give up sleeping."

"The extra few days have been helpful for all of us, but our luck, if you can call it that, may not hold out much longer. If our reconnaissance flights are going to find the Resistance ships at all before they show up here, it's going to happen within the next forty-eight hours. So now that we've reached a minimal level of readiness, I want you to bump crew rest up to the top of your priority list. Well-trained or not, we won't perform if we're sleep-deprived … and you know how I feel about stims," he said, staring into his XO's bloodshot eyes with a furrowed brow.

"Aye, sir. Will do." For her part, Reynolds had never been especially fond of the idea of putting her people on prescribed stimulants either. Fleet Medical's official stance was that they were safe and effective for keeping crewmembers on duty for up to seventy-two hours straight, but only in cases of 'urgent operational necessity.' Although she took more of a pragmatic stance on the issue than her captain, Reynolds hated the way they made her feel. She already dreaded the "detox" period — which usually required a different set of meds to help force her mind out of its chemically-induced state of alertness so that she could finally get some rest. The absolute worst part about the stims, however, was the restless sleep and weird, unsettling dreams that always seemed to follow.

Prescott stared at his XO a moment longer, knowing full well that she had worked herself well beyond the point of mental and physical exhaustion. He knew she was doing what she felt was required, and the last thing he wanted to do was discourage her after the monumental effort of the past several days. Instead, he contented himself with a subtle tilt of his head and a look that he hoped registered his concerns without any implied criticism.

"I know," she smiled, nodding her head and closing her eyes momentarily. "I haven't had one in twelve hours, and I'm hitting the rack right after this briefing."

Prescott nodded his approval without comment, then paused briefly before getting back to the subject at hand. "Logan has been pretty tight-lipped about what he has to show us today, but I gather it's mostly about new systems, particularly getting us up to speed on the shields."

"Uh huh … I think I would appreciate eventually being assigned to a ship that's loaded up with technology that has proven itself reliable over a long period of time. And by 'proven itself reliable,' I mean by someone other than us."

"Oh come on. You have to admit we've been very fortunate along those lines so far. Besides, if the shields don't work properly, we'll be the first to know as soon as someone starts shooting at us again."

"How did Joseph Heller say it? 'That's some catch, that Catch-22.'"

"'It's the best there is,'" Prescott chuckled, completing one of his favorite literary references.

The bridge simulation facility was becoming increasingly crowded as members of all three of *Theseus'* bridge watch crews filed onto the floor of the simulator area itself. Since the room was designed to be quickly reconfigured to mimic the bridge layouts of all four of Fleet's primary ship classes, it was a bit larger than *Theseus'* actual bridge, thus providing a fair amount of standing room around the perimeter. At the same time, an even larger group composed primarily of crewmen from other departments filled the round observation deck perched high above the simulator floor.

Although not designed for the delivery of technical briefings, the room performed admirably well in the role in spite of its minimal seating capacity. Every system present on the destroyer's bridge was faithfully reproduced to the smallest detail. This included a fully functional ship's AI, which, while clearly overqualified for the purpose, made for an excellent audiovisual assistant. Perhaps most importantly, the enormous, wrap-around view screen lining the front of the bridge was visible throughout most of the facility, and was supplemented, where required, by a few additional screens installed around the perimeter of the observation deck.

After a few minutes, *Theseus'* chief engineer, Commander Kip Logan, squeezed his way through the rear entrance of the now-crowded simulator floor and made his way to the open area between the Helm console and the front of the bridge.

"Good afternoon, everyone," he began, playing up his disarming Southeastern U.S. accent as he often did when speaking publicly. "I think most of you know me by now since I've been the guy running around yelling at everyone within earshot for the past several days. In case I haven't yet had the opportunity to yell at you personally, I do apologize, and I'm sure I'll get around to it soon. Anyway, I'm Commander Kip Logan. I was *Ingenuity's* chief engineer until a few days ago, when I was reassigned to the *Theseus*. Now, I'll be the first to admit that I'm not sure being *Ingenuity's* Cheng necessarily makes me qualified to transition immediately into the same role aboard *Theseus*. After all, it's a completely different class of ship, right? The good news is that, even after only a few days of working with her, I can tell you without hesitation that the whole 'mod/com' concept works, and works very well. I was skeptical at first, as I'm sure many of you were, but I have to tell you, folks, I've become a believer in a big hurry.

"On all four of our primary ship classes, parts, systems, and even crew procedures are interchangeable to the maximum extent possible. While it's not one hundred percent, I'd say it's probably about as close as we're likely to ever get. We operational guys tend to beat up on the eggheads at Fleet Science and Engineering quite a bit for being out of touch with real-world requirements, but I think they've truly done a great job in this case. In fact, I think as soon as I can get someone to show me how to start her engines, *Theseus* will be ready to go." Logan smiled and looked around the room in an effort to gauge his audience, but other than a few people clearing their throats or shifting in their seats, his attempt at humor was met with complete silence. Searching for encouragement, he glanced at his captain and XO and saw that each was wearing a lopsided grin while slowly shaking their heads – both clearly enjoying his discomfort.

"Oh, come on, people … that's pretty good comedy as far as engineers go. Trust me when I tell you that I can do a lot worse."

"It's the truth, he can!" Reynolds interjected, which finally drew a smattering of laughter from the impassive crowd.

"Okay, now that I see what I'm dealing with here, I'll move on. Oh, and before I forget, all of you know that essentially everything you see, hear, smell, or touch at the beautiful Yucca Mountain Shipyard is classified, Top Secret, code word MAGI PRIME. Even though the entire facility has been raised to this classification level, Fleet still wants you to be reminded of your responsibilities along those lines when we start talking tech. This is also intended to be an informal presentation, so feel free to interrupt with questions anytime. Most of you look like you're way past due for a nap, so I'll try not to keep you too long today.

"This briefing is primarily for the benefit of *Theseus'* bridge crews, all of whom I believe have now been designated as 'mission ready.'" Logan glanced at Reynolds for a confirmation and received a nod in return. "Alright, that's good. So that means you all have at least a basic understanding of the ship's systems, so I'm not going to spend too much time talking about those today. For those of you coming from *Ingenuity* like me, a good rule of thumb to remember is that many things on *Theseus* are simply three times what they were on *Ingenuity*. That applies to quite a few basic stats like length, displacement, crew complement, and number of reactors, to name a few."

On the bridge simulator view screen, and without prompting from Commander Logan, the AI provided supporting information in perfect synchronization with the briefing. At the moment, multiple views of both ship types were displayed, with specific traits highlighted as he continued to speak.

"The truth is that our 'factor of three' observation doesn't come close to telling the whole story. Even with Earth under the threat of a possible attack, the *Theseus*-class ships were held in port until the remainder of their systems could be fully integrated. I think you'll all agree that this was a huge risk, given the circumstances, right? Well, the reason the Admiralty was willing to take that risk is evidence of the tactical advantages these ships have over all other Fleet vessels at the moment … and hopefully over the bad guys too.

"Quick question … and feel free to shout out your answer. Successful warship design always has and always will come down to one thing — and that's …"

There were a number of answers around the room including "speed," and "big guns," before someone came up with the word "power."

"There it was, finally!" Logan laughed, "It all comes down to power. All of the other answers I heard *depend* on our ability to generate ridiculous amounts of power. All else being equal, the ship with a power advantage tends to win the battle. Now, even though we Humans are new at building *starships*, this is a fundamental tenet of warship design that we have been applying for a very long time. So the first thing you need to know about *Theseus* is that she can generate, manage, and direct power in the general direction of her enemies more effectively than any of our other designs. This is one of the two reasons why I believe the *Theseus*-class is a game-changer for Terran Fleet Command. It's also one of the primary reasons their deployment was delayed slightly so that they could benefit from the lessons learned during *Ingenuity's* shakedown cruise and first operational missions. Going forward, we'll see many of these same improvements retrofitted into our existing frigates, cruisers … even the carriers to some extent.

"So, if you are transitioning from *Ingenuity*, surprisingly little has changed with regard to how the ship operates. Big picture though, where power generation is concerned, that 'factor of three' rule I mentioned becomes a factor of nine. That means *Theseus* should always have an excess of power available to run every one of her systems simultaneously, while still maintaining fully-charged capacitor banks in case 'getting the hell out of Dodge' starts looking like the best option. Having survived a battle aboard *Ingenuity* where we were significantly outgunned, I can tell you that you don't ever want to find yourself in a power-deficient situation. I strongly recommend that all of you, particularly those who were not a part of *Ingenuity's* crew, spend some time studying how that engagement unfolded, with an eye towards what other options we would have had available had we not found ourselves short of power at a critical time." Logan paused and glanced around the room. As was often the case, there were quite a few young officers assigned to the bridge crews. Although he was never one to dwell on the dangers associated with their chosen vocation, he wondered if most of the young men and women present — many of them still just kids from his perspective — had the foggiest notion of what they had signed up for.

"Well, I guess that just about covers everything that's new and exciting about the *Theseus*. Did any of you have additional questions before we all get back to work?" Logan asked, deadpan. In response, the word "shields" erupted from several locations around the room and from the observation deck. "What's that … you want me to talk about grav shields? Astounding. I never would have guessed.

"Alright, here we go," he began again. "First off, let me give you a brief history. Much like what we saw during development of the C-Drive, gravitic shields are in many ways just an extension of technology already deployed aboard all Fleet vessels. Also very much like the C-Drive, their 'discovery,' if you will, was something of an accident."

Precisely on cue, the simulator AI began playing footage of an F-373 *Reaper* aerospace superiority fighter, apparently in the process of executing a low-level attack run against a distant ground target that was not yet visible on the screen. With the exception of the missing engine nozzles that once protruded from the rear of such aircraft, as well as the lack of any visible cockpit canopy, the *Reaper's* appearance clearly portrayed a direct lineage extending back to the late twentieth century and beyond. Although quite large for a fighter, the ship's aggressive, flowing lines and incredible speed mere meters from the terrain below left little doubt that she represented the culmination of over three centuries of fighter aircraft design. Also very much in keeping with top-of-the line fighters of previous generations, the F-373 was, pound for pound, the most expensive aerospace vehicle ever constructed by Human hands.

"And here we have the *Reaper*," Logan said, turning to admire the footage playing on the enormous view screen. “I gotta tell you guys, I’ve been putting together models of fighter aircraft since I was a kid, but the 373 makes all the others look like a bunch of boxy crop dusters. If you can watch something like this without getting fired up about it, I’m afraid you may have chosen the wrong career path. I was lucky enough to be assigned to the first operational starship and then survive the first true space combat twenty-four light years away, but there is still very little in my experience with a higher ‘cool factor’ than an aerospace superiority fighter. Hooyah?”

“Hooyah!” came the enthusiastic, albeit obligatory, response from the crowd.

“Alright then, some of you might actually be awake now. I just have a couple of additional things to say about the *Reaper* before we move on. Military analysts have been predicting the end of crewed fighter aircraft since shortly after they first arrived on the scene in the twentieth century. The problem is that, even as advanced as our AI has become, there are some missions where having a Human in the loop is still seen as either critical, or at least a necessary compromise. There actually is a pilot in there, by the way, although the cockpit is now a heavily armored cylindrical structure — often referred to as the ‘bathtub’ — located in the center of the fuselage. As you can see, there is no canopy and no windows, but once the pilot is wired into the aircraft’s systems, he is literally no longer able to see the aircraft itself. Instead, the AI provides him with a full three-hundred-sixty-degree view of the space around the ship. Any data the pilot needs is projected into his field of view. There is also no longer any need for traditional controls since all of the ship's systems are managed via neural interface, much like those embedded in combat armor and EVA suits. As has always been the case for multirole fighters, every cubic centimeter of internal volume is packed with the most advanced hardware available. With the recent rapid advances in technology, the fact that Fleet has managed to keep a significant portion of the (albeit small) F-373 fleet flying while constantly upgrading components and software is a tremendous accomplishment.

"So what does this have to do with grav shields? Well, first off, I'm sorry to say that it was actually the *Reapers*, not the *Theseus*-class destroyers, with the first operational shield system." This bit of news was met with a smattering of boos from the now-engaged and understandably biased crowd. "Yes, yes, I know," Logan soothed, "but the reason for that is pretty simple. The effect that ultimately led to their development was first discovered by an F-373. This one, in fact." Logan said, turning to gesture once again at the view screen. Thanks to a bit of clever timing on behalf of the simulator AI, the fighter pulled up slightly to gain a few extra meters of altitude before a weapons bay door opened beneath its fuselage, followed by the immediate launch of an HB-7 missile in air-to-ground attack mode. A fraction of a second into the missile's flight, the AI froze the footage, highlighting several items on the screen in brackets with accompanying blocks of textual data.

"Until recently, Fleet had not spent a lot of time planning for ground attack missions — understandably, their primary focus had been developing the capability to successfully attack enemy spacecraft. When they did get around to doing some air-to-ground weapons testing, however, the *Reaper* was the obvious choice. The problem was, every time we sent an F-373 out to the range to attack a ground target, our engineers kept noticing small variances in ordinance delivery. That held true regardless of what type of weapons were being used. Missiles like the HB-7 you see here are generally smart enough to correct the problem for themselves, but when we attempted to drop weapons that don't have their own propulsion systems, we experienced some pretty significant problems. There was even one case where we very nearly lost an aircraft when the lead pilot in a two-ship formation dropped a glide bomb that separated from the aircraft in an unexpected manner and came close to taking out his wingman."

"Anyone know — or care to guess — what the problem was?" Logan asked, looking around the room. "Lieutenant Lau, you were a physics major right? What do you think?"

While paying attention, Lau had not been expecting a direct question and was somewhat caught off guard. "Uh, yes, sir," he stammered as he stood up from his Tactical console. "I don't know for sure, but it pretty much had to have something to do with the gravitic field generators," Lau answered. "I'm thinking it was related to either inertial dampening for the pilot, or the way they manipulate the field to attenuate sonic booms."

"That was two guesses, Lieutenant, and they're both wrong," Logan laughed. "Not bad guesses, though. No, at first, the Science and Engineering Directorate didn't suspect anything related to the grav fields because they should not have been anywhere near strong enough to cause the effects they were seeing at the time weapons were being launched."

On the view screens the AI now displayed a rotating three-dimensional depiction of the F-373, including a spherical bubble surrounding the fighter to represent its gravitic field. "We're obviously not going to delve much into the physics here today, but let me try to give you a grossly oversimplified version of what they found. The gravitic generators aboard all Fleet vessels are active to some extent all of the time. They serve a variety of functions including what everyone refers to as 'artificial gravity' as well as inertial dampening for those of you who prefer to avoid being crushed. When we operate inside the gravity well of a planetary body, those same generators ramp up their power tremendously and create an effect we all like to call 'mass cancellation.' Incidentally, this whole subject area is full of misnomers and technical inaccuracies, but the real physics underlying these systems is so complex that using colloquial terms is generally accepted practice, even among Fleet engineers.

"So you might be thinking, 'But the *Reaper* has wings, so why would it need a mass canceling grav field?' While it does indeed have wings that provide quite a bit of lift when flying in dense, Earth-like atmospheres, it's generally not enough to sustain flight for such a large ship. This thing is a 'hyper maneuverable' aircraft, and there was no way to create the kind of flight envelope its mission required using aerodynamic lift and flight controls. The designers also wanted the ship to have essentially the same capabilities, regardless of what kind of environment it was operating in. To accomplish that, we ended up with a gravitic field that would look a lot like this if you could actually see it," Logan said, gesturing towards the view screen. "What I want you to notice is that, although the field is spherical, it's actually generated in two pieces … two hemispherical domes. That results in an interference area you might describe as a 'seam' running all the way around the field. It actually looks a little like the way two halves of a walnut shell come together. As you can see, the seam circles the ship's longitudinal axis through points above and below the fuselage.

"Alright, Lieutenant Lau, here's your chance to redeem yourself. *Now* what do you think the problem was?"

Lau had just sat back down, but now stood once again to answer the commander's question. "I'd say when weapons are launched from the aircraft, they have a nasty habit of going right through the area of interference."

"Exactly, thank you. Please take your seat and I promise not to pick on you anymore today," Logan smiled. "The engineers discovered that this grav field seam sometimes caused localized, and unexpectedly intense, variations in field strength. Once they figured out that this was the problem, it took several months of testing to accurately model what was going on and come up with a workable solution. During that testing, one of the things they did was fire beam weapons through the interference pattern to see how much accuracy was lost. That testing inspired a gifted and irritatingly lucky doctoral candidate from Missouri S&T — which happens to be my alma mater — to suggest essentially four things: first — that what was going on was actually a form of gravitational lensing, second — that the ship's AI was fast enough to detect and respond to disturbances in the field … and by disturbances I mean things like incoming fire, third — that the AI could be coaxed into producing and controlling the lensing phenomena on demand, and fourth — that the effect might potentially be used in reverse to deflect incoming fire. The rest, as they say, is history."

Logan paused for a moment, correctly assuming that there might be a few questions at this point. The first came from Captain Prescott. "Commander Logan, if I can interrupt you with a question or two …"

"Of course, Captain."

"I think I managed to follow you reasonably well, but I'm not sure I understand how we made the jump from some sort of distortion in the gravitic field to a workable shield system. Can you expand on that subject a bit?"

"I can try, sir. First off, although the technology involved is quite similar to the existing gravitic systems we were already using, some additional hardware was required. To provide some redundancy, additional, dedicated field generators were installed for the shield system. There are also a number of emitters installed at various locations on the hull that allow the AI to control the local intensity of the shield on the fly."

"So we're not talking about completely surrounding the ship with a single field then?"

"No, not at all. The AI literally responds in real-time to place an incredibly intense area of gravitational distortion in the path of incoming fire," Logan replied.

"And what effect does this have on incoming ordinance?"

"That depends on the ordinance. The AI classifies the type of incoming fire, then responds in a different way, depending on what it's trying to defeat. For lack of a better term, energy weapons are 'lensed' or deflected away from the ship. For missiles, the system creates shear forces that tend to either destroy the warhead outright and/or throw it off target. Incoming kinetic energy rounds are usually not possible to destroy, but, depending on their angle of entry, they can be slowed to the point where their effectiveness is degraded significantly. In other cases, they are redirected much like a bolt from a plasma or energy weapon so that they miss the ship entirely. The other great thing about handling it this way is that we can blaze away with our own weapons without the need to disengage our shields. Incidentally, we really don't fully understand how the Sajeth Collective vessels pull this off."

"That all sounds pretty good," Prescott continued, "but what happens when we are being hit by more than one type of weapon from more than one direction?"

"Yes, sir, that was one of my first questions as well. It turns out that, on the time scale we're talking about here, it almost never happens. The duration of most shield system 'events' can be measured in microseconds. They also went on to say that the AI could handle 'a large number of simultaneous events.' That's as much detail as they would provide, and that usually means they don't know for sure."

"Right. I think we're all growing accustomed to incomplete specs at this point. I have two final questions.

Since the function of the shields is primarily to deflect rather than destroy or absorb incoming fire, I assume that means the gravitic distortions are created at a greater distance from the ship than our grav field typically extends. How far out do these shield 'events' occur and does all of this deflected ordinance pose a threat to friendly vessels?" Prescott asked.

"You're making me feel smarter than I actually am, Captain, because I asked those questions as well. The distance at which the gravitic disturbances are created is a function of the size of the ship's hull. It essentially becomes a geometry problem for the AI to ensure that the rounds either miss completely or, failing that, are degraded as much as possible before they impact the hull. I can't give you exact distances, but the maximum distance is something like five times the ship's beam. For *Theseus*, that means the first shield event should be around fourteen hundred meters out. The AI will continue interacting with the incoming ordinance until it's either no longer a threat or it hits the ship. Now, as far as deflected rounds being a danger to friendlies, the short answer is that yes, it's a possibility. The AI is aware of the positions of friendly ships in the vicinity, and will make an effort to avoid sending deflected fire in their general direction, but doing so is not its first priority."

"I suppose that becomes a problem for the other vessel's shields to handle at that point," Prescott smiled.

"Hah, that's exactly right. Hey, it's better than the alternative, right? Oh, one other thing, the AI will purposefully deflect incoming fire towards hostile targets whenever possible, but I suspect it would take a pretty specific set of circumstances for that to come into play."

"Commander Logan," Reynolds said, raising her hand slightly, "do we have any projections regarding what to expect if we come under fire, based on what we know about Sajeth Collective weapons so far? How much damage can the shields take … or prevent?"

"That's the money question, alright," Logan replied, "and the one that none of the engineers want to commit to answering for fear they will be wrong. What we do have is a pretty good profile of the energy weapons and missiles used against *Ingenuity* at Gliese 667. Some pretty sophisticated computer modeling of that entire engagement has already been completed, and, if I can find some wood around here to knock on, it looks like she would have suffered zero hull impacts if grav shields had been in place."

"Wait, you said *zero* hull impacts? As in, nothing at all would have hit us?" she asked, incredulous.

"Can we get a battle damage schematic of TFS *Ingenuity*, please?" Logan asked, prompting the AI to immediately display a slowly rotating image of the battered frigate. After a few seconds, hundreds of colored circles appeared in locations all over the ship's hull. "As you can see, she took quite a beating out there, but her armor held up pretty well, for the most part. The green circles, which make up the vast majority of the hits, indicate superficial damage limited to the outermost layers of her armor plating, so no more than half a meter of penetration. The yellow circles represent more serious hits that penetrated up to one meter. And, finally, the single red circle shows the critical hit from the nuclear detonation. This impact was very nearly catastrophic, penetrating completely through all of her armor layers and down to the inner hull itself."

"That says we took over two hundred hits total."

"Um," Logan said, turning to glance at the view screen briefly before facing the XO again, "two hundred forty-two, yes."

"And you're saying that not a single one of those would have hit our hull if these grav shields had been installed?"

"Please overlay gravitic shield model and show us a time lapse of all incoming weapons fire that originally impacted the hull." The schematic on the screen was now replaced with side and top views of *Ingenuity*, with incoming energy weapons fire highlighted in red as the entire battle was condensed down to a ten-second clip. The result was at once unsettling and reassuring, as huge quantities of directed energy streamed in towards the frigate's hull before glancing off in seemingly random directions in the final fraction of a second before impact. As if the AI intended to heighten the drama, the final portion of the clip was displayed frame by frame as the missile that very nearly destroyed the frigate approached her starboard side. Energy cannon fire from *Ingenuity's* close-in weapon system slammed into the missile — doing significant damage, but failing to halt its progress towards the hull. In the next frame, the AI highlighted the missile in green brackets with 'gravitic shield engaged' displayed in the accompanying text block. Next, what remained of the missile's body visibly distorted before being abruptly deflected at an angle well above its original flight path. Just as before, the warhead's onboard computer switched its small nuclear warhead to proximity mode and detonated, but this time sending its deadly shaped-charge jet of nuclear fire streaming harmlessly away into space.

Near the bottom of the view screen, a counter reported the total estimated hull impacts as zero. The background noise level in the room increased dramatically as excited conversations broke out among those in attendance. After allowing a few moments for the room to settle, Logan raised his hands. "Listen, folks, I'm just an engineer, but I know a lot of you are feeling some uneasiness about finding yourselves in battle for the first time. For what it's worth, I can tell you that the *Theseus*-class is exactly the right ship with exactly the right technology at exactly the right time. The Resistance forces clearly do not expect us to put up much of a fight, if any, but I can tell you that if things go the way we hope, it'll be an unfair fight alright … just not in the way they expect. I think I can speak for all of us who have already seen combat when I say, to hell with a fair fight. Fair fights are for those who didn't plan properly. I'm much more in favor of the kind of battle George S. Patton was referring to when he said 'May God have mercy upon our enemies, because we won't.'"

The room immediately erupted in raucous cheers and applause.

Chapter 11

SCS Gunov, Pelaran Resistance Rally Point
(3.3 light years from Earth)

Sitting at the workstation in his ready room, Commodore Sarafi allowed his mind to wander in spite of the rather urgent task at hand. Like a great many Wek, he considered himself a warrior in every sense, and on Graca, this implied much more than a state of mind or a simple choice of vocation. To be a warrior was to accept life under a strict moral code — one that placed duty above all other considerations.

Duty, he thought distractedly. *Am I truly here out of a sense of duty?*

It was certainly true that there was no duty more sacred than acting as a protector of his people. Sarafi also truly believed that allowing the emergence of yet another puppet of the Pelaran Alliance so near to his homeworld would ultimately lead to its virtual enslavement at best, if not its complete destruction. Exploration and contact with neighboring civilizations had provided plenty of evidence to support just such a conclusion, had they not?

In fact, Sajeth Collective intelligence clearly indicated that the Pelaran Alliance was conducting a great deal of cultivation activity in the small section of the Milky Way Galaxy known as the Orion Spur. At over ten thousand light years in length and three thousand five hundred light years in width, there was plenty of room for multiple cultivated species to carve out their five-hundred-light-year spheres of influence, generally without the worry that they would come into conflict with each other. Unfortunately, the seven civilizations of the Sajeth Collective occupied a large section of space near the center of the spur, putting them in the unenviable position of eventually coming into direct conflict with as many as three Pelaran-cultivated civilizations (including Terra).

It had also become clear that cultivated civilizations tended to choose so-called "militarized" species as their first targets. In every known case of Pelaran cultivation, any worlds with a culture that produced a warrior class, a history that included at least one global war, or even the presence of long-standing professional military forces, were quickly neutralized. As disturbing as this was, Sarafi did have to admit that it made sense from a military, and perhaps even a political perspective. In any event, the Wek people could not allow this to happen … and, therefore, *he* could not allow this to happen.

Recalling the situation that led to his previous train of thought, the Wek officer glanced once again at the latest status report provided by his executive officer, who at the moment happened to be standing at attention just two meters away. The man was a Damaran, which in Sarafi's mind automatically placed him squarely into several categories: entitled, narcissist, arrogant, incompetent, and, worst of all, coward. Looking up from the report, Sarafi regarded his XO for a long moment with an expression of open contempt. Ever since he had first encountered one of their kind, they had reminded him of the Banea, massive herds of which still roamed the plains of Graca. There was little doubt that the Damarans had descended from similar prey animals, and the image of relentlessly hunting the pitiable creature standing before him formed unbidden in the deep recesses of Sarafi's mind. The commodore indulged himself for a moment longer, allowing the accompanying release of endorphins in his brain to wash over him as he relished the thought of a well-earned kill. A savage smile had begun forming at the corners of his mouth before being once again replaced by a more businesslike scowl as he continued with the task at hand.

"In spite of sitting idle at this rally point for two days longer than expected, our forces are still incomplete. We have not heard from the two ships sent to deal with that traitor Naftur and must assume that they have been captured or destroyed. I do not have to tell you what could happen if it becomes generally known that he still lives. Worse still," Sarafi paused, emitting a deep, threatening growl from the center of his chest, "we have been detected by the Humans, losing any possibility of surprise and rendering an attack on our forces a near certainty. Does that just about sum up the situation, *'Commander'* Miah?" he mocked.

The Sajeth Collective's charter recognized that all civilizations in the alliance should be represented in the ranks of its military. Fortunately, the alliance's founders also realized that it would be foolish indeed to guarantee an even split among its member worlds. The Wek, for example, had a fine tradition of professional military service extending back several millennia. The Damarans, on the other hand, while often being quick to advocate the use of military force (as long as someone else was doing the fighting), were generally a passive civilization with virtually no history of organized military activity of any kind. Accordingly, each world was guaranteed a small percentage of the officer corps based on their population. All of the remaining officer billets, as well as the entire enlisted corps making up the Sajeth Collective military, were chosen by means of an incredibly challenging and competitive selection process. At the moment, this meant that the Damarans were entitled to appoint 2.1 percent of the alliance's officers, up to the rank of commander, without their being subject to the same standards as everyone else. Naturally, everyone in the military was fully aware that there were three alliance civilizations that would have no representation at all were it not for the guarantees provided in the charter — leading inevitably to groups of largely incompetent officers who were sorely resented by their peers.

Experiencing feelings ranging from terror to righteous indignation and rage, Commander Woorin Miah felt a cold bead of sweat trace a line from the base of his neck all the way to his waistline. His family, after all, had enjoyed a position of power and influence on Damara for generations. While aware on some level that this had at least something to do with his appointment as a senior Sajeth Collective military officer, he also believed that he had earned the position, or was at least more qualified to hold it than some brutish Wek, particularly the one who had been making him stand at attention for the past five minutes.

"Captain, I …"

"You may address me as Commodore," Sarafi interrupted. "A title you will find that I have earned after decades of *competent* service to the Collective."

"Yes, of course, Commodore. My apologies. Our battlespace defense cruisers made short work of the Human scout vessels, sir. Surely they had no way of sending any sort of distress call other than a direct radio or optical transmission before they were destroyed."

"And do you further assume, then, that the Humans are so inept that they would not notice that two of their scout vessels have failed to report in or return to their base on schedule?" Sarafi spat.

When first approached by members of the Governing Council regarding this mission, Sarafi had quickly bought into the notion that destroying the Humans in a preemptive strike was a moral imperative – and a logical extension of his obligation to defend both Graca and the Collective. Not for the first time over the past month, however, the mission now struck him more as the errand of a fool … and possibly a dishonorable fool at that. Nevertheless, he had given his word that he would see it done, so there was little point in further introspection and debate at this point.

Miah, for his part, at least had the presence of mind to realize that the commodore's question was rhetorical in nature and did not warrant a response.

"Let me tell you what just happened here, Commander, and then I'll predict for you what's *about* to happen. Whether it was through the help of Admiral Naftur, the Pelaran Guardian ship, or just dumb luck, the Humans have managed to precisely locate our task force in a *very* short period of time at well over three light years from Sol. For months, the Governing Council was led to believe, primarily by members of the Damaran delegation, I might add, that the Humans were in possession of a single, unarmed starship based on what they referred to as 'introductory' Pelaran technology. The simple fact that they were capable of a rendezvous with Admiral Naftur's ship at Gliese 667 is an indication that our intelligence — again, from Damaran sources — was wholly inaccurate. The same can be said for the appearance of Human scout vessels at our rally point. If we finally manage to have a little luck ourselves, it will take the Humans a few hours to realize that their scout ships are missing, and perhaps a few more to lay on an attack mission. Either way, make no mistake, they will be coming for us."

"Sir, shouldn't we be more concerned about an attack from the Guardian ship itself?" Miah asked sheepishly.

"When your ship is ripped apart around you and your body exposed to the vacuum of space, it will make little difference whose weapons were used," Sarafi replied in a low, menacing tone. "Based on what we know of the Pelarans, however, their Guardians have a tendency to avoid direct involvement in military actions themselves once the cultivated world begins deploying forces of their own. Unless I miss my guess, it is the Humans we will be facing, not the Pelaran ship."

"Then surely, Commodore, we will be more than a match for their fledgling forces," Miah scoffed.

"I am happy to hear that you believe this to be the case, Commander, because I am about to give you the opportunity to redeem yourself as both my executive officer and intelligence chief. You may sit," Sarafi said, gesturing to the straight-backed, unpadded chair opposite his desk and then sliding a tablet containing his orders in Miah's direction.

"You have orders for me, Commodore?" the XO asked eagerly.

"I do indeed. As you know, our task force has a serious shortage of senior officers at the moment. Most of our acting captains hold the rank of commander — even lieutenant commander in a few cases. In fact, you are the only commander in the task force who is currently not in command of their own vessel."

"You are giving me a ship, sir?" Miah blurted out, his enthusiasm overcoming all discipline and common sense.

Sarafi closed his eyes momentarily and breathed in slowly in an effort to control his temper. "No, Commander Miah, I am putting you in command of a detachment of *four* ships."

The Damaran sat straighter in his chair, raising his chin slightly at the idea of his first independent command. "I won't let you down, sir, thank you."

"Your life will literally depend on that being the case, Commander," Sarafi growled. "This mission is a dangerous one, but I can assure you that it is absolutely critical to our cause. If you succeed, perhaps my report of your performance may improve."

"What is my mission, sir?"

"As I have said, we must assume that an attack on our forces at this location is imminent. While I agree, to some extent, with your sentiment that we have nothing to fear from the Humans, waiting here to engage their forces is not what we were sent here to do. We need every available ship in order to successfully attack Terra itself, so we cannot afford to risk a confrontation until our attack is underway. Unfortunately, five of our ships have not yet arrived, and we have no way of letting them know that we have relocated our forces unless someone remains behind at this location." Sarafi paused, staring into Miah's large, dark eyes in an effort to determine whether he had the vaguest understanding of what he was being asked to do.

Finally, the reality of his mission seemed to dawn on the Damaran. "So I am to remain here at the original rally point with only four ships? What am I to do if the Humans attack with a superior force?"

"Crush them," Sarafi grunted, now beginning to enjoy the conversation as he sensed Miah's fear increasing. "As you said, they are nothing more than 'fledglings' thus far … and certainly not capable of fielding forces that pose a threat to the ships I am placing under your command. We must place our faith in the intelligence reports you have been providing, Commander."

"Can you tell me which vessels will be in my detachment?"

"Of course. I am leaving you with two of our new battlespace defense cruisers, the *Hadeon* and the *Keturah*. While I am reluctant to do so, their network of surveillance drones is already in place. Just remember that two ships cannot defend the area as effectively as four, so you should consider reducing the size of their defensive perimeter accordingly. You will also have two *Shopak*-class heavy cruisers at your disposal, but I recommend you exercise command from the *Hadeon*, since she possesses the most modern command and control systems."

"And when may I abandon the original rally point and rejoin the task force?"

Sarafi could hear that the Damaran's heart rate had nearly doubled since realizing the scope of his mission — the smell of his fear becoming so thick that it threatened to overcome the Wek officer's own self-control. The commodore drew in a deep breath and swallowed the saliva now filling his mouth before continuing, "All five of the remaining vessels are battleships – each one commanded by a senior captain whose experience we desperately need. I am loathe to begin the attack on Terra until they have joined the task force. As each one arrives, you will immediately direct them to the new rally point. Your detachment may accompany the fifth and final ship."

"But what do I do if they …"

"Everything you need to know is contained in your orders, Commander," Sarafi interrupted. "Please take some time to review them and then you may ask any additional questions you have. I will be moving the task force to the new rally point in two hours, so you will need to act quickly. I suggest you shuttle over to the *Hadeon* immediately and take command of your detachment."

"I understand, Commodore. Thank you, sir."

"Dismissed, Commander Miah. Good luck."

TFS Navajo
(Combat Information Center)

With the *Hunter* reconnaissance flights nearing the end of their list of potential Resistance rally points, Admiral Patterson was now well past the point of feeling anxious. For the past several days, he had pushed the question of what to do next in the event of an unsuccessful search to the back of his mind. On an intellectual level, he knew that ignoring the need for a backup plan was in no way based on his confidence that the Resistance ships would be found. The cold reality was that he simply didn't know what to do next. Sure, there were a number of actions that he could and would take: checking the recon locations again with larger search radii, extending his picket line with the remainder of his standard *Hunters*, and overseeing the deployment of a number of additional capital ships expected to come online within the next few days, to name a few. All of these were purely defensive moves, however — the kinds of moves that desperate commanders have made throughout history upon finding themselves in an untenable situation.

Before entering the CIC, Patterson stepped to one side of the corridor and removed a well-worn index card from his wallet. Like the small "cheat sheets" some of his college engineering professors allowed during tests, the card was completely covered with his scrawl. Rather than odious formulas and physical constants, both sides contained motivational quotes and other bits of wisdom he had collected over the course of his career. Interestingly, the words he was looking for this morning were not those of a great military leader … although some Green Bay Packers fans might disagree.

"The strength of the group is the strength of the leader— I am the first believer that Leaders must have the quiet confidence, the certainty, of professional preparation,

and personal conviction that the task can and will be done. If so, it will."

~ Vince Lombardi

Patterson reflected for a moment, then carefully placed the fragile card back into his wallet while reminding himself that *all* leaders struggled with doubt, even fear, on occasion. The key was keeping those emotions in check, and *never* putting them on display in front of those you are trying to lead. That thought in mind, the admiral authenticated his identity and, with renewed resolve, drew in a deep breath, squared his shoulders, and strode confidently onto the floor of the CIC.

"Good morning, Commander," he greeted the young officer staring intently at the holographic display table in the center of the room. "Anything interesting yet?"

"Ah, good morning, Admiral … great timing, actually. It was a pretty peaceful watch until about half an hour ago, but since then there has been quite a bit of activity."

"Unfortunately, that's usually the way that kind of thing works. What's going on?" Patterson asked, now reasonably alert after his self-administered pep talk and five and a half hours of desperately needed sleep.

"First off," the commander replied, selecting two large ships with a gesture that sent a zoomed-in real-time view of each to large view screens nearby, "as expected, *Ushant* and *Philippine Sea* completed their climb to orbit about two hours ago. Neither has begun flight operations as yet, but both are reporting a 'mission effective' status and should begin taking over some of the combat air patrol missions that *Jutland* has been handling within the hour."

Patterson regarded the two carriers with satisfaction while taking a sip of the morning's second cup of "navy coffee," noting absently that it was just the way he liked it — strong, hot, black, and with a pinch of salt. "That's excellent news, but I actually want them taking over *all* of the CAP missions from *Jutland* as soon as possible. Pair each one with a cruiser to maximize their defensive firepower."

"Aye, sir."

"As soon as they get their *Hunters* on station, have *Jutland* recall their entire air wing with the exception of the birds that are out looking for the Resistance task force. Have we heard from her CAG this morning that you know of?"

"I'll check with the bridge to make sure, but I don't think so, sir. That's Captain Zhukov, right?"

"Dmitri 'Deadeye' Zhukov, yes indeed. Have you met him?" Prescott asked, giving the man a sideways look and a raised eyebrow.

"Yes, sir," he chuckled. "I don't intimidate easily, but that guys scares the hell out of me."

The admiral grinned while nodding his head knowingly. "Yeah, I understand why a lot of people say that. He's a pretty intense guy, but probably the finest pilot in the fleet."

"I assumed his call sign referred to the fact that he was a good shot with a pulse rifle or excellent on the gunnery range in his fighter until I met him in person."

While many people still associated Russians with blond hair and gray eyes, those tracing their ancestors to eastern sections of the huge country were much more likely to have dark brown eyes and hair. Captain Zhukov's were, in fact, so strikingly dark that it was often difficult to see any distinction between his irises and pupils.

"Nope, although I'm guessing that's probably true as well," Patterson laughed. "Don't worry about confirming, I'll check in with him directly. The reason I want *Jutland's* fighters aboard is that I want her out of Earth's gravity well and ready to respond when word comes in that we've found that enemy task force."

"Aye, sir. That's actually the next item I have for you," the officer said while reconfiguring the holo table to display the most recent status information from *Jutland's* reconnaissance flights. "As you know, the *Hunters* C-Jump back to the nearest NRD surveillance drone or communications beacon after visiting each reconnaissance location. That means we should hear from them about once every ten and a half hours. As you came in, I was just noticing that this one right here," he said, zooming in on the last known location of "Nail 42" flight, "is running a little later than expected."

"Hmm … well, there's some room for variation there. How much later are we talking?"

"They're just over five minutes off the average at this point."

"I'm sure they're watching the situation pretty closely over in the *Jutland's* CIC, but I'll mention it to Captain Zhukov in just a moment. Anything else?"

“Nothing else out of the ordinary at the moment, Admiral. Our favorite Pelaran elder statesman and superweapon is still right where he’s been for the past week. No change in emissions since its most recent campaign speech ended.”

“Good, hopefully it will stay that way for a while. Thank you for the update.”

“Yes, sir.”

“Ensign Fletcher!” Patterson called without looking in the direction of her Communications console.

“Yes, Admiral!” came her usual, enthusiastic reply. Over the past week or so, the young comm officer seemed to have had the dubious honor of always being on duty while the “old man” was present in the CIC. Since he rarely left the room, however, this was hardly a surprise. What did come as a surprise, especially since she was sure she had made a horrible first impression, was the fact that he actually seemed to have taken a liking to her.

“Good morning, Katy. I’d like to speak with Captain Zhukov aboard the *Jutland*. I’ll take it in conference room two, please,” Patterson said over his shoulder before stopping mid-stride and turning back to Ensign Fletcher. “Also, go ahead and issue a prepare for launch order for TFS *Theseus*.”

“Aye, sir, will do, and good morning to you as well,” she smiled.

Patterson smiled pleasantly in return before heading off once again in the direction of the conference room. The admiral’s three sons were only a little older than the young ensign. Although raising three boys had been more than enough, as far as he and Mrs. Patterson were concerned, he had still always wanted a daughter. *There's always granddaughters,* he thought, *assuming I don't screw all this up.* The CNO's job was stressful under the best of circumstances, but taking personal command of Earth's defenses had allowed the full burden of his responsibilities to bear down on him like nothing he had ever experienced before. Perhaps more so than any single person in Human history, Kevin Patterson had the weight of the world on his shoulders. *Please, God, don't let me screw this up*, he thought, silently repeating the G-rated version of astronaut Alan Shepard's famous prayer from three centuries before.

By the time he managed to close the door and take a seat at the table in the small conference room, a chime, accompanied by a textual notification on the wall-mounted view screen, indicated that the commander of *Jutland's* air wing, still generally referred to as the "CAG," was standing by. "Open the channel please," Patterson ordered, to which the AI responded with a slightly more urgent-sounding chime, followed immediately by the appearance of Captain Zhukov on the screen.

"Good morning, Admiral. I take it you noticed that one of our *Hunter* formations is past due."

"Good morning to you, Dmitri Nikolayevich," Patterson began, using the officer's given name followed by the patronymic based on his father's first name. Although the patronym had fallen out of common, everyday use, even in Russia, it was still seen as a sign of polite respect — especially when used by a superior officer from another country. "I did see that. Any chance it's a coincidence?"

"I would say that with each passing minute a coincidence becomes less likely. If we hear nothing within the next half hour, we must conclude that the formation is most likely lost. Of course, this does not necessarily mean that they were destroyed by hostile forces, but …"

"But it doesn't mean they weren't, either," Patterson interjected. "Do you have a strike package ready for me?"

"Yes, sir. We prepared three different options, but the one I recommend that we execute first is more of a reconnaissance in force. We begin by sending in one of our *Reaper* squadrons — twenty-four aircraft — configured for an anti-ship strike with C-Drive-equipped missiles."

"That's a more conservative approach than I would have expected from you, Captain. Tell me what you're thinking."

"I do not believe I have ever been accused of conservative combat tactics, Admiral," Zhukov smiled, "but, as you know, we are in a bit of a tenuous situation. Assuming the missing *Hunters* were destroyed by the Resistance task force, this seems to imply that either: a) they jumped directly on top of the enemy formation; or b) the Resistance ships have deployed sophisticated defensive measures covering a large region of space surrounding their rally point. It is also possible that we are dealing with more than one rally point, so I would like to continue the *Hunter* reconnaissance flights even after we locate some of the enemy task force."

"I agree wholeheartedly. How many *Hunters* do you have in action at the moment?"

"Ah, I'm glad you asked that, sir. Fifty-six are in operation at the moment, including the two that may have been lost — that's nearly half of the C-Drive-equipped *Hunters* we have available at the moment. Please recall that the decision was made to embark *all* of the available C-Jump-capable *Hunters* aboard the *Jutland* before she launched since, at the time, we did not know how long the other two carriers would be delayed. Now that all three are in space, I suggest we divide the RPSVs evenly so that each ship will have forty available, in addition to one hundred fifty-two with sublight capability only."

Admiral Patterson swore silently to himself, then closed his eyes and massaged the bridge of his nose between his thumb and index finger as if trying to ward off a particularly bad headache. "Yes, of course, Captain. You're absolutely right, and I realize now that I've issued a couple of orders that did not take that into account. I appreciate your compensating for my oversight, but please don't hesitate to ask a question if I tell you to do something that doesn't make sense. Yes, please make it as you say. Once you get the RPSVs redistributed, let *Ushant* and *Philippine Sea* take over the local CAP missions as well as the long-range reconnaissance flights. Since we have probably lost any potential of surprising the Resistance ships, we also need to beef up the local patrol missions quite a bit. Admiral Naftur seems to think they are waiting for the arrival of several additional ships, but if we have spooked them, they may decide to attack with the forces they have available. I also want the *Jutland* out of Earth's gravity well and paired up with the *Navajo*. As the situation develops, we'll need as many ships as possible ready to move — and hopefully dedicated to offensive combat operations at some point. Please pass all that along to Captain Donovan when we are finished here."

"I will do so immediately, Admiral. Regarding the strike package, economy of force is our primary concern. With all of the Block 2 upgrades underway, we have only six active squadrons of F-373s available — and we had to strip all of our planet-side bases to get those. Two squadrons are now deployed aboard each carrier. Getting back to your original question, there are far too many unknowns at the moment, so I am reluctant to commit a significant portion of our tactical strike forces until we have a better idea of what we are up against."

Patterson stared off to the side for a moment, slowly nodding his head as if testing Zhukov's reasoning against his own set of assumptions. "Everything you said sounds reasonable to me. And I also agree that it seems likely the Resistance ships have some pretty intense anti-ship defenses set up around their perimeter. So I assume your plan is to C-Jump into the general area of the missing *Hunters'* last recon location, but allow yourself some room to maneuver or retreat in case it's too hot to conduct your attack."

"That is correct, sir. The Operations Order calls for two flights of twelve *Reapers* to C-Jump into the area simultaneously at a distance of one light minute either side of the *Hunters'* last destination. We have no way of knowing where the Resistance ships were located relative to this point in space, but dividing our forces should minimize the possibility of sending the entire squadron into the middle of an enemy formation. Each flight's first priority will be using their passive sensor suites to gather as much information as possible regarding the enemy task force's disposition, strength, and composition. Each flight commander will then evaluate the situation to determine whether to press the attack or return to base. Unlike the RPSVs, our *Reapers* are capable of multiple, consecutive C-Jumps, if necessary."

"Very well, Captain. I have a couple of additional things in mind, but I'm going to need real-time comm out there — surveillance too, if I can get it. Are any of your fighters rigged to deploy a surveillance drone?"

"Not at the moment, sir, but we do have a few crews who have completed deployment missions before. The drone or beacon enclosures can be fitted to an external hardpoint and simply released at the desired location."

"Can a single ship complete a deployment while remaining undetected?"

"Unlikely, sir. Not with a surveillance drone, since the pilot would be required to transition into normal space to deploy the second half of the system. Under the circumstances, I believe a communications beacon is the better choice, since doing so without detection should be possible. While its capabilities are limited to the relay of data, it would function in much the same way as a surveillance drone as soon one of our ships arrives in the area."

"The fighter would remain in hyperspace for the entire deployment mission, then?"

"Yes, sir. C-Jump to the deployment location — drop the beacon — C-Jump home. Seems simple enough, yes? Although we have no way of knowing if the Resistance ships have the capability of detecting vessels in hyperspace."

"No we don't. What we *do* know, however, is that *we* have no way of doing so ourselves unless we hammer the area with active sensor scans, and even then it generally only works for frigate-sized or larger vessels that remain stationary for an extended period of time."

"Correct. If we assume the Resistance vessels possess a similar level of capability, it is unlikely our fighter would be detected."

"That doesn't sound like a particularly sound assumption, Captain," Patterson grumbled, "but I believe it's a gamble worth taking. I have two more questions for you and then I need you to get with Captain Donovan and make all of this happen as quickly as possible. Number one, can you disperse five of the beacons around the area to give us the best chance of providing something like real-time coverage, and, number two, how quickly can you get all of this done?"

Zhukov glanced momentarily at a schematic showing the F-373's ventral hardpoints, then nodded slowly as he responded. "The comm beacon launch enclosures are small, so I believe it will be possible for the *Reaper* to carry five, yes."

The concept of 'stealth' had changed radically in recent years as designers grappled with the implications of adapting military tactics to faster-than-light spacecraft. Since the early twenty-first century, for example, strike fighters like the *Reaper* had primarily relied on internal bays to conceal their often blocky and decidedly unstealthy weapons. While such concealment was still beneficial for some specific mission types, it was largely unnecessary for others — particularly those where the ship was able to remain in hyperspace for most of the approach to its target. As a result, designers had quickly returned to the practice of attaching external ordinance and other specialized equipment on pylons beneath the fighter's wings and fuselage.

"As for real-time communications coverage," Zhukov continued, "we must make some educated guesses regarding the most likely location of the Resistance task force based on the information we have. If we assume the *Hunters* were destroyed in the immediate vicinity of the enemy ships, we may be able to establish NRD communications with only minimal delay. How much delay depends on the location of our ships with respect to the beacons once they transition into the area, of course. I can get a ship rigged and ready within the hour as long as our engineering staff can prepare the beacons for deployment that quickly. If you will permit me …" Zhukov paused, issuing several commands via his tablet. After a few moments, he looked back up at Patterson. "A fighter is being prepared for launch as we speak. I will be able to provide an estimated time to launch within the next few minutes."

"Excellent. That's exactly what I wanted to hear," Patterson replied with a broad smile.

"One more item regarding the reconnaissance in force mission … with your permission, the two flights will be led by myself and Commander David Waffer."

The admiral regarded the CAG through narrowed eyes for a moment, then softened his expression a bit before answering. "You know exactly what I'm going to say, Dmitri. I absolutely cannot afford to lose you or your Air Boss. At the same time, I recognize that you are both superb pilots and I trust your judgment as well as anyone else I could name." Patterson took in a deep breath and sighed to himself before giving his answer. "Do *not* get yourselves killed."

"Yes, Admiral. I will add this new requirement to the OPORD," Dmitri laughed.

"See that you do. Now, just one more thing …," Patterson said, his face taking on a piratical grin. "Let me tell you about a hunch of mine that may change a couple of items in your mission plan."

Chapter 12

TFS Theseus, TFC Yucca Mountain Shipyard Facility

"Commander Reynolds," Lieutenant Dubashi said over her shoulder from the Communications console, "Admiral Patterson just issued a prepare for launch order."

The XO had upgraded the destroyer's status to "mission effective" immediately after the entire crew had completed their minimum required training rotation. This had the immediate effect of requiring *Theseus* to begin operating much more like a ship of war than an ongoing construction project. All six of the ship's reactors were now online, her weapons and stores loadouts complete, and her bridge manned by a designated officer of the deck twenty-four hours per day. At the moment, Lieutenant Dubashi happened to be on duty, but Commander Reynolds, like competent executive officers since time immemorial, always seemed to be everywhere onboard at the same time.

"Is that all the order contained?"

"Yes, ma'am. There were no other details attached. The flagship has indicated that they will be attempting to use a new form of quantum cryptography for message traffic requiring the highest levels of security. They believe our standard encryption methods have been compromised, but they are continuing to use them for most routine communications. I suppose they consider that an attempt at deception, but I have my doubts it will make much difference where the Guardian in concerned."

“I see. Well, details or no, the admiral obviously believes something is about to happen,” Reynolds said. “I guess one good thing about being at Yucca Mountain is that we don’t have to worry about the crew wandering very far from the ship. Please confirm our status when you acknowledge the order, then go ahead and issue a general recall. As soon as you do so, we are granted a three-hour grace period. After that, we are required to be airborne within one hour of receiving an actual launch order, so things are about to get very busy around here.”

“Aye, ma’am, but I’m not sure I remember things ever not being busy,” Dubashi laughed.

“True enough,” Reynolds smiled, then looked at the ceiling out of habit before continuing. “Captain Prescott to the bridge,” she said aloud for the benefit of the ship’s AI.

Within seconds, the captain had been located and summoned back to the ship, resulting in an immediate call via the ship’s comm system.

“Reynolds, Prescott.”

“Reynolds here. Go ahead, Captain.”

“I’m in Captain Oshiro’s office at the moment. Did we get a prepare for launch order?”

“Yes, sir, we did.”

“I have been expecting that for a little while now. Admiral Patterson mentioned that he would like us to do a sort of ‘mini shakedown cruise,’ but I’m not sure if there is anything else going on or not. I assume you’re flying the Blue Peter?” he asked, referring to the traditional naval flag signal for “P,” signifying that the vessel was about to depart and that all personnel should report aboard immediately.

“Yes, sir. Most of our people are already onboard, but everyone else has at least acknowledged the recall order. I’m not sure how much good a short shakedown cruise will do at this point, but the AI seems to think all of our major systems are in the green and ready for departure. Overall, I think we’re in pretty good shape. The extra couple of days have been a godsend.”

“Glad to hear it. I’ll be along shortly. Prescott out.”

SCS Hadeon, Pelaran Resistance Rally Point
(3.3 light years from Earth)

Commander Woorin Miah strode onto *Hadeon’s* bridge for the first time in what he believed to be a manner befitting an officer commanding his own squadron of ships on detached duty. He was already a bit annoyed that there had been no honor guard present when his shuttle arrived and had also noted that the ship’s AI had failed to properly announce his arrival. Now that he had reached the bridge — *his* bridge — he was absolutely incensed by the apparent lack of respect. The Wek brute guarding the bridge entrance had not even bothered to call the room to attention when he entered. He stopped momentarily to glare at the Marine who, even without his combat armor, outweighed the Damaran by at least sixty kilograms and towered over him by thirty centimeters or more.

“I am Commander Miah,” he seethed. Although it was rare that anyone addressed the young enlisted man while on guard duty, he immediately came to attention per his training. With his eyes focused straight ahead, however, he was barely able to see the top of the commander's head in his peripheral vision. "You will see that your commanding officer contacts me regarding your failure to follow protocol after you complete your duty hours today."

"Aye, Commander," the Marine responded smartly, in spite of having no idea what he had done to irritate the little Damaran.

Miah regarded the man for a moment with a look of disapproval before spinning on his heels and continuing in the direction of the command chairs lining the rear of the bridge. In spite of the scene he had just created in the entryway, the Wek bridge officers on duty had not noticed his arrival. Instead, their attention had been focused on making adjustments to their defensive perimeter required by the imminent departure of their two sister BD cruisers.

Stopping squarely in front of the console reserved for the ship's commanding officer, Miah turned and stared down its current occupant — a commander who was busily issuing instructions via the Command console's touchscreen. After completing his task, the officer looked up from his screen, offering what any Wek would consider a polite smile accompanied by a low purring sound from the center of his chest.

"Good afternoon, Commander …" he paused while reading the Damaran's nameplate, "Miah. I am Commander Yuli Takkar. How can I help you?"

"You can begin by addressing me as 'Captain Miah!'" he snapped, this time raising his voice to ensure the entire bridge was aware of his presence, and causing several heads around the room to immediately turn in their direction. "I am now in command of this vessel, as well as the other three that will be remaining here to secure the task force's original Rally point."

"I beg your pardon, Commander Miah, but we have received no instructions along those lines from the Flag. Perhaps it's just an oversight due to the haste with which we have been forced to relocate most of the task force. If you would like to have a seat here for a moment," he said, gesturing to the empty Command console to his left, "I will be happy to confirm my instructions with the *Gunov* before she departs. My executive officer will also see to your accommodations aboard as well as anything else you might need during your stay."

"I *relieve* you, sir," Miah growled with barely contained fury while holding his ground directly in front of the Wek commander's chair.

Commander Takkar was feeling less hospitable by the moment and, in fact, would probably have already taken grave offense to the Damaran's abusive behavior under different circumstances. The situation struck him as so odd, even vaguely entertaining, however, that he managed to hold his temper in check for the moment. *Is it possible this impudent whelp is telling the truth?* he wondered. It was exceedingly rare that Damaran officers ever rose above the rank of commander — and they generally only reached that rank as a result of Governing Council fiat. It was also unusual for a member of their species to be given command of a single vessel, let alone a small squadron. Something about all of this didn't seem quite right, but the Wek officer cautioned himself to avoid jumping to any conclusions just yet.

"I'm waiting," Commander Miah said impatiently.

Takkar glanced at his second-in-command in the chair to his right, but received only a noncommittal expression along with what he was sure was a hint of amusement forming at the corners of his eyes. *Fine, let's see where this goes*, he thought, chuckling to himself as he rose to his full height. At just over two meters in height, Takkar dwarfed the Damaran almost as effectively as the Marine sentry in combat armor. "I stand relieved, sir. I will, of course, remain on the bridge and assist you in any way I can."

"I will require your services in acting as my second-in-command. Handling the more mundane tasks of managing this ship and her systems will remain your responsibility, Commander Takkar," Miah sneered without bothering to look at the Wek officer. "I have been tasked with guarding the original rally point until our remaining five battleships can arrive and be safely directed to join the rest of the task force."

"Captain Takkar, I have an incoming transmission from Commodore Sarafi aboard the *Gunov*," a Wek lieutenant announced from the Communications console.

Miah had just taken his seat, but immediately stood again to address the entire bridge crew. "Commander Takkar has been relieved as acting captain. I am Commander … excuse me, *Captain* Woorin Miah. I have taken command of this vessel as well as three others that will be remaining at this location until the remainder of our forces arrive."

Wearing a look of surprise and confusion, the lieutenant glanced at Commander Takkar for confirmation. Having already reached the point where amusement had transitioned to anger mixed with grave concern, Takkar simply nodded in reply before taking his seat at the command chair to Miah's left.

"Let's not keep the commodore waiting, Lieutenant," Miah scolded.

Within seconds the face of Naveen Sarafi appeared on the bridge view screen. "Ah, Captain Miah," he greeted "I trust you have found the condition of the *Hadeon* satisfactory and are settling into your new command?"

"There are a few deficiencies, Commodore, but none that I won't be able to handle," he replied haughtily.

"I'm confident you will," Sarafi replied, a smile spreading across his face.

Although lost on the Damaran, the manner in which the commodore was conducting himself provided further evidence for Commander Takkar's growing suspicion that something was amiss. Like many of his contemporaries, he had been won over to the Resistance cause by the fiery rhetoric and saber rattling from several members of the Sajeth Collective's Governing Council over the past several months. While covered around the clock by news outlets across the entire alliance, their lofty speeches were specifically crafted to appeal to the Wek population's natural sense of duty and integrity. As a result, many had become convinced that the solemn oaths they had sworn to protect the Collective demanded that they take action to address the growing threat posed by the Humans and their Pelaran masters. While he agreed in principle, Takkar had been optimistic that some way could be found to simply eliminate the Pelaran Guardian spacecraft. Perhaps then, the Humans could be shown the folly of allowing themselves to become an instrument of Pelaran aggression. He sincerely hoped that this could be achieved without resorting to an all-out attack on Terra, but he did believe that some sort of temporary occupation of the planet might be required. Not for the first time since joining the Resistance, the Wek commander questioned whether he was being used in much the same way as the Humans — the only real difference being the identity of his master.

"The rest of the task force will be leaving momentarily, Captain," Sarafi continued. "Before we depart, I wanted to take a moment to reiterate the importance of your mission. We simply cannot proceed without the remaining five battleships, especially given the experience level of their captains. Frankly, I still do not believe that the Humans possess any forces capable of posing a serious threat to your detachment of ships. Having said that, I admit that I also did not anticipate the arrival of their scout ships. Remain at your highest level of alert, Captain Miah. Any ships not transmitting Sajeth Collective identification codes should be considered hostile and attacked immediately. Do you have any questions?"

Commander Takkar considered asking the commodore why he would risk such an unnecessary division of his forces when there were other secure methods available for directing the battleships to the new rally point. He knew without asking, however, that the commodore was well aware of this fact — although probably not this fool of a Damaran. He also knew that asking such a question would be treated as something approaching mutiny by both, although for very different reasons, he suspected.

“No questions at this time, sir. Rest assured, I will have the crews of all four of my ships whipped into shape by the time we rendezvous with you.”

“Of that, I have no doubt,” Sarafi smiled. “Good luck, *Captain* Miah,” he said with an ironic tone noted by every Wek officer on the bridge.

The commodore’s image was replaced by a view off the *Hadeon’s* starboard bow, which currently included several task force warships. Without further comment, Miah began his first act as captain by passing the time remaining until the task force’s departure overriding Commander Takkar’s preferences at the Command console.

“Captain, the task force is transitioning to hyperspace,” the comm officer reported after a few minutes had passed.

On the view screen, the starfield surrounding each ship’s hull appeared to blur momentarily, followed by a flash of gray light as each ship departed in rapid succession for the secondary rally point. Miah shot a disinterested glance at the bridge view screen before returning his attention to the Command console. After a few moments, he noticed an odd tension in the room that made the hair on the back of his neck stand on end. Looking slowly up from his touchscreen, he saw that every Wek officer in the room was staring directly at him from their individual workstations. Miah felt the familiar tinge of panic form in the back of his mind as the reality of his situation slowly dawned on him. He was utterly alone … and, unless his usually keen hearing was failing him, he was sure he could detect low, threatening growls from at least three locations in the room.

TFC Comm Beacon Deployment Flight "Gamble 22," Near the Pelaran Resistance Rally Point
(In hyperspace - 3.3 light years from Earth)

In the adjacent dimensionality commonly referred to as hyperspace, a single F-373 *Reaper* had just completed deployment of the first of its payload of five communications beacons. Since it was assumed that the missing *Hunter* reconnaissance flight must have transitioned into normal space in close proximity to the enemy task force, the corresponding location in hyperspace had been chosen for release of the first comm beacon.

The pilot relaxed for a moment as he waited for confirmation that the beacon had stabilized and begun the process of synchronizing with the next closest nodes on the NRD network, just over three light years distant. He was in no particular hurry at the moment. There was virtually no chance that his ship would be detected as long as it remained in hyperspace. And since it was critical that all five of the beacons be brought online successfully, it made sense to sit tight at each deployment location and wait for the beacon to come online before moving on.

That wouldn't have been an option just a few weeks ago, but the Combat Communications Division of the Fleet Science and Engineering Directorate had reportedly made significant improvements in the beacons' routing software. Once again managing to improve significantly on the Pelaran-provided design, the developers had introduced an algorithm based on the latest commercially deployed networks in use on Earth. Several beacons released within the solar system with the updated software had shown a nearly tenfold improvement in network convergence time. If the same held true here, real-time communications with the rest of the fleet should be available in a matter of minutes.

With nothing more than the black void associated with remaining stationary in hyperspace displayed via the ship's optics, the lieutenant decided to spend a few moments manually cycling through a few of his ship's other passive sensors. He realized that this activity was largely symbolic, and served more to occupy his own mind than contribute in any meaningful way to what the fighter was already accomplishing without his help. Though the *Reaper* was designed to carry only a single pilot, it was always understood that the complex task of operating the fighter and its myriad of systems was well beyond the capabilities of a single Human … or several Humans for that matter. Accordingly, the AI was designed to shoulder much of the burden without any assistance whatsoever from the pilot. When direct interaction *was* required, however, the ship's user interface behaved in a much more interactive style than those deployed aboard larger Fleet vessels. So while the neural interface provided incredibly efficient communications between ship and pilot during combat, most of their routine interactions were conversational — closely mimicking the manner in which pilots had traditionally worked in concert with a navigator or radar intercept officer (RIO).

“Anything unusual showing up on the passive array?” the pilot asked aloud.

“Define ‘unusual,’” the AI answered in a casual, joking tone. “Just about everything we see and do every day is unusual.”

“Yeah, I guess you got me there,” he laughed. “I was just thinking that it’s entirely possible that we are essentially superimposed at the same location as the Resistance task force ships. We know how to detect ships in hyperspace from normal space using a combination of active sensors, but it would be damned helpful if we could do the same thing from hyperspace using only the passive array.”

“Indeed it would,” the ship answered in a thoughtful tone. “We, of course, have nothing approaching the sensor capabilities of our larger warships, but if something obvious happens, we should be able to detect it.”

“Obvious, huh? Well, right back at you, smart guy, you go right ahead and define ‘obvious’ for me,” the lieutenant chuckled.

“Hah, well I guess I mean if something so definitive happens that we could hardly fail to notice. You know, like a big, neon sign with an arrow that says ‘enemy ships, exit here.’” The AI paused momentarily as it continued to monitor vast quantities of data streaming in from its sensors. “By the way, looks like the first comm beacon is up and running. Estimated time remaining for sync with NRD net: zero five minutes.”

“Whoa, that’s very good news, thanks. Since the new software appears to be working as advertised, we might as well hang out here until it syncs up. We have a preprogrammed pattern for deploying the other four beacons, but if we were to detect something, we might change …"

"Contacts!" the AI interrupted excitedly.

"*Contacts?* Where away? Clarify!" the pilot commanded. To his knowledge, no Human vessel had ever detected *anything* while in hyperspace, let alone something that could be classified as another ship. *Then again*, he thought, *it's not like we have a lot of experience in this area.*

"Unable to classify the contacts at the moment, sir," the AI answered. "It's a previously undetected phenomena characterized by massive particle emissions."

"Source?"

"Precise sources unknown, but I can confirm twenty-four distinct events, all occurring within a span of zero eight seconds."

"Okay, is it possible we're seeing ships transitioning either into or out of hyperspace?"

"The pattern is consistent with current hyperdrive theory for ships transitioning from normal space into hyperspace. The same would not be true if the ships had been transitioning back into normal space. I have sufficient data now to pinpoint the source coordinates of all twenty-four events. You should be able to see them plotted to port."

"Yeah, I see them," the lieutenant replied, looking off to his left at the grouping of red ovals pulsing urgently within his field of view. "Is there anything else you can tell me?" he asked, shaken by the sudden realization that he was perhaps not as isolated and concealed as he had believed just moments before.

"I'm still processing data. Can you please be more specific?"

"Sure, yeah, sorry about that," he breathed, trying to calm and refocus his mind. "Can you tell if there are twenty-four enemy warships sitting at those locations?"

"Again, keep in mind that we're breaking new ground here to an extent. I'm filling gaps in the observational data from our sensors with some theory-based hypotheses."

"Fine, whatever. Give me your best guess," the lieutenant replied, beginning to lose his patience. Interaction with the fighter's AI was often so Human-like that it was easy to forget that he was dealing with a machine. "Conversations" like this one brought the reality of the situation back to the forefront of his mind in a manner that was as jarring as it was irritating.

"I believe that I can not only assert that the ships have left the area," the AI replied, as a series of red lines extended from the contacts displayed within the lieutenant's field of view, "but I can also project their direction of flight."

Chapter 13

TFS Navajo
(Combat Information Center)

While he had never been one to micromanage his people, Admiral Patterson had taken the unusual step of insisting that the pilot of Gamble 22 be patched directly through to the *Navajo's* CIC as soon as the first comm beacon came online. He was fully aware that the pilot would likely have little if any useful information to convey at this point. Still, he considered the act of establishing real-time communications with one of his ships in what he hoped was the vicinity of the enemy to be a pivotal first step — one he hoped would ultimately lead to a successful defense of Earth.

"Admiral," Ensign Fletcher called from her Communications console, "the first comm beacon is operational, and I have Gamble 22 on the line."

"Outstanding. Designate the coordinates of the first comm beacon as Location Dagger," Patterson ordered, selecting a word that he liked from a list of randomly generated code names on his tablet. "How are we set for crypto?"

"It's the latest and greatest based on the new software hand-delivered by the Combat Comm guys yesterday," she replied, raised eyebrows revealing her skepticism. "They seem to believe it's 'unbreakable.'"

"I'm pretty sure I've heard that before, but I guess we'll see. It's not like we can just stop communicating with our ships," he groused, while donning a nearby headset. "Put the pilot through, please."

“Aye, sir,” Fletcher replied, issuing the required commands at her console before nodding to indicate a live audio connection.

“Gamble 22, Gun-shy.”

“Gun-shy, go for Gamble 22,” came the immediate reply from 3.3 light years away with more than sufficient clarity to detect the nervousness in the young lieutenant’s voice.

“We’re happy to hear from you, Gamble. How do you read?” The traditional question and response regarding signal readability and strength had little relevance in digital communications, but was still sometimes used more as a greeting than for the purpose of confirming the audio connection.

“Five by five, Gun-shy. You should be getting data as well.”

“Understood. Stand by one.” Patterson waved to get the attention of the commander at the holographic display as he turned and walked in the direction of the table. The admiral pointed at his headset then back to the holo table, which was all the young tactical officer needed by way of instructions. A few seconds later, all of the information currently displayed in the cockpit of Gamble 22 was projected in exquisite, three-dimensional detail above the surface of the table.

“Alright, son, we’ve got your feed. Very nice job so far. Explain to me what I’m seeing.”

“Roger, Gun-shy. The contacts you see appeared immediately after release of the first comm beacon. The AI classified them as probable outbound hyperspace transitions from twenty-four individual vessels in the directions indicated by the course projection lines.”

“Did the AI make any guess as to their destination?”

“Negative, sir. The signatures appeared to be consistent with standard hyperdrives, so there is no way to tell when they intend to disengage their engines. The AI did note, however, that if they had been C-Jump signatures, it might have been possible to project their destination based on power output.”

“Great work, Gamble, that’s a bona fide major discovery,” Patterson replied, making a mental note to follow up with Science and Engineering about the treasure trove of information this short mission had already provided. “We’re going to rework your target package based on this new data. Sit tight for a few minutes and we’ll transmit new orders for you. If anything else happens in the area, let us know immediately.”

“Understood, Gun-shy. Gamble 22 out.”

“Alright,” Patterson began, energized by the fact that he finally had some hard intelligence to work with, “show me where we were planning on placing the remaining four comm beacons.”

“Aye, sir,” the commander replied, entering a series of commands on his tablet to access the information. Before he could finish, the *Navajo’s* AI anticipated his request — pulling the relevant data directly from the fighter’s AI. Three pulsating, green spheres appeared above the table to indicate the original deployment locations.

“Okay, let’s move number two to this location,” Patterson said, physically grabbing one of the three spheres and dragging it to a location closer to the hyperspace transitions detected by Gamble 22. “Number three looks pretty good as is. Four is pretty close too, but let's just pull it in a bit and get a tighter grouping since we now have a better idea where their rally point is located."

"Begging your pardon, Admiral, but can we not assume that those twenty-four hyperspace transitions were the Resistance ships *leaving* their original rally point?"

Patterson looked up at the youngish commander, wearing the kind of smile he might have given one of his sons when he knew they were right on the cusp of grasping some new skill he had worked hard to teach them. "We might indeed, Commander. We might even be tempted to assume that they have abandoned their original rally point and won't be back. Consider, however, that we have a number of other pieces of information that don't quite add up. For one, their course vectors do not indicate they were on their way to Earth, right?"

"No, sir. They're not even heading in our general direction," he said, feeling as if he had become privy to a diabolical practical joke that was just about to be put into motion — at someone else's expense.

"Now keep in mind that I may be the one who's being had here, but in my mind, that was a missed opportunity on the part of their commander."

"Because …" the commander paused as the implications ran rapidly through his mind, "if they thought there was any chance we might detect their departure, heading in the general direction of Earth would have put us on the defensive, even if their intent was to move their task force only a short distance."

"Right. It's all about maintaining the initiative, especially when you can do something simple that just might succeed in throwing your enemy off balance. The fact is that they probably had no reason to suspect we would detect their departure. If you put yourself in their commander's place, though, wouldn't you be looking to move your task force?"

"I'd get the hell out of there in a hurry, sir. It looks like our *Hunter* recon flight must have transitioned right on top of them. So he knows their original rally point is compromised."

"He does indeed. In fact, he has a number of new pieces of information with which he must now contend. He knows that his task force has most likely lost any possibility of a surprise attack, he knows that our capabilities are likely more formidable than he was led to believe, and he knows that it is entirely possible that we, or perhaps old GORT out there, might decide to mount an attack in short order." Patterson paused and stared at the display for a moment, wondering if it was he who was missing something obvious. "Here's something else to consider," he continued. "Why the delay? Why had they not already attacked Earth before our *Hunters* arrived?"

"I'd have to say for the same reason he didn't head in our direction just now. He's not ready."

"That would be my guess as well. And if he's expecting more ships, he has no capability to contact them if they are en route, just like us. In fact, their long range comm requires their ships to remain in normal space and stationary for an extended period of time, right?"

"Yes, sir, although we're not entirely sure how long. It's apparently something Admiral Naftur has been careful not to reveal."

"I can't say I blame him. A smart commander will take a comm advantage over one in raw firepower any day of the week … within reason, of course," Patterson said. "In any event, it's probably a safe bet that there will be more ships arriving at the original rally point. And that makes it a pretty important piece of real estate for us to control if we can."

"Got it, sir. Thank you for taking the time to explain all of that to me," the commander said.

"Hah! You can thank me after we see if I was right," Patterson laughed. "If we manage to live long enough to find out, that is."

The tactical officer raised his eyebrows, surprised by the admiral's rather unusual candor … or was that dark humor? "One other thing I noticed, Admiral," he continued, "aren't we missing the location for deployment of the fifth comm beacon?"

"I just don't think we can see it at this scale. We probably need to zoom out to include about a five-light-hour radius," Patterson replied, pinching the space above the table to make the necessary adjustment. On the far edge of the display, an additional pulsating green sphere came into view.

"Surely that's an error, sir. That one won't provide us any additional coverage sitting way out there."

"Nope, that looks about right to me as well. Go ahead and transmit the new deployment orders to Gamble 22. Tell him to stay put and await further orders once he's finished. Then notify Captains Zhukov and Donovan aboard the *Jutland* of our changes."

"Aye, sir," he replied, shooting Patterson an expectant look.

"Don't worry, Commander, that last location will make sense to you soon enough," the admiral said, winking as he turned to head for the *Navajo's* bridge.

TFS Theseus, TFC Yucca Mountain Shipyard Facility

"Captain on the bridge!" the Marine sentry barked as Prescott made his first "official" appearance via the aft entrance near his ready room. Looking around, he noticed that Commander Reynolds had asked the standby bridge crew to step in for the occasion … and the sight of all of his officers and the young Marine standing at attention produced an unexpected stream of emotionally laden thoughts. It occurred to him that he did not remember his first formal entry onto *Ingenuity's* bridge ever being announced in this manner. He assumed that was probably because an opportunity had never presented itself amid the chaos of her shakedown cruise, commissioning, and immediate transition to operational status. This time around, Fleet had opted to skip the shakedown cruise altogether, and he couldn't help but wonder whether reliance on AI-based testing and evaluation would prove sufficient to avoid unpleasant or, worse yet, tragic surprises. As his brief stream of consciousness concluded, Prescott allowed himself to pause briefly and enjoy the moment. After all, his crew had performed admirably thus far, and they had every reason to take pride in their accomplishments — both aboard *Ingenuity* and in preparing *Theseus* for departure. Taking a deep breath, Prescott moved on with the business at hand.

"Stand easy for a moment, everyone. I very much appreciate the courtesy. As you all know, that kind of thing rarely makes much practical sense on the bridge of a starship, so thank you for taking advantage of the opportunity. I know it goes without saying, but, once we are underway, it will not be necessary to call the room unless Commander Reynolds or I specifically tell you otherwise. For those of you I have already served with, I'm proud of your performance to date and happy to have you aboard once again. For those of you who are new," he laughed, shading his eyes with one hand as he looked around the room, "and I think that's limited to Lieutenant Lee at the moment … welcome aboard. Commander Reynolds went out of her way to irritate all of the other destroyer captains by cherry-picking some of their very best crewmembers. Unfortunately for you, that means she'll have the bar set pretty high to make sure you're worthy of all the favors she owes for stealing you away.

"Now, while I wish we had more time to get acquainted, both with each other and with our new ship, we were at least fortunate enough to get a few extra days of training and prep time before being sent out on our first mission. Hopefully, you're all reasonably well-rested and ready to go, because our so-called 'grace period' is just about to expire, and I suspect we will be getting underway shortly thereafter. On that note, I'm going to let Commander Reynolds go over what we know so far regarding our first assignment. Commander."

"Thank you, Captain. First watch crew, you can all take your seats. Standby crew, please remain with us for just a moment, if you would. This won't take long," she said as she walked around to the space between the Helm console and the bridge view screen. "I see that you have all reviewed the pre-mission briefing materials," she began, taking a quick glance at her tablet, "so I'll just hit the highlights and then give you the opportunity to ask questions. As you know, Admiral Patterson believes we have located the site of the original Pelaran Resistance rally point, which is now being referred to as Location Dagger." Reynolds turned to confirm that the AI was displaying the appropriate imagery, knowing, even as she did, that it was wholly unnecessary to do so. "One of TFS *Jutland's* fighters has managed to deploy comm beacons in these locations, so the entire area now has excellent comm coverage. We expect that our role will be to transport Sajeth Collective Admiral Rugali Naftur to the area and attempt to make contact with Resistance forces. Lieutenant Commander Schmidt, did you have a question?"

"Yes, ma'am. Sorry for the interruption. Does Admiral Naftur expect the Resistance forces to be receptive to opening some sort of dialog?"

"I think the most honest answer to that question is that he thinks doing so offers our best chance of avoiding a military confrontation, so it's at least worth a try. The Resistance crews are expected to be made up almost entirely of Wek personnel, and I think it's safe to say that Admiral Naftur is widely known and respected among their military forces. He believes there are likely to be many among them who would also prefer to avoid bloodshed, if at all possible — especially if we can convince them that Humanity does not pose a threat to the Sajeth Collective. The question, of course, is whether attempting to communicate in this fashion will provoke at least some of their forces into attacking us immediately."

"And do we have some way of letting them know that we are proposing a parley? A signal of some kind?"

"Yes we do, and their forces do have a historical context for such meetings, just as we do. Admiral Naftur has indicated that it would be considered a grave breach of their rules of war to execute an attack during a parley. Then again, one could argue that the entire Resistance movement is operating outside the bounds of their legal command authority structure," she said. "That brings us to our contingency plan. A full squadrons of F-373s will be standing by for our signal here," she said, turning to point to the comm beacon now indicated by a pulsating red oval by the ship's AI. "The comm beacon where our fighters will be waiting has been designated Location Willow and is approximately five light hours from Location Dagger. That should be well outside the detection range of the Resistance ships, but the fighters will remain in hyperspace, just in case. If our, uh, negotiations are unsuccessful, they will immediately join us and assist in whatever actions are deemed appropriate at that time. Captain Zhukov and Commander Waffer from the *Jutland* will lead the two flights of *Reapers*, but Captain Prescott will be in overall command of the mission."

“Ma’am?” Ensign Fisher said, raising his hand to get her attention. “If the fighters remain in hyperspace, how will we call them if we need their help? I thought we couldn’t communicate with ships in hyperspace.”

“That’s a better question for Commander Logan, or Lieutenant Dubashi, but the details will have wait for another time. My decidedly nontechnical understanding is that the beacons are indeed point-to-point, real-time links … almost like telegraph stations alongside an old-fashioned railroad track. So, from a practical standpoint, it’s true that you can’t communicate with a ship traveling in hyperspace — just like the telegraph operator couldn’t communicate with the train once it left the station. A ship can, however, still communicate directly with the comm beacon, just as we do in normal space. That’s where the physics get way over my head. Bottom line, as long as you’re in the immediate vicinity of the comm beacon, it works fine.”

“Commander Reynolds,” Lieutenant Dubashi interrupted, “we have received an authenticated launch order from the Flag. Admiral Patterson says he needs two minutes alone with Captain Prescott and yourself, but he wants us underway immediately thereafter.”

“Thank you, Lieutenant,” Reynolds replied, then paused as if considering how best to wrap things up quickly. “Believe it or not,” she began again, “I have already covered most of what I had planned to show you anyway. Clearly, we continue to find ourselves at the center of a historic and rapidly evolving situation. So far, our success has depended less on detailed planning than it has on our ability to think on our feet and give each other our absolute best … and I have no reason to believe that will change on this mission. All of you are ready. *Theseus* is ready. Let's get this done." Even with only eleven crewmembers and a Marine sentry on the bridge, Reynolds received enthusiastic applause and expressions of approval as she joined Captain Prescott on the way to his ready room. "Lieutenant Commander Schmidt, you have the bridge," she ordered. "Notify Engineering to expect an immediate departure and work on getting us cleared for launch with Yucca Control."

"Aye, ma'am," he replied, moving to take his place at one of the Command consoles while being immediately replaced at Tactical 1 by a lieutenant from the standby crew.

"Good brief," Prescott said as he and Commander Reynolds reached the privacy of the ready room.

"I've always said there should be a three-minute limit. Anything longer than that needs to be handled some other way. A lot of our youngsters struggle to keep their attention on one topic for even *that* long," she said as Prescott entered the required commands to pull up the vidcon stream with TFS *Navajo*.

"Did you read that the spooks seem to think our encrypted comm is secure again?" he asked.

"I did. Long may it last … and I only mean to sound a little cynical when I say that," she replied as Terran Fleet Command's official service seal appeared on the view screen, followed a few seconds later by the obviously tired but smiling face of Admiral Kevin Patterson.

"Good morning to you both," he said cheerfully. "I trust you've enjoyed your extended R&R at the Yucca Mountain resort and are ready to get back to work."

“Good morning to you as well, Admiral. Sir, I’m just glad you’re not sitting here with us, since having my XO cooling her heels in the brig for slugging you wouldn’t be particularly helpful at the moment,” Prescott laughed.

“I’ve been slugged for a lot less, I can assure you,” Patterson replied mischievously. “In all seriousness, while I do wish we had located the Resistance task force rally point several days ago, it’s good that you had a little extra time to prepare. I know even six days was nowhere near sufficient, but I’m sure you’re much better off now than you would have been a few days ago. I also congratulate you both for achieving ‘mission effective’ status so quickly after transitioning out of *Ingenuity*. Don’t get me wrong. I expected nothing less from you two, but it’s excellent work nonetheless.”

“Thank you, Admiral,” both officers replied in unison, grateful that their CNO actually did understand and appreciate the Herculean effort required to prepare *Theseus* for her first mission.

“I’ll keep this short. I know you are fully briefed on the mission to Location Dagger. What you may not have had time to notice over the past week, however, is just how unstable things have become, politically, in the wake of the Guardian’s entrance onto the world stage. And, by the way, we will *not* be calling that damn thing Griffin, Tom, Dick, or Harry for that matter. It’s a foolish affectation in my opinion, and we’ll have no part of it unless, God forbid, the Leadership Council orders us to do so. If that happens, I’d personally be more comfortable addressing it as we would any other ambassador … which would at least prevent us from sounding like a flock of mindless sheep.”

Both Prescott and Reynolds smiled and nodded approvingly as the admiral continued.

"Admiral White's folks over at Fleet Intelligence have put together some good summary documentation regarding the political situation that you should probably read through when you have a moment. I guess if I had to provide a one-word description of world affairs at the moment, I'd use 'chaotic.' Classified information has been leaking like a sieve for a full week now. All of that can probably be traced back to the Guardian in one form or another, but I suppose that's neither here nor there at this point. Some nations are up in arms that we would ever even consider membership in the Pelaran Alliance. Others are incensed that we allowed representatives from the Sajeth Collective to come aboard one of our vessels, let alone be granted diplomatic status by TFC. Pretty much everyone is angry for being kept in the dark about the true state of our fleet … although I suppose most of them are able to see some benefit in not being completely defenseless in the face of a possible Sajeth Collective attack on Earth. I'm just scratching the surface here, but you get the gist. Things are a real mess at the moment, but I'm sure they will settle down after the immediate threat has passed."

"Will Admiral Naftur be shuttled over to us before we launch?" Prescott asked.

"No, and that gets to the heart of why I just summarized the current political situation for you. The Leadership Council has largely been in continuous session since the first direct contact from the Guardian a month ago. Council sessions have always been a little on the contentious side, but over the past week, things have gotten especially tense among the representatives. While it's generally not appropriate for Fleet personnel to comment on how the Council conducts its business, the Admiralty has serious concerns regarding some of what we have been seeing. For the sake of our discussion, I'll simply say that Chairwoman Crull has been behaving in a manner we believe is inconsistent with the TFC charter. Under normal circumstances, I think we would probably expect to see someone calling for a vote of no confidence in her leadership, followed shortly thereafter by her being removed as Chair and perhaps as the Central and South American Union's representative. Unfortunately, that's not what's happening. Somehow, she has managed to put together a fairly solid voting block composed of seven of the fifteen members … not a majority, for the moment, but enough where she manages to get her way on pretty much every issue that comes up. That's all well and good, but right after the first Guardian speech, she began what appears to be a well-planned campaign to 'demilitarize' TFC Headquarters."

"I wasn't aware that HQTFC was a military installation before," Reynolds commented.

"It was not by any means … and that was intentional. Part of the reason why that was the case was to support the original cover story that TFC was not a true military organization. Beyond that, even though defending the Earth has obviously always been at the top of our priority list — developing Pelaran technology and the peaceful exploration of space are primary missions as well. As you both know, we are also dedicated to the idea of civilian control … civilians who are duly elected representatives of our member nations."

"Is the Admiralty concerned that this voting block the chairwoman has put together is the result of some kind of election fraud?" Prescott asked.

"No. Frankly, I'm not sure what we collectively think at the moment, so let's not go down that path. The first element of her campaign to 'demilitarize' the headquarters campus, however, was to replace the Marine security contingent with a private security force. Other than a few Marines assigned to provide security for a few key admirals, notably Sexton and White, the rest have all been reassigned. From what we can tell, there are at least one hundred civilian guards in the new security force. We don't know much about them, other than the fact that they are armed to the teeth and appear to have at least some level of special operations training. There are several large private military corporations with significant interests in the governments that make up the Central and South American Union, so it's a safe bet that these firms are providing the troops and their equipment. We are still looking into how all of this took place so quickly, but clearly it had been in the works for some time."

"Well it certainly doesn't sound 'demilitarized' now," Reynolds observed.

"Precisely, Commander, and that's just one of the reasons we are concerned. In any event, I tell you all of this because we need Admiral Naftur aboard the *Theseus* immediately for your mission. Ordinarily, we would have shuttled him back to Yucca Mountain before your departure, but late yesterday, a contingent of HQSEC —

that's what they're calling themselves — security guards showed up at Sexton's office. They demanded that both Admiral Naftur and Nenir Turlaka be turned over to them for what they referred to as 'protective custody.' Admiral Sexton refused, of course, but he suspects they won't be put off for long. Sexton is now concerned that if he attempts to fly our two Wek out onboard a shuttle, they'll just end up being detained. At that point, we will have not only lost access to Naftur, but also relegated them both to an uncertain fate. There are many who already refer to them as enemy combatants. I'm sure I don't have to tell you that if anything happens to either of them, they might as well *have* been enemy combatants. They'll be coopted as martyrs for the Resistance cause, and the entire Sajeth Collective will almost certainly declare war on Humanity."

Prescott furrowed his brow and stared intently into Admiral Patterson's eyes. "Sir, this is starting to sound like you are asking us to perform an extraction."

The CNO sat back in his chair and sighed wearily. "No, Tom, I'm not. I'm telling you that I am about to send you into an ambiguous and potentially dangerous situation. All I'm asking you to do is use your heads and be aware that all of this is going on behind the scenes. Get there, evaluate the situation on the ground, and get both Naftur and Turlaka aboard *Theseus* and out of harm's way, as quickly as possible. So far, no order has been given by the Leadership Council that would prevent us from doing so within the bounds of our ongoing operations against the Pelaran Resistance. I'm afraid, however, that this could very well change as early as this afternoon when the Council reconvenes. Once that happens, our choices will become much more limited."

"Either proceed without Naftur or commit an act in open defiance of the Leadership Council," Prescott concluded.

"I believe we generally refer to that as mutiny, Captain. If possible, I would prefer to avoid putting ourselves in a situation where we might feel obliged to do such a thing in order to fulfill the promises we made when we took our oaths of office."

There was a long moment of silence as all three officers struggled to come to grips with what might be required of them … and all *before* they even set out to meet the enemy.

"There is an access tunnel linking the Marine barracks to the Admiralty Building. At the moment, it appears that HQSEC either hasn't discovered it yet, or just isn't using it for whatever reason. The barracks is less than a kilometer from the only suitable landing location in the immediate area. It's a heavily reinforced concrete pad that was built by TFC for that purpose. Believe it or not, it's so large that there wasn't room on the campus itself, so it was constructed on leased property outside the main boundary fence. Admiral Sexton will meet you there with Naftur and Turlaka. All of the pertinent data has been uploaded to your AI. Any questions?"

Prescott glanced at Reynolds, who had the look of someone with a number of unanswered questions, none of which she was inclined to ask at the moment. "No sir. We will be on our way shortly and contact you when we reach orbit."

“Be safe and be smart, you two. Patterson out.”

There was a period of uncomfortable silence after the display returned to a view of the five other *Theseus*-class destroyers in the berths immediately to starboard. It was Prescott who finally broke the silence.

“Here’s the thing, Sally. It looks like we’re going to be navigating some very murky waters here, and it’s going to be *very* important for the two of us to stay on the same page. I honestly don’t know what to say about any of what we just heard, other than the tired old platitudes about holding each other accountable and trying to do what we think is right.”

“Uh huh, that’s fine, but if I’m going to participate in a coup, I’d prefer to do so on the winning side,” she said.

Prescott stared back at his XO, incredulous. “You amaze me sometimes. That didn’t rattle you at all, did it?”

“It’s not that it didn’t rattle me, it’s just that I tend to take things like that as nothing more than additional background information. Is it important to keep in mind? Sure. Is it likely to change much about how I conduct myself? Offhand, I’d say not really.” She stopped and stared back at her captain for a moment, narrowing her eyes as she began again. “As to our being on the same page … I’ve always read how command of a ship of war can become extremely isolating for a captain, so please allow me to respectfully remind you of something I’m sure you knew before you ever sat in the big chair. I don’t follow you — respect you — push myself to ridiculous feats of endurance for you — because it’s my job. I could do *much* less and still be doing my job … and doing it well. I do those things because I know you, because I trust your judgment implicitly, and because you have *earned* it. In over two years of working together, I have never seen a day when I didn't think you deserved my very best. Rest assured that if that day ever comes, I'll be the first to let you know."

Understanding at a fundamental level that there was nothing he needed to say in response, Prescott simply nodded and smiled appreciatively.

"Now," Reynolds continued, "can we please get out of here and pick up our Wek friends before someone decides to tell us we can't?"

Chapter 14

Terran Fleet Command Headquarters
(Admiralty Building access tunnel)

"I expect Captain Prescott will arrive shortly to take you aboard the *Theseus*, so this may be the only opportunity I have to apologize to the two of you for the manner in which things have degenerated over the past few days," Admiral Sexton said as he escorted Wek Ambassador Turlaka and Admiral Naftur down the long corridor leading to the TFC Marine barracks facility. "I don't recall ever witnessing a more disgraceful breach of protocol and general lack of good sense. I hope you will bear in mind that this situation does not reflect how we normally treat our guests."

"My dear Admiral Sexton," Nenir purred with an amused grin, "to my knowledge, we are Terra's *only* visitors to date, so isn't it fair to say that this *is* the way you normally treat your guests?"

Sexton stopped dead in his tracks at this and looked Ambassador Turlaka in the eyes. Both she and Naftur lasted only a few seconds before both of their faces took on the rather savage-looking smiles that Sexton had come to appreciate, followed by the usual rumbling growls that he now knew was the Wek equivalent to a good laugh at his expense.

"Oh, that's good, you two. I appreciate very much that you can both manage to find some humor in this situation," he chuckled before resuming their progress towards the barracks. "I'm not sure I would be so gracious if our roles were reversed."

“You have been a most courteous host, Admiral Sexton,” Naftur replied. “I’m sure Ambassador Turlaka would agree that we have been treated with the utmost respect and hospitality throughout our stay. I very much hope to have the opportunity to return after things settle down, and I have every confidence that they will do so once the current crisis has passed. The political unrest is no surprise, after all. Fomenting this sort of global fear and turmoil is very consistent behavior for the Pelarans.” Naftur breathed deeply and let out a long, weary sigh. “In any event, I would like to return to Terra in an unofficial capacity in hopes that I might be able to do some exploring.”

“I would like that of all things. Once it is safe for you to return, you have an open invitation to do so. I will personally see to it that you have the opportunity to experience every wonder our world has to offer. We are deeply in your debt, sir.”

“Thank you, Admiral, but I am afraid that remains to be seen. If you still believe that to be true four weeks hence, I will happily allow you to serve me more of your stimulating carbonated soft drinks.” Both Wek had been given the opportunity to sample a variety of Human cuisine during their stay, in addition to a number of different beverages — both alcoholic and otherwise. Although they both seemed to enjoy several types of wine, coffee, and even beer, Coca-Cola had been their hands-down favorite.

Very few TFC Marines remained on the headquarters campus at this point, and the Leadership Council’s recent insistence on demilitarizing the facility had placed strict limits on the manner in which they were allowed to conduct themselves. Only two Marines had been available to accompany Admiral Sexton's small group for the rendezvous with *Theseus*. Under normal circumstances, a pair of TFC Marines in full combat armor and armed with pulse rifles would be more than adequate to protect their group from anything less than a full-on assault from a platoon-sized contingent of HQSEC troops. The Marines were now better equipped for office duty than combat. Since Crull's edicts had taken effect, they had been restricted to wearing their basic black TFC fatigues and were allowed to carry only their sidearms.

Now, as they reached a point roughly thirty meters from the end of the corridor, the Marine in the lead position raised his right hand in a fist to signal a halt. He then turned and signaled the group to hold their position before jogging ahead alone to check the room at the end of the hallway. Not expecting trouble at this point, Sexton wasn't entirely sure this precaution was necessary, but stopped nonetheless. He was keenly aware that the current rules of engagement did not allow the Marines to use force unless their 'principals' were openly attacked — which he thought extremely unlikely. The more probable scenario was that Chairwoman Crull and her allies on the Council would issue new orders in response to his refusal to turn over Naftur and Turlaka the previous evening. If and when that happened, her large contingent of HQSEC troops would quickly realize that he and the two Wek were not where they should be. He felt sure this would immediately lead to something resembling a full-scale manhunt across the entire Headquarters facility. If he could manage to get them safely aboard *Theseus* before that happened, however, it would be a fairly straightforward exercise in bureaucratic spin to delay their return to Earth until the current, volatile situation came to some sort of resolution.

The lead Marine glanced in both directions through the small windows set in the double doors at the end of the corridor, then, with his back against the wall, slowly pushed one of the doors open before proceeding into the barracks facility. The first room was really nothing more than an extension of the access tunnel, with two elevators on the right-hand side. Straight ahead, a double staircase led up to the first floor before intersecting a long corridor running parallel to the front of the building. Hearing nothing, he proceeded quietly up the stairs to make a quick check of the main hallway.

After two full minutes had passed, the second Marine approached from the rear. He quickly put a finger over his lips for silence, then signaled the group to crouch down below the line of sight from the doorway ahead. Without any means of communicating with the other guard, he was unsure why his partner was taking so long, but he felt certain that something was amiss.

"Sir," he whispered to Admiral Sexton. "Sergeant Hicks should have been back by now. I'm afraid we may be compromised."

"Agreed. I think we need to assume that HQSEC has been mobilized to find and detain us at this point. You know where the LZ is, Sergeant. Do we have any other options for getting there from here?"

"Not good ones, Admiral, no. If we turn back, we're going in the wrong direction. Besides, I'd say back at the

Admiralty Building will be the first place they'll start looking for us. Also, if we assume they just grabbed Sergeant Hicks, the fact that they didn't come running down those stairs up ahead leads me to believe they may be waiting for backup."

"That sounds logical to me. What do you propose?"

"I'm guessing we're only dealing with a couple of guys, so they are probably sitting tight up there in the main corridor. Let's move out as a group and see if we can manage to get ourselves into one of the elevators just on the other side of those doors. If we go up to the third floor, we can take the skyway over to the JAG Building next door. If we're lucky, we can get out the back door before they figure out where we've gone."

"That's right, there's a picnic area back there that adjoins the wooded area next to the landing pad. Good plan … let's move."

"Sir, what about Hicks?"

"He'll be fine. Detaining him is one thing, but I can't imagine they would be dumb enough to do anything to hurt him. We'll find him as soon as we get these two out of here."

"Aye, sir. Everyone stay low, keep quiet, and follow me."

With that, the Marine moved over to one side of the corridor and hurried off in a crouch towards the double doors. Upon reaching the end of the corridor, he allowed everyone to catch up, signaled again — quite unnecessarily at this point — for quiet, and then slowly pushed the right-hand door open. Seeing no one on the stairs or in the hallway intersection beyond, he quickly ushered the group through the doorway before allowing the door to close silently behind them. Realizing that the slightest sound would attract unwanted attention, the young sergeant turned to face his three companions and mouthed "*Ready?*" before holding up his hand and flashing a three-count; he then pressed the up arrow to call the elevator. As he had hoped, the elevator was already on their level, but, as he had feared, the doors immediately clattered noisily open, accompanied by a mind-numbingly loud BING.

Before the doors were even halfway open, several things seemed to happen at one time. The Marine sergeant pivoted to place himself between the stairway and the rest of the group as they quickly boarded the elevator. From the hallway above came the sound of footsteps hurrying in their direction, followed immediately thereafter by a confusing combination of clattering metal and muffled swearing as a single HQSEC guard came stumbling into view before falling face-first onto the hard tile floor. Before the guard could manage to pick himself up and continue after the group, the elevator doors rumbled closed.

Even with skyscrapers routinely topping two kilometers in height around the world and paired with wondrously fast elevators for whisking their occupants into the heavens with remarkable speed, the elevators in smaller office buildings had changed very little over the past three centuries. Now safely inside, the Marine sergeant, Sexton, Naftur, and Turlaka stood facing the doors, staring passively as the digital indicator above slowly changed to display their current floor. Overhead, a tinny-sounding speaker softly played an ancient, instrumental version of "Memory" from the Andrew

Lloyd Weber musical *Cats*. Only a few seconds into their seemingly endless journey to the third floor, a low, threatening growl could be heard radiating from the center of Admiral Naftur's chest.

Stricken by the comic and rather surreal nature of the situation, and unable to control himself any longer, the young Marine burst into a fit of uncontrollable laughter, and was immediately joined by all three of his charges. He assumed neither of the Wek had any idea what had set him off, but the fact that they were laughing fully justified his momentary lapse in military bearing as far as he was concerned.

Fortunately for the four of them, the single HQSEC guard who had been lucky enough to surprise Sergeant Hicks had been generally inept otherwise. The fall they had witnessed had been caused by a combination of his headlong rush down the corridor towards the sound of the elevator door and a heavy metal stand normally used for holding a TFC Marine guidon. With the taste of blood in his mouth, one Fleet Marine already in custody, and reinforcements on the way, he had made no further attempt to give chase.

When the elevator doors finally opened on the third floor, the Marine sergeant held the door and listened momentarily, then quickly checked the immediate area before moving to the intersection with the main hallway. Seeing nothing, he motioned for the others to follow and trotted off in the direction of the skyway leading to the TFC Judge Advocate General Building.

"Are you two doing okay?" Sexton asked the two Wek in a low voice from the rear of the group. Both Naftur and Turlaka had already begun picking up a surprising amount of conversational English, sometimes even managing to preempt the tablets they still carried for translation services.

"We are doing quite well, Admiral Sexton, thank you," Turlaka whispered in English, the corners of her mouth turning upwards in a satisfied smile. She then paused for a moment, furrowing her brow before deciding to let the tablet handle her next sentence. "As long as no one starts shooting at us, this is actually quite stimulating."

While smaller than average compared to other planets Humanity had long referred to as 'terrestrial,' Earth's iron/nickel core resulted in a density that was significantly above the norm. This, of course, also meant that Earth's mass was quite high for her size compared to other habitable worlds. Contrary to popular belief, a given planet's surface gravity was not necessarily higher than another's simply because it was physically larger. While surface gravity did indeed increase with a planet's mass, it actually decreased with the square of the planet's radius. The Wek home world of Graca, for example, while possessing nearly double the Earth's land mass and a planetary diameter roughly twenty percent larger than Earth's, had a surface gravity of only 7.85 m/s^2. This was largely due to the fact that the planet's density was closer to that of Mars — a full one-third less than that of the Earth.

The twenty-percent increase in gravity coupled with a slightly lower atmospheric pressure and oxygen content made heavy physical exertion a bit of a challenge for the two Wek. Fortunately, both were in excellent overall physical condition and had been on Earth long enough to begin the process of adapting to the environment. Although breathing heavily, neither had much difficulty keeping pace with their Human companions.

"Will the neighboring structure be occupied at this time of day?" Naftur asked as they paused at the entrance to the skyway leading across to the JAG facility.

"Normally, I would say no," Sexton replied, "but with everything that's been going on with the Council, it wouldn't surprise me if there are a few people already in the office. I doubt a few lawyers and custodial staff are what we need to be worried about at this point, though. Sergeant, I think you were probably right about the HQSEC guards downstairs. It was probably just a random patrol … maybe even just one guy."

"Yes, sir. Otherwise, I think they would have been right on our heels. The bad news is that they will have help on the way by now, so we need to keep moving. At the other end of the skyway, hang a left and head towards the stairwell — it will be the last door on the right at the end of the hallway. There should be an external door on the ground floor that will allow us to exit behind the building. We can run the length of the skyway ahead, but I need all of you to stop before we reach the end so that I can clear the intersecting hallway."

Run they did — loudly. Upon reaching the halfway point, Sexton realized that something about the structural properties of the skyway had the effect of magnifying the sound of their crossing into something approaching that of a herd of wildebeests in a mad rush to escape a pride of hungry lionesses. While the irony of such a comparison was still forming in his mind, he noticed that both Wek had removed their shoes at some point, and, unlike the two Humans' pounding gaits, their footfalls were virtually silent.

The Marine sergeant slowed to a brisk walk as he approached the hallway ahead, then strolled as casually as possible around the corner to the left while motioning with his head for the others to follow. Although a few voices could be heard coming from some of the offices, no one seemed to pay particular attention to their passing, and they were soon in the stairwell heading down to the ground floor.

"Alright, everyone," Sexton said, risking a more conversational volume upon reaching the external door, "I honestly don't think there is much point in making a run for it once we are outside. We have to cross a relatively open common area for the first fifty meters or so behind this building, and I think the four of us running will do nothing but get us noticed. Do you agree, Sergeant?"

"Well, sir, the problem is that we're likely to stand out this time of day no matter what we do, but, yes, I think we should avoid looking any more suspicious than we have to. Once we reach the tree line, we should have some pretty good cover all the way to the LZ."

"Very good. Everyone ready?" Sexton asked. Since the encounter with the HQSEC guard back in the Marine barracks, his mind had been preoccupied with the moral ambiguity of the current situation. Arranging for the two Wek to leave TFC Headquarters before any orders to the contrary had been issued was one thing, but now that it was clear that the Council's security contingent had been given orders to detain them, it would be much more difficult to justify his actions. Was this what mutineers always felt like when in the act of defying their superiors? Could he trust his own judgment in a case like this? He wasn't sure it mattered at this point, and he was certain that he didn't give a damn either way. The Commander in Chief, TFC had gone through this particular scenario in his mind countless times over the past week, and, right or wrong, believed that his duty was clear. He would see the two Wek safely aboard the *Theseus* because he firmly believed that Admiral Naftur offered the best chance — perhaps the only chance — of preventing an attack from the Resistance task force. *That*, he believed, was the single course of action he could take that best supported TFC's most important mission of defending the planet. He would leave it to the historians to determine if he had made the right call.

Receiving nods all around, Admiral Sexton opened the door and proceeded outside. It was a frigid, April Fool's Day morning with a heavy white frost covering the grass-covered common areas behind the JAG Building. As they walked, the water vapor in their breath condensed into small, puffy clouds in front of them. Looking off in the direction of the landing pad, Sexton also noted that Headquarters was socked in with heavy fog, resulting in something approaching zero visibility.

Trying their best not to give the impression that they were running from something, the small group followed the diagonal path leading towards the picnic pavilion located near the center of the park-like common area behind the JAG Building. They walked two by two, with the Humans even attempting a bit of small talk in an effort to seem as unremarkable as possible. As they passed the pavilion, a low-flying formation of Canadian Geese crossed the sky having recently — and rather optimistically, Sexton thought — begun their trip north for the summer months. The surprisingly loud wingbeats and flight calls as the birds passed overhead briefly distracted all four members of the small party. Not even the keen hearing possessed by the two Wek detected the faint clicks and whining sounds as over forty pulse rifles were powered up and trained in their direction.

Chapter 15

TFS Theseus
(On standard autodeparture from the Yucca Mountain Shipyard Facility)

"We are clear of the entrance tunnel and free to maneuver, Captain," Ensign Fisher reported from the Helm console as TFS *Theseus* took to the sky for her first operational flight. To ensure adequate in-flight separation from commercial air and space traffic during their short trip to TFC Headquarters, Theseus' AI had coordinated with both Los Angeles and Denver Air Route Traffic Control. Although the ship was still required to file a flight plan similar to those used by other aircraft, TFC starships generally received priority routing and were granted much more autonomy to choose their altitudes and flight paths — as long as they could do so without posing a danger to other aircraft or those on the ground. Aboard *Theseus*, the result was a graphical display of exactly where the destroyer was and was not allowed to fly, updated in real-time on the massive wrap-around view screen lining the front of the bridge.

"Very good, Ensign. Proceed as filed," Prescott replied with the calmest and most professionally detached tone he could muster at the moment as the warship made the transition from AI-control to being 'hand flown' for the first time.

The autodeparture had been uneventful, from the standpoint of nothing unexpected having taken place, but nerve-wracking nonetheless for everyone involved. This included Yucca Mountain Control, which had technically still been responsible for the ship until control authority was passed to her crew. The entire departure — from the first, tentative application of reverse thrust to exit Berth Ten until her dramatic passage through the massive blast doors at the end of the two-kilometer-long entrance tunnel — had taken less than two minutes. Now, as Fisher pointed the ship's bow forty-five degrees above the horizon, *Theseus* leapt effortlessly into the morning sky above the Amargosa Valley, the breathtaking scale of her power beginning to tell for the first time.

"Dear God," Fisher muttered under his breath, already feeling like the ship was getting a little ahead of him only seconds after leaving the shipyard. "This thing really does scare the hell out of me."

"Easy, Blake," Prescott soothed, "just another day at the office. Her flight characteristics should be almost identical to *Ingenuity's*, right?"

"Yes and no, sir," Fisher replied, manually rocking the massive warship along her longitudinal axis in an effort to get a better feel for how she responded to control inputs. "For lack of a better term, the 'feel' is just … different. For one thing, there's no lag at all. *Ingenuity* was responsive, sure, but this thing responds instantly — no hesitation whatsoever. I also can't feel the ship's movements in the seat of my pants quite like I could with *Ingenuity*."

"Ah, well that part does make sense. The gravitic systems have dramatically more power available, so you shouldn't expect to feel the same delay you did with *Ingenuity*. When you make a control movement and place a G-load on the ship, inertial dampening should happen in near real-time. We should also be capable of more aggressive maneuvers without exceeding the 6-G crew limit internally."

"That all sounds great, sir, but right now I'll settle for her and me coming to some kind of an understanding," Fisher laughed.

"Captain," Reynolds reported, "Lieutenant Lee — Marine First Lieutenant Jackson Lee, that is — reports that his two squads are suited up and ready to deploy. They will be waiting in two of the *Gurkha* ASVs until you give the go order."

"But they're not actually deploying in the *Gurkhas*, correct?"

"That's correct, sir. With their new combat EVA suits, they prefer not to mount up for short-range deployments. That way, they don't all bunch up in one spot and become a single target of opportunity. Two of the *Gurkhas* will still deploy with the Marine squads for fire support, however. While the squads are waiting on the hangar deck, the ASVs provide a convenient place to strap themselves in until they get a 'green deck' signal."

"Understood. With any luck, their services won't be needed, but I'm pretty sure two squads of Marines — well, *these* two squads of Marines in particular — should provide quite a deterrent in case we run into any problems."

"We've got enough problems waiting for us topside, sir," Reynolds said. "I'd appreciate having at least one part of our mission turn out to be a cake walk."

"That reminds me … Lieutenant Lee," Prescott called, raising his voice so that the young lieutenant at the Science and Engineering console could hear, “we need to come up with some way to refer to you and your brother so that everyone knows who we’re talking about.”

Although TFC had a relatively short history, as well as relatively few installations to which young officers could be assigned, it was still unusual for two siblings to share a duty station, let alone be deployed aboard the same ship. Strangely enough, TFC Navy Lieutenant (Junior Grade) Jayston Lee and his fraternal twin brother, TFC Marine First Lieutenant Jackson Lee, were originally from Alice Springs, Australia, less than forty kilometers from the Pine Gap Shipyard Facility. Pine Gap, along with the nearly identical facilities at Yamantau Mountain in Russia and Yucca Mountain in the U.S., had been the construction sites for all of Fleet’s capital ships. The only exception had been *Ingenuity*, which had been constructed with great fanfare and in full view of the public near Tokyo, Japan as part of the massive disinformation campaign surrounding the MAGI PRIME program. After receiving his commission as a TFC officer, Jayston’s first assignment had been to join the crew of the *Theseus* at Yucca Mountain to assist in her fitting out and then ultimately deploy with the destroyer. Jackson, on the other hand, ended up being assigned to a “black” engineering project working on a prototype for a new type of combat EVA suit being put through its paces at Camp Lejeune, North Carolina. The fact that the two brothers had ended up aboard the same ship had been purely coincidental, as was the fact that, like *Theseus* herself, today’s mission would be the first operational use of the new combat EVA suit.

“I was thinking we could call your brother ‘Lieutenant Jackson,’ or maybe ‘Lieutenant Jacks,’” Reynolds said. “Do you think he’d have a problem with that?”

“Oh, we should definitely go with ‘Jacks,’ ma’am. Our mum tried that one time and he absolutely hated it,” Lee laughed.

“Well, there’s a ringing endorsement if I ever heard one,” Prescott said with a smile.

“No, in all seriousness, Captain, it won’t be a problem. Believe it or not, we had an instructor at the Defense Force Academy come up with the same solution, and it has stuck with him ever since. In fact, I’m sure his platoon already calls him Jacks … to his face at least.”

“Alright, there you have it,” Prescott chuckled. “Please let our Marine platoon commander know that he is officially dubbed ‘Lieutenant Jacks’ until further notice. We’ll give him a chance to air his grievances later.”

“Aye, sir,” Reynolds replied, reflecting that it might have been a better choice to pick on the Navy lieutenant rather than the Marine one.

Whenever possible, military air and spacecraft were required to attenuate their sonic boom footprint during overflights of populated areas. For today’s flight, *Theseus’* AI calculated that the ship’s gravitic fields could prevent its sonic booms from reaching the ground as long as her airspeed remained under two thousand six hundred kph. This rather leisurely pace also allowed ground-based controllers to more easily keep the massive ship clear of other traffic during its transit. After quickly reaching her relatively low en route altitude of forty-five thousand feet and at just over Mach two, *Theseus* covered the one-thousand-kilometer distance to HQTFC in just under twenty-four minutes.

As the ship neared its destination and began its descent, Prescott somewhat uncharacteristically stood and walked around to the front of the bridge. "Listen up for just a moment, everyone. Without going into too much detail, I feel it's important to give you an idea of what's going on at Headquarters, and why we are taking the ship there to pick up Admiral Naftur and Ambassador Turlaka rather than simply shuttling them over to meet up with us. The political situation worldwide has become unstable in the wake of the Guardian's, uh … shall we say 'invitation' for Earth to join the Pelaran Alliance. Unfortunately, that instability appears to be affecting TFC just as it is all other governmental bodies around the world. Recently, a number of decisions have been handed down by the Council that threaten to undermine our ability as a military force to provide for Earth's defense. You should also be aware that the contingent of Marines who normally provide security on the Headquarters campus were dismissed last week and replaced with what you might refer to as a private military force. Frankly, it is unclear whom these troops are taking orders from at this point, so it is difficult to predict how they might respond to our arrival. I don't want to sound alarmist or dramatic, but there is at least a chance that they may try to prevent us from accomplishing our mission of evacuating the two Wek. We cannot allow this to happen. As you know, Admiral Naftur, as well as the TFC Admiralty, believe that putting Naftur in direct contact with the Resistance forces offers our last, best chance of preventing an attack on Earth.

"Why am I telling you all of this? Well, that's where things might get a little dicey. Ultimately, our military forces take their orders from the Leadership Council, and we absolutely recognize their authority to issue lawful orders per the TFC charter. We don't have time for me to deliver a lecture on duty and professional ethics at the moment," he paused, smiling wanly, "so let me come straight to the point. The situation with the Leadership Council has become so unstable that it is unclear — to me at least — that they are currently in a position to issue lawful orders. If, therefore, I am ordered by anyone not in our TFC military chain of command to stand down and not retrieve Naftur and Turlaka, I do not intend to comply."

Prescott paused to allow the gravity of what he was saying to weigh on his officers for a moment, then continued. "Please understand that it is not my intention to use force to extract the two Wek unless it is absolutely necessary, and, even then, we will endeavor to use nonlethal means as long as doing so does not endanger this ship and her crew.

"If any of you is uncomfortable with what I am about to do, please relieve yourself of duty immediately so that we can replace you before our arrival. You have my word that there will be absolutely no repercussions of any kind if you make this decision for yourself. Let me remind you, however, that if you do decide to stay, our oaths of office say absolutely nothing about following the orders of our superiors. That kind of language typically appears only in the oaths used by enlisted troops. This has been the case for most professional military forces around the world for centuries and the reason for it is simple. As officers, we are expected to think for ourselves and exercise sound judgment at all times. As you have all heard a thousand times, 'I was just following orders,' is never a valid excuse for misconduct of any sort."

Prescott paused again to look around the bridge in an effort to gauge the reactions of each of his young officers. Seeing a room full of poker faces, he decided it was time to move things along. "So there you have it. We still have a few minutes remaining, so please take a moment to consider what your captain may be about to do, then follow your conscience and decide for yourself. Any questions?"

There was a long, uncomfortable silence during which no one seemed to be willing to speak — or even look around the room — for fear of committing themselves one way or another. Finally, irritated by the drama and unwilling to tolerate the silence any longer, Lieutenant Lau spoke up. "Captain Prescott, I believe I heard you say that *if* the Council orders us to leave the Wek admiral and ambassador here, you would violate their order. I assume that means such an order has not yet been issued," he said, stating the fact as a question.

"That is correct. It was Admirals Sexton and Patterson's hope that we might be able to get in and out before that happened, but there is certainly no guarantee either way. Look, I understand your question, Lieutenant, and I share your hope that we beat them to the punch, but I need you to make your decision as if you will be *knowingly* violating an order from the Council."

"Captain," Lieutenant Commander Schmidt said, raising his hand slightly to get Prescott's attention. "I'll speak for myself, but I'm betting everyone here feels the same way I do. We understand the significance of violating an order from the Council, but in a combat situation, wouldn't it be a little unusual for us to start getting direct orders from them anyway? Their role is to set strategy, not start issuing operational orders. Besides, that seems like more of a question for the attorneys to debate after we're all safely back home and no longer under an immediate threat of annihilation from the Resistance. I'm sure we all appreciate your giving us the opportunity to consider the consequences for ourselves, but there is no way anyone here is going to take you up on an offer to sit this one out."

There were emphatic nods and expressions of agreement from the other four officers, each of whom were eager to end the tedious discussion and get on with the business at hand.

Prescott looked directly at each one, making sure there were no signs that they were simply going along with the group in spite of their own personal convictions to the contrary. "Very well," he finally replied, heading back to his command chair without further comment on the issue. "Lieutenant Dubashi, status please."

"All systems in the green, Captain," she reported immediately. "Both standard and C-Drive transitions are available. C-Jump range *98.7 light years* and stable. We are on our final approach to the target — just over zero two minutes from the planned drop zone."

“You’ve been waiting to report that C-Jump range, haven’t you?” Prescott grinned.

“Yes, sir, every time I look at it, I think it’s an error of some kind,” she replied, shaking her head in wonder.

“Hah! Don’t jinx us, Dubashi,” he chuckled.

The notion that mystical forces like “fate,” or “luck” had a very real impact on life aboard ship could be traced back across thousands of years of maritime history. The only thing that had really changed in more modern times was that such things were rarely discussed openly for fear of ridicule (or from an unspoken fear that doing so was bad luck in and of itself). After all, such things were nothing more than foolish superstition … were they not?

“Tactical?”

“Lots of civilian traffic within fifty kilometers of the target, Captain,” Schmidt reported, “but they’re all at a safe distance for the moment. Otherwise, the threat board is clear.” Schmidt and Lau had already devised a system by which they could share the workload across the two Tactical consoles, including who should speak up to deliver status updates to the captain, without verbally communicating with each other. It had taken only a few minor modifications to their user interface, and really wasn’t much of a challenge for young officers long accustomed to dealing with a continuous stream of complex communications without ever saying a word.

“I’m really not expecting any airborne threats, but if you see any fast-movers heading in this direction, even if they are a thousand kilometers out, I want to hear about them immediately.”

“Aye, sir.”

“Lieutenant L—.” Prescott checked himself, then started again. “Lieutenant Jacks, bridge,” he announced. The ship’s AI seamlessly inferred the intended recipient of the captain’s call based on his recent conversation and routed the call accordingly.

“Lieutenant, uh, Jacks here. Go ahead, Captain.” It was obvious by the tone of the young officer’s voice that, while he was still a little surprised that the bridge had decided on a name change, he understood that now was not the time to question why. Besides, he was pretty sure that his ‘little brother’ (born five minutes later) was in some way responsible. The Marine had long since grown accustomed to the name “Jacks” anyway, and didn’t really mind it. Nonetheless, he took solace in the thought of evening the score with his brother when the time was right.

“Just over zero one minute remaining, Lieutenant. Remember, we want zero casualties on this op. Do not fire unless fired upon. The use of lethal force is *not* authorized at this time. Understood?”

“Understood. No worries, Captain.”

“Let’s make this quick. Good luck. Prescott out.”

“Sir, the AI is running the approach from here, but I’ll be on the controls just in case,” Fisher reported. “Rapid deceleration in zero seven seconds. Use of the Anti-G Straining Maneuver should not be necessary.” Shortly thereafter, the background noise of *Theseus’* sublight engines increased slightly in pitch and volume, accompanied by a noticeable, but not uncomfortable increase in G-forces as the ship smoothly transitioned its nearly five hundred thousand tons into a hover over the preselected drop zone.

"Drop zone reached, sir," Fisher continued. "We are stabilized in a two-hundred-meter hover. Gravitic fields have been reduced to minimum extension and are clear of the flight deck."

"Wow," Reynolds muttered to herself, astounded by the almost routine, businesslike manner with which her ship was accomplishing feats that still looked and felt like the stuff of science fiction.

"Green deck, XO," Prescott said calmly.

"Aye, sir. Executing," she replied, entering commands on her touchscreen to relay the appropriate orders to both the flight deck and the two Marine squads hunkered inside their *Gurkha* assault shuttles.

***

Marine First Lieutenant "Jacks" and his second-in-command, Master Sergeant Antonio Rios, had just completed a final set of equipment checks for each of their two squads when the go order was received. Side and rear cargo doors opened immediately on both *Gurkha* assault shuttles, both of which were already positioned for launch on *Theseus'* aft flight apron. In just seconds, each of the ASVs had disgorged its squad of fourteen troops, then released the clamps holding them in place as their controlling AIs prepared to follow the two groups of Marines to their target location.

Although he was the most experienced combat veteran assigned to the platoon, Rios was the only Marine who had not received extensive training in the new, "universal" version of the combat EVA suit. Priding himself as (by far, in his opinion) the toughest man in the unit, he would never, under any circumstances, admit to being afraid of anything at any time. So it was with no small amount of irritation that he was forced to overcome a brief feeling of apprehension as he followed his squad at a dead run off the aft flight apron to begin a brief free-fall through the chilly morning air ten kilometers from Terran Fleet Command Headquarters.

Chapter 16

TFS Theseus
(10 km from TFC Headquarters landing zone)

"The Marine squads are away, Captain," Reynolds reported. "Flight deck secure."

"Thank you," Prescott replied. "Lieutenant Lau, are we in range of Admiral Sexton's beacon?"

"Yes, sir. Our drop zone is just inside the beacon's maximum range, but that can vary quite a bit, particularly in weather like this. It doesn't have a lot of power, so with all of the electronic countermeasures in place on the Headquarters campus, we may not be able to isolate the signal until he's pretty close to the LZ."

During the discussion between Admirals Sexton and Patterson the previous day, the two officers had considered various methods of communicating with *Theseus* during her approach. Handheld comm devices were generally useless anywhere near HQTFC, but Sexton had nonetheless agreed to try one of the small signal beacons sometimes used by spec-ops Marine units to mark their position during an extraction mission. Roughly the size of a small pocketknife, the device had a battery life measured in years rather than hours and a transmission range of approximately ten kilometers. Whether it would be useful for today's mission remained to be seen, but the beacons had already saved countless lives in the field by eliminating situations where would-be rescue teams passed repeatedly within a few hundred meters without ever seeing their target.

“Understood,” Prescott replied. “I doubt there is much to see yet, but please show us a combined sensor feed of the area around the LZ.”

Lieutenant Lau issued a series of commands at his console, after which a detailed overhead view appeared on the right side of the bridge view screen. The landing pad itself was centered on the left edge of the video feed, bordered by the wooded area immediately to its east, and then finally ending with the common area and rear of the Judge Advocate General office building just over five hundred meters away. As usual, the imagery was produced using a wide variety of data sources. Everything from existing satellite imagery, to blueprints retrieved from TFC archives, to live sensor feeds were combined by the AI to produce the most accurate, real-time view possible. At the moment, however, there was little if anything displayed that would give the impression of live data. In fact, the image looked like nothing more than a static, overhead view of the area surrounding their landing zone.

“Are we getting any data from the *Gurkhas* or the Marines’ EVA suits?” Prescott asked, immediately chiding himself for allowing a hint of impatience to creep into his voice.

“Yes, sir. We’ve got good data feeds from all twenty-eight Marines and both *Gurkhas*. The LZ is obscured by cloud cover and heavy fog, so that’s enough to defeat the optical sensors. Throw in some heavy electronic countermeasures, and we’re just not detecting much of anything at the moment.”

“Hmm … well, it doesn’t surprise me the suits aren’t picking up anything. Their sensors are optimized for short-range tactical combat. They tend to *receive* most of their data from other sources rather than act as a source themselves, in fact. The *Gurkhas*, on the other hand … I honestly did not realize that our Headquarters ECM systems were this effective. We're displaying infrared data as well?"

"I'm afraid so, sir. Based on what we're seeing so far, I'm wondering if we will also lose the Marines' data feeds once they reach the perimeter of the campus."

Prescott sat back in his command chair, taking in a long breath and commanding himself to relax before continuing. "Alright folks, I realize we're not talking about a hot LZ in enemy-held territory here, but I'd still very much prefer to avoid going in blind," he stated flatly. "Recommendations?"

"Captain," Lieutenant Commander Schmidt interjected, "I know our mission profile has us holding here until the Marines secure the LZ and our guests, but if we position the ship so that we have a direct line of sight, I'm betting our sensors will stand a much better chance against the countermeasures. The closer we get, the more we should be able to see."

"Ensign Fisher, do you think you can move us any closer to the LZ without attracting too much attention?" Prescott asked.

The location of the drop zone had been selected to minimize the number of people likely to notice the *Theseus* while the two Marine squads went about the business of locating Admiral Sexton's party and escorting them safely to the landing zone. While keeping a six-hundred-and-twenty-five-meter-long destroyer concealed only a short distance from several heavily populated areas was perhaps the most futile of exercises, her low altitude, the time of day, and the current weather conditions were all working in their favor at the moment.

"We've got good terrain masking behind this ridge line, Captain, and the fog is helping quite a bit as well. There is a solid cloud deck at about five hundred meters, though. I think if we get back above the cloud cover, we can go ahead and start heading in the direction of the LZ. I doubt anyone on the ground will notice us unless they know exactly what to listen for."

"Excellent. Do it," Prescott responded.

Marine Squad "Savage 2"
(On EVA approach to TFC Headquarters landing zone)

"Rios, Jacks."

A distant corner of Master Sergeant Rios' mind registered the call from his platoon commander, but at the moment, he had his hands full. Having completed countless missions wearing previous versions of the EVA combat armor, he had developed his own personal list of settings and checks that he accomplished in near ritualistic fashion at the beginning of every mission. Although generally not recommended, and indeed beyond the skills of most of his contemporaries, one part of his routine involved using the suit's neural interface to momentarily take manual control of the suit in flight. It was a reasonably quick method of testing virtually every major system at one time, and Rios always found that the mental discipline required put his mind in the required, almost Zen-like, state also allowed him to better focus on the mission.

With *Theseus* at an altitude of only two hundred meters above the terrain, the mission profile had called for a very brief free fall, after which the suit's Cannae thrusters would engage to both arrest his descent and begin a high-speed, very low-altitude approach to the landing zone ten kilometers away. Accordingly, Rios had taken manual control immediately after jumping from the ship — and had been largely out of control ever since.

While any deviation from controlled flight at such a low altitude was potentially dangerous, the suit's AI was unlikely to allow him to make a fatal error. Hundreds of thousands of times each second, the AI made minor corrections to prevent him from going completely out of control — much like a parent nudging a child from each side to maintain their balance while they learned to ride a bicycle without training wheels. Nevertheless, his uncharacteristically erratic flight path was being monitored with interest by members of his unit nearby, and by the suit itself.

"What the hell is your problem this morning anyway, Rios?" his EVA suit's AI asked, using perhaps the least colorful language it had uttered since they had left the relative safety of *Theseus'* flight apron. "The boss is on the line and you're still flailing around like some kind of snot-nosed rookie. Here's what we're gonna do. I'm gonna fly for a while and you're gonna talk to the boss. Then you're gonna take a few seconds to pull your head out of your keister before you get us both killed. Then — if you think you can handle it — you can take over again, kapish? Sheesh, kid, you gotta get it together before somebody sees you, for chrissake."

The identity of the synthetic voice Rios used for his EVA suit was a closely guarded personal secret. First and foremost, he figured it wasn't anyone else's business, but he was also aware that far too many people spent far too much time looking for reasons to be offended. So what … he just happened to be of mixed Italian and Latino descent and also just happened to like the idea of going into battle feeling like he was an early twentieth century mafioso. What of it? What Rios had no way of knowing was just how unrealistic and stereotypical a portrayal the voice truly was compared to the real thing (sounding more like a poor imitation of Joe Pesci than the actual Charlie "Lucky" Luciano — the origin of the nickname he used for his AI).

"Yeah, okay, fine. Take over for a sec." His flight path instantly stabilized, after which he breathed deeply for a moment before answering the lieutenant's call. "Rios here. Go ahead, LT."

"Hey Top, you doing OK over there? It looked for a second like you might be having a little problem with your suit."

"Sorry about that, sir. No, I'm fine … just having some trouble with the neural interface. It doesn't seem to want to respond like my old suit for some reason."

"Alright, no problem, Sergeant. Oh, hey, you did have the AI import your old preferences and mod them for atmospheric flight, right?"

Muting his mic with a quick thought, Rios rolled his eyes and swore loudly at himself, knowing full well that this was indeed the problem. It was, in fact, a simple, but incredibly dumb oversight that never would have happened if he had not allowed himself to become complacent when running his armor's pre-mission checklist. A rookie mistake to be sure, and because it represented a potentially serious safety issue, one that would have prompted him to cheerfully take the head off any member of his platoon if they had done the same thing (Lieutenant Jacks included). Worse yet, the fact that the LT had suggested a fix made it painfully clear that he had known what the problem was before he even asked. He had even been *nice* about it, which somehow added insult to injury.

"Rios copies. I'll check the settings again, sir. Thanks."

"You do that, Top," Jacks replied with a tone of barely contained amusement. "We still have six zero seconds until show time, so you're good. Jacks out."

"Hey Lucky," Rios said, addressing his AI again.

"Yeah, I'm right here. I already checked and the boss was right. It should be fixed right about … okay, it's fixed."

"Seriously? Mr. Super-Advanced AI, but you weren't able to warn me about a simple setting?"

"Hey, what do you want from me? I did exactly what you told me, didn't I? What, now I'm supposed to do what you *meant* for me to do instead? *Get* the hell outta here!"

Rios just shook his head, realizing that, somehow, there was a kernel of undeniable logic in "Lucky's" comments.

"Alright, alright. You're right, I screwed up. Now, give me a status update and let's try the neural interface again."

"All EVA systems nominal. Power level ninety-nine percent. Pulse rifle integration complete. On course for the LZ — ETA two one seconds. Manual control restored in 3 … 2 … 1 …"

Rios knew immediately that all was now well with his EVA suit. The improper settings had apparently even been preventing its synthetic musculature from completely conforming to his body, which he now both heard and felt taking place. Thinking back, he also realized that things hadn't felt quite right, even before leaving the ship. At the time, he had foolishly chalked it up to the muscle fibers and armor not being fully "broken in," and the fact that he should have known better made that realization all the more irritating. The good news was that his new suit now felt pretty much identical to his old one. The most obvious difference, of course, was that the old model was capable of "flight" only in the microgravity environment of space. This new one … came as close as he imagined Humans would ever come to turning a mere mortal into a super hero.

Marine Squads "Savage 1" and "Savage 2"
(Over the landing zone)

"Savage 1 squad, hold position over the landing pad," Jacks ordered as all twenty-eight members of his small but powerful force arrived silently at their target location, followed closely by their two, AI-controlled *Gurkha* assault shuttles. "Savage 2, split your squad into two sections, proceed three hundred meters north and south from the center of the landing pad, then move slowly east."

"Savage 2 copies," Master Sergeant Rios replied. The command interface of his suit allowed him to quickly designate the members of each new section of his squad and then assign their respective areas of responsibility. In seconds, his new orders appeared within each of his Marines' fields of view, and the two sections headed off toward the north and south ends of the huge landing pad.

"Be advised that since we don't have eyes on the target, neither does *Theseus*. We might also lose contact with the ship after we cross the boundary fence," Lieutenant Jacks said. If there was one thing he hated during a mission, it was a bunch of unnecessary chatter on the radio. He had already been forced into saying more than usual on this op, but it couldn't be helped. His Marine special operators were accustomed to operating in an "information-rich" environment, after all, but the unusual circumstances created by TFC's countermeasures and today's poor visibility had them going in almost blind.

"Savage 2 sections in position," Rios reported from the northernmost group. "Moving east."

Without responding verbally, Jacks commanded his squad to begin their sweep eastward at the same moment, adjusting the altitude of both squads to fifty meters as he did so. He had hoped to be in contact with Admiral Sexton by this time, or at least have acquired a signal from his beacon. So far, there had been no contact – no signal from the beacon, no thermals, nothing. Now, the young lieutenant monitored the sensor readouts projected in his helmet display intently as his two squads of Marines moved forward in a line stretching nearly one kilometer from end to end. *It shouldn't take us long to find them,* he thought, a*ssuming they're where they're supposed to be, that is.*

The wait did not last long. Like many of the other electronic countermeasures designed to foil any attempts to eavesdrop on TFC Headquarters from the outside, the thermal masking systems formed a dome-shaped barrier surrounding the facility. As soon as the first Marine penetrated this barrier, the short-range passive sensor suite built into his suit instantly located and classified every Human (and Wek) signature on the campus. Fortunately, the tactical comm gear built into the EVA combat armor suits was specifically designed to penetrate even the heaviest signal jamming and still provide short-range communications between the troops. Each of the twenty-eight Marines was immediately presented with a comprehensive tactical plot of their battlespace projected seamlessly within their field of view. Their comm links back to *Theseus*, however, had now been severed.

Shit! Jacks thought, instantly ordering the two squads to halt as his mind raced to take in the situation unfolding on the ground a scant two hundred meters in front of him. He had literally gone from zero information to full situational awareness in an instant, and, unfortunately, there was far more going on than he had hoped to see. Focusing his attention on what he believed to be his targets, Admiral Sexton's signal beacon was clearly visible — and apparently in his right front pocket judging by the pulsing red ovals projected in Jacks' field of view. In spite of their masking devices, the AI also identified the two Wek by their distinctive bio-signatures as well as what appeared to be another Marine who was not wearing combat armor and carrying only his sidearm. All four of them were currently hurrying down a stairwell inside the southern end of the JAG Building.

Finding the admiral and his party, however, was no longer the problem … the problem was dealing with the forty-seven HQSEC troops taking up positions atop the building and just inside the line of trees to the west.

TFS Theseus
(5 km from TFC Headquarters landing zone)

"Captain, we're finally starting to get some data from the infrared sensors," Lau reported from Tactical 2, although he need not have done so with the huge image on the right side of the view screen finally displaying some movement for the first time. "We shouldn't put too much faith in what we're seeing on the combined sensor view just yet, though, sir. The AI has the sensitivity dialed up to the max, so some of the thermal sources displayed may just be transients from the surrounding area."

"Understood," Prescott replied, nevertheless staring intently at the live feed on the view screen. "What do you think?" he asked, leaning towards his XO without shifting his gaze.

Reynolds cocked her head to one side and narrowed her eyes. "I don't know *what* to make of that, actually. I'm not used to seeing the AI display raw sensor data like this, but my first impression is that it looks like an awful lot of heat signatures for that part of the campus this early in the morning."

"Yeah, that's exactly what I was thinking. Ensign Fisher … keep us above the cloud deck for now, but go ahead and get us over to the LZ as quickly as possible." Prescott checked himself, realizing that "as quickly as possible" might well have an entirely different meaning for Ensign Fisher than he had intended. "Belay that. Please move us over to the LZ as quickly as possible while observing all applicable regulations governing our speed and altitude."

"Aye, sir. Smartly and safely," Fisher responded, smiling to himself.

"What, you didn't want him to C-Jump us over there?" Reynolds asked under her breath while entering the necessary commands at her touchscreen to prepare the ship for landing.

"For a split second, I actually did consider it, but as far as I know, a low-altitude transition has never been attempted by anything larger than a fighter. I've seen a computer model for this ship, though. Over structures and people on the ground, the absolute minimum altitude would need to be two thousand meters. The shock wave would probably still break a lot of windows in the area and seem like the end of the world if you were unlucky enough to be caught in the open underneath us at the time."

Prescott paused to reconsider the situation momentarily as the ship's AI announced General Quarters for landing. As the announcement concluded, the lighting on the bridge took on a blue color. "I hate to give a conflicting announcement, but let's go ahead and add possible combat ops to the General Quarters status."

“Aye, sir. That won’t be a problem,” she replied as a single additional keystroke on her screen caused the lighting on the bridge to dim slightly. Shortly thereafter, the blue hue indicating an imminent landing became mixed with the eerie red tint associated with combat operations. While the AI announced the updated status, crew members throughout the ship hurried to their action stations. Just forty-three seconds later, all departments had reported their readiness, exceeding their captain’s standing expectation by two seconds on their first real-world attempt.

“All six reactors available and operating at one hundred percent. All weapons charged. We are at General Quarters for landing with possible combat ops, Captain. Should we configure the ship for landing?” Commander Reynolds asked.

“Very good, Commander, thank you. Not just yet I think,” Prescott replied, still staring at the combined sensor view of the area around the landing zone.

“We’ll be directly over the landing pad in zero one minute, Captain,” Fisher reported.

“Hold position above the cloud deck once we get there, Ensign.”

“Aye, sir.”

As good as the electronic countermeasures employed by TFC Headquarters were, *Theseus* was equipped not only with a powerful array of sensors, but also an AI capable of sifting through incredible quantities of data in an effort to uncover seemingly inconsequential patterns. Patterns that, in this case, finally resulted in the discovery of a weakness in the facility’s thermal masking systems.

On the bridge view screen, the view of the landing zone resolved into perfect clarity, with a variety of raw sensor information now used to produce a photo-realistic representation of the situation on the ground. A situation that looked as if it could quickly spin out of control.

Chapter 17

Terran Fleet Command Headquarters
(Approaching the wooded area behind the JAG Building)

"Stop!" Nenir exclaimed in a hoarse whisper that brought the four members of their party to an abrupt halt. "We are not alone here."

Hearing nothing, but feeling the hair on the back of his neck stand on end from the urgency of the Wek's warning, the young Marine immediately motioned his small party back up the path in the direction of the picnic pavilion. He knew there was very little cover available unless they made it all the way back to the JAG Building, which did nothing but take them farther from their destination.

"Everyone relax," Sexton said calmly as all four took the short walk back to the pavilion, stopping between the rows of tables under the center of the structure.

"Did anyone actually see any movement?" the Marine asked, looking back towards the line of trees as casually as possible. "Could it have been our people coming from the landing pad area?"

"I have seen nothing," Admiral Naftur replied, "but I smelled them as soon as Nenir spoke. I trust you will understand that I mean no disrespect when I tell you that Humans emit a most peculiar scent when under stress," he smiled. "My senses are not as sharp as they once were, but there is definitely a large party nearby."

"Thirty," Nenir said flatly. "Perhaps more."

"Maybe so, but if they have thirty HQSEC troops waiting for us in the woods, what are they waiting *for*?" the Marine asked.

"I think we're about to find out," Sexton said, nodding back in the direction of the JAG Building as a small armored personnel carrier (APC) bearing HQSEC's emblem on both sides rounded the northwest corner and headed in their direction. "It's alright. Just stay calm and let me handle this," he said, holding up both hands in a pleading fashion. "We haven't violated any orders that have been issued so far, so there is no reason for them to prevent us from taking you to meet the *Theseus* as far as I know."

The lightly armored vehicle stopped at the halfway point between the building and the picnic pavilion, its small caliber railgun traversing in their direction as the side and rear doors opened to reveal several HQSEC troops armed with pulse rifles and a woman in civilian business attire. In the distance, more guards could now be seen both in the line of trees to the west as well as along the top of the JAG Building. There was absolutely no doubt that such an overwhelming show of force was intended to remove any thought of resistance or escape.

"Admiral Sexton," the woman called out with a commanding tone. "I am placing you under arrest for dereliction of duty as well as providing aid and comfort to two enemy combatants. There is no reason for anyone to be injured, but I need you all to throw down any weapons you might have, lock your fingers behind your heads, and kneel on the ground in front of the pavilion. Headquarters Security will then place you in restraints before taking you into custody."

“It grieves me to hear it, Madame Chairwoman, but I can assure you that no such crime has taken place,” Sexton replied. He had felt an involuntary chill run down his spine the moment Crull emerged from the troop carrier. Had some sort of coup already taken place in the Council chamber, or would history record that it had been he who had attempted a coup? At the moment, he knew only that his best option was to play for time in hopes that help would arrive in time. “As is my sworn duty, I will be happy to submit to any lawful order issued by the Leadership Council. Has an order for my arrest been issued?”

Crull furrowed her brow and scowled at Sexton through narrowed eyes. “*I* have issued such an order, Admiral. As the Chair, you know very well that my orders carry the full authority of the Council.”

“With all due respect, ma’am, I do not believe that to be the case. No single person on the Council is in my direct chain of command,” Sexton replied in a carefully measured tone. Crull was always a bit dramatic, but there was now something almost … unhinged in her demeanor that he had never before witnessed. “Before we go any farther down this path, perhaps you and I should appear before the Council together. If what you say is the will of the full Council, they can issue a duly authorized order for my arrest at that time. Once that happens, you have my word that I will comply.”

“Give me your weapon, Sergeant,” she ordered the nearest HQSEC guard.

“Uh, ma’am?” he stuttered, unsure how he should respond.

"Idiot! What part of 'give me your weapon' don't you understand?" she screamed, wheeling on the young NCO and physically ripping his pulse rifle from his grip. With a surprisingly practiced hand, Crull checked the weapon's status, disabled the safety, and aimed it directly at the center of Sexton's chest. "You will comply *now*, Admiral! At least one of your crimes is a capital offense, so I'll execute you on the spot if need be."

As she steadied her aim and prepared to fire, Crull heard a distinct THUMP somewhere in the distance off to her right. The sound was not one she recognized … almost like something heavy and metallic had impacted the ground not far away. The fact that she had *felt* the impact as much as she had heard it caused her to take her eyes off the admiral and look in the direction of the sound. Within a few seconds, the THUMP was repeated, this time from somewhere behind her. Now wholly distracted, Crull lowered her weapon and turned completely around to stare back in the direction of the most recent sound.

Watching from above and slightly behind, but still completely obscured from the ground by the heavy fog, Lieutenant Jacks issued a flurry of orders to several of his troops only four hundred milliseconds after the muzzle of Crull's rifle started moving towards the ground. Before she had even managed to turn in the direction of the Marine who had executed an intentional hard landing just to her north, five others dropped with the same intimidating but bone-jarring impacts near the picnic pavilion. Each did his best to place himself in the line of fire between the chairwoman and Admiral

Sexton's group, taking quick aim at both Crull and the HQSEC personnel surrounding the APC.

Since the "universal" EVA combat armor was intended to fulfill a variety of mission types, including crowd and riot control, if necessary, its designers had realized that a voice amplification system might be useful in certain situations. In some ways as dangerous as the pulse rifle itself if used incorrectly, the "VA" system was always a favorite during training exercises. When atmospheric conditions were just right, troops could sometimes use the system to yell to other members of their squad located as far as fifteen kilometers away in a voice that could reach one hundred twenty decibels (roughly the same volume as a clap of thunder). In addition to amplifying the user's own voice, the system also provided a "command voice" option, which produced a psychologically-profiled tone which had a tendency to compel most Humans into immediate compliance. It was with this voice that Lieutenant Jacks now addressed Chairwoman Crull and her HQSEC troops. It was a voice without an apparent source, thundering from the leaden sky above as if God himself had decided to intervene in the current situation.

"Chairwoman Crull and all HQSEC personnel. You are interfering with an active Terran Fleet Command military operation. For your own safety, you are required to stand down immediately. Lower your weapons, step slowly into the open, and lie face down on the ground. Comply immediately and you will not be harmed. Marine special operators will be relocating Admirals Sexton and Naftur as well as Ambassador Turlaka aboard transport. Once we are clear of the area, you may resume your normal security operations."

During the time it had taken Jacks to make the announcement, Master Sergeant Rios had seen to the deployment of the remaining Marines. Rather than slamming into the ground for effect, each now touched down in complete silence, quickly taking up key positions to cover HQSEC troops located on the roof of the JAG Building, in the vicinity of the APC, and inside the line of trees to the west. Although the HQSEC force significantly outnumbered the Marines, none were wearing anything more substantial than standard-issue body armor. Perhaps even more importantly, none were TFC Marines.

This being the first operational appearance of the universal combat armor, none of the HQSEC troops had ever seen the like. Each was a truly terrifying merger of man and machine — with an unspoken promise to become the embodiment of rapid, violent death to any who chose to stand against them. Not only could the Marines fly, but the overwhelming power of their presence, along with Lieutenant Jacks' earth-shattering voice, was more than enough to convince every member of the security force to quickly follow instructions. Only seconds after the first TFC Marine had landed, all but one of the HQSEC troops lay face down with their hands interlocked behind their heads. Only Chairwoman Crull — who had once again taken aim at Admiral Sexton — and the commander of the HQSEC detachment — who appeared to be calmly trying to convince her to hand over the rifle — remained standing.

Crull, seeing that she had a clear shot, and desperate to regain control of the situation, squeezed the trigger.

Situations of this type have always had a tendency to take on a life of their own — the simultaneous actions and reactions of multiple, independent yet wholly intertwined participants coalescing to chart an entirely new course for the events that followed. In the seconds leading up to this point in time …

— Lieutenant Jacks had been about to order one of his men to take down the chairwoman with what would have (hopefully) been a nonlethal shot from his pulse rifle. Doing so always involved significant risk for the target, however, so upon seeing the HQSEC commander's attempt to disarm her peacefully, he had delayed his order momentarily.

— Master Sergeant Rios, believing that Crull was more likely to open fire with every passing second and knowing that there was insufficient time to issue orders to one of the five Marines near the pavilion, raised his own weapon, selecting the "plasma channel" setting as he prepared to fire.

— Admiral Naftur, sensing the very beginning of the minute series of muscle contractions he knew would inevitably lead to Crull firing her rifle, moved with a quickness well beyond the capabilities of his Human companions. Springing powerfully to one side, he shouldered Admiral Sexton out of the path of the incoming directed energy bolt before the weapon had even discharged.

Thanks entirely to Naftur's quick response, Crull's shot missed Admiral Sexton entirely, tearing instead through the Wek admiral's chest and nicking the aortic arch above his heart. The compressed bolt of plasma continued its path of destruction until its lethal cargo of energy had been expended, finally dissipating just before it had passed completely through his body to exit his back.

Less than one second later, Rios' pulse rifle fired a beam of directed energy, striking Crull squarely in the center of her chest. The beam, while doing no damage on its own, created an invisible channel of ionized air between the weapon and her body, acting like a virtual wire. Sensing that a conductive path now existed between itself and its target, the rifle released a lower energy form of plasma — amounting to a fist-sized ball of lightning — which covered the distance to its target at just shy of the speed of light. Upon impact, the chairwoman's nervous system was temporarily disrupted, causing an instantaneous loss of consciousness. Already moving to disarm Crull after she had opened fire, the HQSEC commander at her side grabbed the rifle even as her lifeless body dropped to the ground. Uninterested in suffering the same fate, he immediately threw down the weapon and willingly joined Crull and the rest of his troops face down on the frost-covered grass.

TFS Theseus
(Above TFC Headquarters campus)

"Savage 1, *Theseus*-Actual."

Although there had been frustratingly little Prescott could do to alter the events transpiring on the ground, the confrontation with the HQSEC troops had led him to forgo the landing cycle altogether and instead move the destroyer close enough to reestablish communications with his two squads of Marines. The ship now hovered at the lowest altitude Ensign Fisher had deemed safe — her looming bulk a dark shadow in the fog that seemed to stretch to the horizon in both directions.

"Savage 1 here, Captain," Lieutenant Jacks responded, happy to hear Prescott's voice again. "Sir, we have a medical emergency. Admiral Naftur is critically wounded and requires immediate evac. We have a corpsman working to stabilize him, but he's lost a lot of blood."

"Understood. We need you to get him loaded into one of your *Gurkhas* and onboard *Theseus* as quickly as possible. Once you finish with Naftur, I need you to get Admiral Sexton access to a comlink."

"Aye, sir. Jacks out."

There were a number of trauma units just minutes away in the assault shuttle, but none of them were any better equipped than the medical bay aboard the *Theseus*. More importantly, the warship had the added benefit of Doctor Jiao Chen, who was — by virtue of having been assigned to TFS *Ingenuity* when their species was first encountered — arguably the world's leading authority on Wek anatomy and physiology.

"Doctor Chen, bridge," Prescott announced.

"This is Doctor Chen. What can I do for you, Captain Prescott?" she replied, clearly in the middle of something. Although he always enjoyed working with the chief of his ship's medical staff, Prescott often noted the contrast between his conversations with her and other members of the crew. Had he already become accustomed to an underlying level of deference that she, unlike most everyone else onboard, did not feel obliged to offer? He certainly hoped not, but Chen *was* a civilian after all, and a world-class surgeon to boot — an elite among an elite class of doctors to be sure — a class not generally known for their deference to others.

"Admiral Rugali Naftur has been hit by pulse rifle fire and is gravely injured. He will be arriving on the flight deck momentarily via shuttle."

"I've already spoken with the Marine corpsman who has been working with the admiral and we are prepping for surgery now," she replied, obviously anxious to finish the conversation and attend to the urgent business at hand. "If she is not too traumatized, I would like Doctor Turlaka to scrub in."

"*Doctor* Turlaka," he repeated. "I had completely forgotten that she is a former surgeon. I'm confident she will do so if she is able."

"She's not just a surgeon, Captain, she's a *Wek cardiothoracic* surgeon. Her help may mean the difference between saving him and not."

"Understood, Doctor. I cannot stress to you enough the importance of Admiral Naftur's survival. All of our lives may literally depend on it."

"Rest assured that every patient is treated as if that were the case, Captain. Chen out."

Prescott sighed deeply as he turned to look at his XO. "I'm afraid things may have just gotten quite a bit more complicated."

"If anyone can save him, Jiao Chen is the right doc for the job," she replied with more confidence than she felt at the moment.

“If she doesn’t, our options for handling the situation with the Resistance task force may be reduced to a very short list.”

“Captain,” Lieutenant Dubashi announced, “I have Admiral Sexton, sir — audio only.”

“Put him through, please.”

After a brief delay, a chime indicated that an active comm channel had been established and encrypted. Hearing nothing for several seconds, Prescott spoke up first. “Admiral Sexton, Prescott here. Are you receiving us, sir?”

There were some muffled sounds on the channel, followed shortly thereafter by the Commander in Chief’s voice. “Sorry about that, Captain. Things are still a bit chaotic down here at the moment.”

“How can we help, Admiral?”

“Well, first and foremost, provide your medical staff whatever resources they require to save Admiral Naftur. You can be anywhere on the planet in a matter of minutes, if need be. You have absolute authority to bypass whatever rules you need to in order to make that happen.”

“Will do, sir. I’ve already spoken to Doctor Chen. She believes having Ambassador Turlaka assist her in the surgery may tip the balance in their favor. Do you believe she will be too traumatized to do so?”

“Traumatized? No I wouldn’t say that. I pretty much had to tackle her to keep her from shredding Chairwoman Crull to ribbons. She’s on her way up to you now and I’m sure she will do whatever is required to help.”

“What is the situation with the Leadership Council?”

"Frankly, I have no idea. Right before speaking to you, I drafted a priority message to be hand-delivered to Lisbeth Kistler and Samuel Christenson — two Council members I know and trust. I attempted to summarize the situation and offered to surrender myself into their custody if that is indeed the will of the Council. If that happens, I expect Admiral White will be taking over as Commander in Chief."

"I can't imagine it will come to that, sir. Don't you think Crull was operating pretty much on her own at this point?"

"To an extent, yes. Then again, the Council has approved some very unusual orders over the past couple of weeks. Speaking of that, while I still have the authority to do so, I have declared the Headquarters campus an active emergency operations area until things are back under control. Until you depart, I want *Theseus* sitting right over the center of the facility to make that fact abundantly clear. There will be a full battalion of Marines taking over security here by the end of the day. In fact, I expect the first elements to begin arriving in less than fifteen minutes. I'll release your Marines from guard duty as soon as their replacements arrive."

"Understood, sir. Hopefully, that will provide Doctor Chen enough time to determine if she needs anything else."

"It will have to be enough time, Captain. We cannot afford to delay the reconnaissance mission out to Location Dagger any longer than absolutely necessary. As soon as you are finished with me, update Admiral Patterson and let him know you'll be prepared to depart shortly."

"Aye, sir."

"And say a prayer for Admiral Naftur. He already saved my life today. If he pulls through this, I hope you can provide him the opportunity to save us all."

***

The operating room aboard TFS *Theseus* was truly state of the art, which in many ways implied that it was at least a decade ahead of most of those in planet-side hospitals. Here, the very latest in Pelaran-enhanced robotics was coupled with one of the most powerful AIs available anywhere in the world. Even with all of this technology at their disposal, however, many of the most delicate procedures — including the repair of Admiral Naftur's aorta — still came down to the skilled hands of a gifted surgeon. While Doctors Chen and Turlaka worked, the OR's dedicated gravitic and environmental conditioning systems would prevent even the destroyer's most aggressive maneuvers or impacts to her hull from affecting what was taking place on the operating table. Indeed, as long as the ship stayed generally in one piece, there would be no transient G-forces, no interruptions in power, not the slightest tremor.

"The captain wanted to make sure we planned on doing our best work with Admiral Naftur," Chen said, shaking her head and smiling behind her surgical mask. "Hopefully I managed to get across how offensive that was without being too snippy."

"I'm sure he meant well," Turlaka replied. "Oh … hold … clamp right there, please."

"I got it. I'm very happy you're here, Doctor. I might have been able to pull this off alone, but …" Chen paused, breathing deeply. "I'm just very glad you're here."

"I can't imagine I'd be anywhere else," she chuckled, "but I'm more than a little rusty, as you can see. Please keep a close watch on what I'm doing."

"Nonsense, you're doing beautiful work. Unfortunately, there's a lot of work here to do. I'm still not entirely happy with some of what I'm seeing," Chen commented as she once again paused to allow the sterile field to be cleared of blood. "They have offered to acquire any additional equipment or help we might need, but I honestly don't know of anything we don't already have … can you think of anything?"

"Some music might help," Turlaka replied, "but otherwise I agree. We should have everything we need."

Nurse," Chen announced, "please let the bridge know that Admiral Naftur is in surgery and stable, for the moment. I don't believe we will require any additional equipment or assistance, but the procedure is likely to take a couple of hours."

"Yes, Doctor," the OR nurse replied as she turned to leave the room.

"AI, Chen. Please provide us with some Bach. The *Brandenburg Concerto* Number Three should do nicely." The room was instantly filled with the sound of the London Symphony Orchestra. The music was reproduced with such astounding clarity that it actually caused her to pause momentarily. "Wow," she remarked, "that sounds fantastic."

"It's perfect. Thank you," Turlaka replied. "As to Captain Prescott's comments, I have to admit to feeling a little of that sentiment myself. I can't go into detail, so please don't ask me to elaborate, but I don't mind telling you that Rugali is a very dear and influential man. In fact, I think it's safe to say that both of our worlds are relying heavily on him at the moment. We simply cannot allow ourselves to lose him."

As the AI finished translating Doctor Turlaka's last sentence, Doctor Chen glanced up to look her Wek colleague directly in the eyes. *No pressure, though,* she thought wryly.

Chapter 18

TFS Navajo
(Combat Information Center)

"Contact!" the young commander announced loudly from the holographic display in the center of the room.

For the past couple of hours, Admiral Patterson had been dividing his attention between ongoing preparations for the mission to Location Dagger and the rapidly evolving situation at Terran Fleet Command Headquarters. Since the successful comm beacon deployments near the Resistance rally point, his morning had deteriorated under the weight of a steady stream of bad news. What he dreaded hearing most, however, was the worst case scenario — the unexpected arrival of a large force of Resistance ships that would immediately shower the Earth with weapons of mass destruction before he had any hope of mounting a defense. On hearing the commander's announcement, he rose quickly from his Command console and made his way back to the holo table.

"Just one, Commander?" Patterson asked anxiously.

"Yes, Admiral. Looks like a single, so far. The range is just over nine million kilometers — thirty light seconds or so. It popped up pretty close to one of our surveillance drones, so confidence in the data is high at this point. We should have video shortly …"

The display had quickly been reconfigured to provide an all-encompassing view of the battlespace surrounding the *Navajo* out to a distance roughly double that of the new contact. As usual, the admiral's formation of Fleet assets in and near Earth orbit were displayed as blue icons designating them as friendly units. At Patterson's insistence, the Guardian spacecraft, having still not proven itself as a "friendly" in his opinion, but also not openly hostile, was represented by a purple icon. Finally, the unknown contact — which the AI had now classified as a destroyer due to its size — was displayed with a yellow icon, which now flashed to indicate that a live video stream was available.

Leaning over the table, Patterson selected the new contact's icon, and with a simple gesture indicated that he wished to see the video feed on one of the large view screens nearby. What he saw, while not entirely unexpected, was of grave concern given the proximity of the Guardian spacecraft. Almost immediately thereafter, the *Navajo's* AI came to the same conclusion as the admiral, updating the identifying text block displayed next to the contact and changing its icon to blue.

After a week-long journey at her maximum speed from Gliese 667, the *Gresav* had arrived in the Sol system.

TFS Theseus
(Initial climb to orbit)

With all her personnel back onboard, and having finally been cleared for departure by both Admiral Sexton and the two surgeons working diligently to save Admiral Naftur's life in the medical bay, TFS *Theseus* rotated her bow silently to the east and began her first climb to orbit.

"All systems in the green, Captain. Both standard and C-Drive transitions are available. C-Jump range 99.3 light years and stable. Denver Air Route Traffic Control has cleared us for an unrestricted climb from our current location and we are clear of all traffic," Dubashi reported from the Communications console, still adjusting to some extent to doing double duty as both comm officer and navigator.

"Thank you, Lieutenant," Prescott replied. "Ensign Fisher, as usual, it's your show. Please keep in mind what's going on in Medical. In theory, what the ship is doing shouldn't affect the operating room, but let's do our best not to test those systems, if we can help it."

"Aye, Captain. Standard climb underway. The AI has a number of pre-established performance profiles set up as part of our so-called 'abbreviated shake-down cruise.' This specific one isn't all that aggressive, though. We will briefly achieve .002 *c*, but it shouldn't cause a problem for the grav systems. ETA to our rendezvous with the *Navajo* is just under three minutes."

"Understood. Discontinue immediately if we start to feel any lag in the dampeners."

"Aye, sir. Will do."

Since Admiral Naftur had been brought on board, an uncharacteristically somber mood had taken hold on *Theseus'* bridge. Her first climb to orbit, which would normally have been a time of nervous excitement coupled with a fair amount of apprehension, instead took on an air of the routine. While still very much engaged in their work and performing their duties in expert fashion, the members of the bridge crew said little, each one a study in introspection as they dealt with the uncertainty of the situation in their own way.

"How do you expect Admiral Patterson will alter the mission to Location Dagger?" Reynolds finally asked, looking for anything to lighten the increasingly oppressive mood.

"I doubt he will change a thing," Prescott said. "We may not have Admiral Naftur's help, but Patterson is not one to tell his commanders precisely how they are supposed to accomplish a mission."

"And the mission hasn't really changed ..."

"No, not really. He'll expect us to attempt to make contact with the Resistance commander, if possible. If we don't have Naftur available, which seems likely at this point, perhaps Ambassador Turlaka can fill that role. Failing that ..."

"Failing that, we execute the 'force' component of our 'reconnaissance in force.'"

"Maybe so, but I think the bottom line is that it's going to be up to us to assess the situation and determine the best course of action based on what we find."

"Contact," Lieutenant Lau announced from Tactical 2. "Unknown contact, range: nine million kilometers. The AI is classifying it as a destroyer-size vessel."

"Did our sensors pick it up, or are we getting it from the Fleet data feed?" Prescott asked.

"It's about thirty light seconds out, so it's an NRD surveillance drone contact so far, but I suspect our own sensors will pick it up shortly."

"Ah, well, if it's a surveillance drone contact, we should have video shortly."

“Yes, sir, it’s coming in now,” Lau replied, opening a window on the right side of the view screen to display the video feed. The distinctive profile of the previously unidentified vessel was instantly recognizable to every member of the bridge crew.

“Sir, it’s the *Gresav*!” Lau reported, officially acknowledging what everyone had already seen for themselves.

It took only a few seconds more for both Prescott and Reynolds to realize the potential implications of the Wek ship’s arrival.

“This could be a big problem,” Reynolds said, immediately calling up a real-time feed of the Guardian spacecraft and placing it in a window next to the image of the *Gresav*.

“It could be. When we left the *Gresav* at Gliese 667, we had no reason to expect that the Guardian would have openly declared itself and be sitting in the immediate proximity of the Earth by the time they arrived. In fact, Admiral Naftur thought that having her transition relatively close to Earth and then join up with one of our cruisers was probably the safest bet for avoiding the Guardian’s attention. Surely it realizes that attacking without provocation won’t be particularly helpful for its PR campaign.”

“I’m not so sure about that, sir,” Reynolds replied. “One thing we *do* know is that thing is a master of propaganda. It would probably just pass it off as another example of how it continues to protect us from the evil alien hordes bent on our destruction. So if it *does* attack, how should we respond?”

Prescott stared thoughtfully at the screen for a moment without answering. "Lieutenant Lau, have we seen any movement or changes in emissions from the Guardian?"

"None whatsoever, sir, but unless it has broken our new crypto, it shouldn't be getting any NRD data. As far as we know, that means we still have a few seconds before *Gresav's* light reaches the Guardian's location."

Prescott scowled and shook his head, realizing that he had once again found himself in a difficult situation as a direct result of his relationship with the Wek admiral fighting for his life in *Theseus'* med bay. It took him only a few seconds to make his decision, then quickly make the mental shift from deliberation to execution. "If it attacks without provocation, Commander Reynolds," he replied resolutely, "we will do our best to defend the ship that defended us. Set General Quarters for combat ops. Dubashi, plot an intercept C-Jump to the *Gresav*. I don't want to have to chase her down, so put us along her path without getting us into a collision."

"Aye, sir," both officers responded crisply.

"Sir, the Guardian is moving!" Lau reported excitedly. On the view screen, the Guardian rotated smoothly in the direction of the *Gresav*, engaged its sublight engines, and began to accelerate.

"Captain," Lieutenant Dubashi reported. "The *Navajo* has been attempting to hail the Guardian spacecraft, but there has been no response. They are now trying the emergency Guard frequencies."

"Let's hear it," Prescott ordered.

With a few quick keystrokes from Dubashi's Communications console, the voice of Ensign Katy

Fletcher aboard Admiral Patterson's flagship blared from the bridge's overhead speakers. "Guardian spacecraft, Guardian spacecraft, this is Terran Fleet Command flagship *Navajo* broadcasting in the blind on Guard. Stand down, stand down, stand down. Incoming spacecraft is a friendly unit. Do not engage. Repeat … incoming Wek vessel is a friendly. Stand down, hold your position, and do *not* engage."

Prescott drew his hand across his throat, signaling Dubashi to terminate the audio broadcast.

"Intercept plotted and transferred to the Helm console," she announced as relative silence returned to *Theseus'* bridge.

"Alright, everyone, it doesn't look like the Guardian is planning to transition to hyperspace, that could mean it's using the situation to test our resolve more than to actually threaten the *Gresav*. I doubt either of our ships would put up much of a fight if it decides to attack, but we can at least force it to commit itself to open hostilities with TFC if we put ourselves between it and the *Gresav*. Let's just hope that's not something it is prepared to do."

"Captain, all six reactors at one hundred percent, weapons charged, shield systems online, C-Jump range 99.3 light years and stable. The ship is at General Quarters for combat ops," Reynolds reported.

"Very well. Ensign Fisher, after we transition, you may maneuver as required to put us between the Guardian and the *Gresav*. I want a one light-minute emergency C-Jump plotted at all times. Clear?"

"Yes, Captain. Ready."

"Execute your C-Jump."

Without delay, the AI's synthetic voice began a ship-wide countdown. "Capacitive hyperdrive engaged, transition in 3 … 2 … 1 …"

In the center of the bridge view screen, waypoint brackets were displayed around the location of the distant Wek ship. As the hyperdrive engaged, there was no apparent change in the background stars, but the Earth and Moon slid quickly out of view on either side of the display as the AI provided a smooth representation of the instantaneous, nine-million-kilometer journey. The previous surveillance drone feed of the *Gresav* was automatically removed from the right side of the screen as a live, optical view of the actual ship quickly expanded to fill the center of the display.

"Transition complete, Captain. Securing from hyperspace flight," Lieutenant Dubashi reported. "All systems in the green. Sublight engines online, we are free to maneuver. Both standard and C-Drive transitions are available. C-Jump range still 99.3 light years and stable. We are less than one meter from our expected arrival point."

"Thank you, Dubashi. You may discontinue reporting hyperdrive availability and arrival point accuracy unless you see something unusual."

"Guardian ship still accelerating, sir," Lau reported from the Tactical 2 Console. "If it continues to do so at the current rate, its projected ETA is five minutes."

"Thank you, Lieutenant Lau," Prescott replied. "Dubashi, try hailing the *Gresav* with the new comm security protocols in place. Hopefully, the two AIs will manage to work out the encryption algorithm between them."

"Aye, sir. Hailing."

After a very brief delay during which the *Theseus* and *Gresav* easily established an encrypted channel and synchronized for real-time translation, the youthful-looking face of Wek Flag Captain Musa Jelani filled the center of the view screen. "Hello again, Captain Prescott and crew," he smiled fiercely. "We had just detected the presence of the Pelaran spacecraft when your … rather aggressive-looking, I must say … warship transitioned nearby. I was very much relieved to see that it was you."

"Good to see you again as well, Captain Jelani, welcome back to the Sol system," Prescott replied. "As you noted, the Pelaran Guardian ship has detected your presence and is headed in this direction. It arrived at Earth immediately after our return. So far, it has shown no hostile intent towards any of our ships, but I am not sure that the same will apply to a Sajeth Collective spacecraft."

"I suspect not, Captain. What do you suggest?"

"How quickly can you transition back to hyperspace?"

"We have been driving our engines beyond their maximum rated power for several days. As a result, our chief engineer was forced to take the hyperdrive offline temporarily to correct a problem with one of our reactors. While potentially serious, the fix should not be difficult or time-consuming. We expect to be able to transition again within three to five minutes."

"If our luck holds, that should be quickly enough. Our communications officer is sending you a set of coordinates we are referring to as 'Location Willow.'" Prescott said, nodding to Lieutenant Dubashi. "We believe it to be near the location of the original Resistance task force rally point. As soon as you are able, proceed there at your best speed. Before arrival, adjust your hyperdrive to allow your ship to remain in hyperspace. Do *not* transition to normal space until you hear from one of our ships, or you may be attacked by Resistance forces. We believe the bulk of them have now left the area, but we also believe they may have left some of their ships behind to wait for additional reinforcements."

"Understood, Captain. We have the location. We will arrive in just over twenty-six hours."

"Very good. We should be there well before you and hope to have the area secured prior to your arrival."

"Would you be so kind as to allow me to speak with Admiral Naftur before we depart?" Jelani asked.

Prescott had sincerely hoped that this particular complication would not have time to come up before the *Gresav's* departure. There simply wasn't time to explain the situation adequately, and he knew that a misunderstanding here could quickly unravel the fragile trust they had just begun building over the past month. He breathed deeply, allowing his face to take on a very sincere look of concern. "No, Musa. I am afraid that's not possible at the moment. I am very sorry to have to inform you that Admiral Naftur was seriously injured earlier today and is currently in surgery. I regret that we do not have time for me to adequately explain what happened, but I can tell you that his injury was sustained when he pushed our Commander in Chief, Admiral Sexton, out of the path of an incoming pulse rifle round, saving his life in the process."

Captain Jelani stared intently at Prescott for a long moment, then, seeming to find what he was looking for, glanced down and closed his eyes momentarily as if offering a prayer. “I am gravely concerned to hear this news, Captain,” he began again, “but I have no doubt that Rugali Naftur was doing exactly what he believed was required of him at the time. Is Nenir Turlaka assisting with his care?”

“Yes she is. She is assisting our own Doctor Chen in the surgery as we speak. So far, they have indicated that his injury is serious, but not necessarily beyond their skills. We should hear from them again within a couple of hours. I am sorry that you will be unable to receive an update until your arrival at Location Willow, but rest assured we are doing everything within our power to save his life.”

“And I likewise assure you that I have no doubt that this is indeed the case. Otherwise, our conversation would have taken quite a different path,” Jelani smiled, a hint of bold defiance flashing in his eyes.

“Captain, the Guardian is transitioning to hyperspace!” Lieutenant Lau bellowed from Tactical 2 just as the image of the Pelaran ship on the right side of the view screen blurred slightly before disappearing in a faint flash of blue light.

“I’m afraid we’re out of time, Captain,” Prescott said as calmly as he could manage under the circumstances. “I will maneuver to keep my ship between you and the Guardian. Please stay behind us and make your transition to hyperspace as quickly as possible.”

“Understood. Thank you and good luck, Captain Prescott. Jelani out.”

"Alright, Lau, how much time do we …"

"Contact, close aboard to starboard!" Lau yelled.

"Helm, block its line of fire!"

Although Prescott had responded immediately, his order came well after Ensign Fisher — growing increasingly comfortable with his ability to work seamlessly with *Theseus'* AI — had rolled the ship into a left bank while simultaneously increasing power to come between the Guardian and the *Gresav*.

"Well done, Ensign. Keep that up until *Gresav* is away."

"I'll try, sir," Fisher replied, trying to think several maneuvers ahead and realizing that the task would ultimately prove impossible.

At fifty meters in length, the Guardian was only marginally larger than an F-373 fighter and, although maneuverability had not been high on its Pelaran "makers'" list of priorities, it was still significantly more maneuverable than the two destroyers. What followed was like an oddly choreographed dance routine between two blue whales and a single tiger shark as the Guardian spacecraft attempted to place itself in a position that would allow a clear line of fire to the *Gresav* without hitting *Theseus*. Initially, at least, each of its movements was quickly countered by a combination of move and counter move by the Human and Wek destroyers.

"It's playing with us, Captain," Schmidt announced from Tactical 1 after the third such series of maneuvers. "It has had several clear shots at this point." To underscore the point, Schmidt opened a window on the left end of the bridge view screen displaying an overhead tactical plot of the current encounter in a quick playback loop. Each time the Guardian's weapons could have been brought to bear, the AI highlighted the path from the beam emitter to the point of impact on the *Gresav* in an angry, flashing red.

"Looks that way, doesn't it," Prescott answered absently, his attention focused on the *Gresav*, which he sincerely hoped would be on her way shortly. "As I said, I suspect this whole encounter is a test of some sort. In the process, the Guardian gets an opportunity to confirm its suspicions about our relationship with at least part of the Sajeth Collective, while also learning more about our ship's capabilities."

"Meanwhile, we are unwitting participants in its little test," Reynolds added.

"Well, maybe not unwitting, but definitely unwilling," Prescott laughed. "It's not like we felt like we had much of a choice in the matter, and I'm certain the Guardian knows enough about how we think to have made that calculation."

"By the way," Reynolds asked, "do we even know if our shields can take a hit from that thing's beam weapons?"

"I had Logan look into that, but the best he could get out of the Science and Engineering Directorate was a definite maybe. Most of them seem to think that they would hold out for at least a few hits, but beyond that it's anyone's guess. One thing they were able to tell us with absolute certainty is that our armor cannot."

"Inspiring," Reynolds replied cynically.

"The good news is that I think if it were going to fire, it would have already done so," Prescott said, a wry grin on his face.

"Sir, the *Gresav* is transitioning to hyperspace," Lau reported as the starfield surrounding the Wek destroyer blurred momentarily before she disappeared entirely in a flash of gray light.

"Glad to hear it. Tactical, power down the weapon systems for now. XO, we will remain at General Quarters — most likely for some time — please let our people know we will be maintaining a state of readiness so that they can plan their rotations accordingly. Helm, give us a gentle turn in the direction of the *Navajo*. Comm/Nav, plot a C-Jump back to the general area near the flagship, just in case, then request a vidcon with Admiral Patterson."

"Aye, sir," all four officers replied.

Just off *Theseus'* port side, the Guardian spacecraft joined up in formation, almost as if the entire encounter had been nothing more than a routine training exercise between allied forces.

"Sir, the Guardian is hailing us," Dubashi announced.

Prescott hesitated, thinking that under the circumstances, any communications should be handled by Admiral Patterson. Looking to his XO for her opinion, however, he received only a shrug and a facial expression that clearly conveyed a simple question, "Why not?"

"Alright, this ought to be interesting at least," he replied, shaking his head. "On-screen, please."

"Aye, sir, opening channel."

Seconds later, the Guardian's now familiar Human avatar appeared on the view screen, this time seated at a virtual Command console. Although "Griffin" had swapped his typical sport coat and slacks for what looked suspiciously like a TFC flight suit, his smiling visage was otherwise unchanged from his regular appearances on Earth's mass media. "Ah, the heroic Captain Prescott, I presume," he began. "I'm honored to finally get the opportunity to speak with you in person."

"Thank you," Prescott replied flatly, unfazed by the Guardian's typically disarming tone. "I don't mean to be rude, but unless you require our assistance, I believe it would be more appropriate for you to speak with Admiral Patterson or members of the Leadership Council."

"Oh no, I'm perfectly fine, thank you. I'm a little confused as to why you would refer me to the Leadership Council, however. Didn't your vessel participate in removing the duly elected Chairwoman of that august organization from office earlier this morning?"

Prescott stared at the image on the screen, reminding himself that, while not Human or even biological, it represented an advanced and incredibly dangerous potential adversary. "We were indeed at our Headquarters facility earlier today, and were present when Chairwoman Crull was taken into custody for the attempted murder of Admiral Duke Sexton, TFC Commander in Chief."

"This is the same Admiral Sexton who was, himself, being taken into custody at the time for dereliction of duty and providing aid and comfort to two enemy combatants, one of which, I believe, was seriously injured in the process." Griffin paused to offer a maddeningly pleasant smile before continuing. "My, how fond you Humans are of leaving out certain key pieces of information when they do not support your version of events." He paused again, seemingly to provide Prescott an opportunity to respond, but received only a blank stare. "No matter," he continued airily, "I must confess, however, that I am curious as to why you would put your ship and crew in danger to protect an enemy Sajeth Collective vessel. This is, after all, the very same alliance that even now gathers forces in preparation for mounting an attack on your homeworld."

"I am no politician," Prescott finally responded after a long silence, "but it seems to me that you are painting with a very broad brush. It is true that we have had only minimal time to begin forming an opinion of the Sajeth Collective, one way or another, but our experience thus far has *not* shown their alliance to be openly hostile towards us on the whole. Would the Pelaran Alliance have us behave in a hostile fashion towards *all* civilizations we encounter for the first time?"

"Only if your species wishes to survive, Captain," the Guardian replied in an uncharacteristically menacing tone. "You have a great deal to learn, and should be grateful that we have chosen to grant you the opportunity to do so in relative safety. Had we not, I assure you that your period of blissfully ignorant isolation would have already come to an abrupt and violent end."

Unwilling to engage in further meaningless debate, Prescott said nothing, but simply inclined his head politely and waited for the Guardian to continue. When it finally did so, its bright, casual tone had returned.

"In any event," it said dismissively, "I suppose there was no harm in allowing the Sajeth Collective vessel to depart the system. As for your Leadership Council, I am sure that Chairwoman Crull's actions will be deemed wholly appropriate upon further investigation. It also looks as if Terra will be taking her rightful place as a member in the Pelaran Alliance very soon. Once that happens, I will be much more at liberty to share what we know of interstellar politics and the projection of naval power. In the interim, please do be careful to choose your friends wisely." The Guardian narrowed his eyes as the corners of his mouth turned upwards in perhaps his most pompous facial expression to date. "Griffin out."

There was a brief period of silence during which Ensign Fisher could be heard letting out a long sigh as he released some of the tension from the encounter with the Guardian. "Jeez, what an ass," he muttered to himself.

"Mm-hmm," Lieutenant Lau agreed in a low voice that only Fisher could hear.

Chapter 19

TFS Navajo
(CIC conference room 2)

"I'll say one thing for you, Prescott," Admiral Patterson said, leaning back in his usual CIC conference room chair, "when you're in the area, things rarely turn dull. I don't think I've ever encountered a man who stumbles into more situations where he's forced into making far-reaching, life or death decisions without anyone else's input."

"Oh, I get input, Admiral. Just this morning I sought out the counsel of my wise and experienced XO and got a solid 'Why not?' in response. With advice like that backing me up, how could I go wrong?" Prescott smiled, winking at Reynolds as he did so.

"You're lucky to have her, and I'd say that sometimes that *is* the best possible advice," the older man chuckled. "Honestly, though, I don't have much to say about the incident with the *Gresav*. There really wasn't any way we could prepare for her arrival, given all the things that have changed since you left her a week ago. You just happened to, once again, be in the right place at the right time, and you did exactly what I would have asked you to do if I had been given enough time to do so. I don't know that I would have sent them to Location Willow, but I don't know that I wouldn't have either. It was their data that helped us find the Resistance rally point in the first place, and whatever we're about to do will probably be over by the time they get there anyway. Are you ready to depart?"

“I believe so, sir. We’re hoping to hear an update on Admiral Naftur’s condition from our medical bay shortly, but even under the best of circumstances, I don’t think he will be in any condition to assist us during our parley with the Resistance.”

“That definitely complicates things, but it doesn’t change the essence of what you’re going out there to do. When Ambassador Turlaka is available, perhaps she can stand in for the admiral. Based on what I’ve seen so far, I’m convinced that the Resistance task force was thrown off their game a bit by the arrival of our *Hunter* recon flight. The fighter that deployed our comm beacons detected two additional outbound hyperdrive signatures not long after the original twenty-four, so I’m sticking with my theory that we’re seeing late arrivals trickle in and then get forwarded on to a different location.”

Patterson paused, looking as if the discussion had led to him to some new conclusion that he had just noted for later. “In any event,” he continued, “your two flights of *Reapers* departed half an hour ago and are standing by for your orders at Location Willow. Don’t hesitate to call them in if things start to turn sour. I don’t have to tell you that this is a potentially volatile situation that could degenerate from a parley into a knife fight in short order. Don’t get me wrong, I am hopeful that your negotiations will be successful, but let’s not lose sight of the fact that they came here with hostile intentions in the first place. They are a dangerous, rogue faction from a potentially hostile alliance. I think it’s safe to say that the best we can hope for at this point is to convince them to return home in the hopes that cooler heads will eventually prevail.”

"Understood, sir."

"Keep in mind that I'll have a full tactical view of the battlespace as soon as *Theseus* transitions to normal space at Location Dagger. If we find ourselves in a fight, it's obviously my preference to do so out there rather than here in the system where we will be forced to commit the bulk of our forces to defense. If I see an opportunity where sending you some additional help might prove decisive, I'll do what I can, but, for the moment at least, I have precious few C-Jump capable ships at my disposal. Unfortunately, most of our capital ships are a twenty-hour flight away, and I can't justify the risk of not having them available to defend the Earth, if necessary."

Patterson paused and studied both of their faces. He knew full well that *Theseus* was the only realistic option he had for this mission, but he was also painfully aware of the unrelenting stress that her captain and crew had been under for the past month … not to mention what they had already been through just this morning. *One more month,* he thought. *If we had had just one more month before all this hit the fan ...*

"Do either of you have any last-minute questions for me?" Patterson finally asked.

"No, sir," both Prescott and Reynolds replied in unison.

"Well then, Commodore … Commander … *Theseus* is hereby authorized to hoist a broad pennant and depart immediately. Good luck and Godspeed."

TFS Theseus

“Commodore on the bridge,” Lieutenant Commander Schmidt announced as Prescott and Reynolds emerged from the captain’s ready room. This being the first time their captain had officially been in command of a squadron of ships on detached duty, all six officers and the Marine sentry stood at attention as he made his way back to his Command chair.

“Thank you all,” Prescott said quietly. The admiral mentioning the occasion had been one thing, but something about having his bridge crew make this seemingly simple acknowledgment struck him with an unexpected wave of emotion. He swallowed hard before attempting to say anything else, feeling that now was hardly the time for a display of foolish sentimentality. “I appreciate that very much … more than you know, in fact. When we at last reach the point where we are no longer responding to the crisis of the day, every one of us — every member of our crew — has much to celebrate. I promise you when that happens, we *will* celebrate … and we’ll do so in a way that’s worthy of our accomplishments.”

“First and best, sir,” Commander Schmidt said proudly.

“First and best,” Prescott replied, smiling broadly. “By the way, let’s just stick with ‘Captain’ for now, if you would. I’m afraid if you all suddenly start calling me ‘Commodore,’ I might miss something important. Are we ready to go?”

“Yes, sir. All systems in the green. The ship is at General Quarters for combat ops and ready to C-Jump,” Schmidt reported as he made his way back to the Tactical 1 console.

"Very good … Commander Logan, bridge."

"Logan here. Go ahead, Captain."

"If you're having doubts about any of our critical systems, particularly the shields and the C-Drive, now would be a good time to say so."

"As much as I hate to tempt fate by answering that question, everything down here is exceeding expectations so far, sir. That short C-Jump provided some data that allowed us to dial the C-Drive in a little tighter, so you should be able to expect good positional accuracy and the full one-hundred-light-year range. In fact, you might see a little more than that if the current trend holds. As far as the shields go, they are almost completely managed by the AI, so there isn't much either of us can or should do other than hope they work when we need them."

"We aren't going far, but it wouldn't surprise me if we get a warm greeting at first when we arrive. If you see the slightest indication that the shields are not going to hold, I need to know immediately."

"Aye, sir, you'll be the first to know."

"Thank you, Commander. Stand by for C-Jump followed by possible incoming fire. Prescott out."

SCS Hadeon, Pelaran Resistance Rally Point
(3.3 light years from Earth)

"Perimeter drone contact!" a Wek lieutenant called from one of *Hadeon's* four Defensive Operations workstations. As if to further emphasize the lieutenant's announcement, the sound of the battlespace defense cruiser's reactors increasing their power output was clearly audible on the bridge as she automatically opened fire with her starboard energy weapons banks. "Only one ship this time, and in almost exactly the same location as the previous two scout ships. The AI classified the contact as a probable Terran warship and has already engaged."

"That much I can hear for myself. Who gave the order to fire?" Captain Miah demanded, furious not because of the attack so much as the idea that anyone would presume to take action without his expressed permission.

"Captain," Commander Takkar said, leaning over and speaking in a low voice in an attempt to save the pompous Damaran from further embarrassment, "the task force's standing rules of engagement allow the battlespace defense AI to autonomously attack hostile targets if there is sufficient data to classify them as such. The system was designed to provide force protection over a large area of space. Removing the need for manual intervention is a key …"

"I'm fully versed on the design of the *Keturah*-class BD cruiser, Commander," Miah interrupted with such a vehement tone that Takkar pulled quickly away — his mind instinctively preparing his body to defend itself, if necessary.

The massive Wek commander's reaction caused an equally involuntary chill to run down Commander Miah's spine. Realizing that he was perilously close to crossing a line that might yield an unpredictable response from this simple-minded barbarian, he immediately moderated his tone.

"Apologies, Commander. I am not sure the original rules of engagement should still apply, given the dramatically diminished size of our current force. That, however, is a discussion for later. In the meantime, does it make sense to you that the Humans would send a single vessel back to the precise location where they lost contact with two of their scouts?"

"I prefer not to speculate, Captain Miah, but the Terrans might simply be looking for their missing ships," Takkar said, furrowing his brow. "It's also possible they know we are here and wish to communicate with us."

"If that were the case, I assume we would have received their hail by now. Besides, I'm sure they are intelligent enough to realize that our immediately opening fire on them is a strong indication that we are not here to chat," Miah sneered.

"The Pelarans seem to be in the habit of sending in a single ship … one with such an asymmetric technological advantage that additional ships are simply not required," Takkar said as he called up a real-time video feed of the intruder from the closest surveillance drone. He had offered this final explanation not because he believed it to be the case so much as he knew that it would both irritate and terrify the Damaran.

"Nonsense! There is no indication the Humans have done much more than putter around in the immediate vicinity of the Sol system with a few small scout ships and maybe a frigate or two," Miah scoffed. "Surely you don't mean to imply they have anything that might pose a serious threat to several of our warships at one time."

Commander Takkar, having long since grown tired of Miah's seemingly endless stream of insulting comments, simply nodded towards the view screen in reply. The light-amplified and thermally enhanced image of the approaching Terran warship was rendered with a stunning level of clarity, and it was with no small degree of satisfaction that Takkar detected a renewed stench of fear from his so-called captain.

TFS Theseus, Location Dagger

Since the primary objective of *Theseus'* mission was contingent on the Resistance task force agreeing to a parley, there was no particular need for subtlety upon her arrival at Location Dagger. In fact, Prescott had intentionally chosen their transition point to coincide with the final recon location of the two missing *Hunter* RPSVs in the faint hope that it might provide some indication of their intentions.

"Four contacts," Lieutenant Lau reported immediately from Tactical 2. "Passive sensors only so far — approximate range: three million kilometers — four Sajeth Collective cruiser-class warships. They'll have us in six seconds, Captain."

"Understood. Designate as Charlie 1 through 4 and bring up a tactical plot on the starboard view screen, please," Prescott replied calmly. "Dubashi, begin transmitting Admiral Naftur's parley request hail in a continuous loop until we get a response."

"Aye, sir," both responded as the somewhat intimidating tactical plot appeared on the right side of the view screen. With the exception of Lieutenant Lee, every member of the bridge crew had witnessed firsthand the huge volume of firepower even a single cruiser could bring to bear, and each now struggled to steel themselves for the potential battle to come.

Sensing the tension in the room, Prescott spoke up in as confident a tone as he could muster. "Everyone take a deep breath and relax. We may well get fired on shortly, but we'll be just fine. Keep in mind that we're here to defend our home, and while we would prefer to avoid a fight if we can, we've brought exactly the right ship for the job if a fight turns out to be what's required."

"Hooyah, sir," Lieutenant Lau replied.

"I'm sorry, what was that?" Prescott asked.

"Hooyah!" every member of the bridge crew shouted as one.

As if on cue, both Tactical consoles emitted a series of warning chimes indicating that the threat posed by the nearby warships had increased to critical levels, requiring the crew to take immediate action.

"They have opened fire with energy weapons, sir," Lau reported. "It's a little wide … almost like they are still working up a firing solution … or maybe just trying to bracket our position."

"The AI says it's also a little early," Schmidt added from Tactical 1.

"Now *there's* some actionable information," Prescott replied eagerly. "Patterson suspected they were using something similar to NRD surveillance drones as some kind of wide-area fleet defense network. See anything nearby?"

"Not yet, sir, but it would have to be close … they opened up almost immediately after we transitioned."

"We're here to talk, but we don't have to sit here and allow ourselves to be an easy target for them. Use an active spherical scan at maximum power and let the AI know what it's looking for. Take it out as soon as you find it."

"With pleasure, sir," Schmidt said.

Working feverishly at her own touchscreen, Commander Reynolds opened a tactical assessment window on the port side of the bridge view screen. Multiple views of each of the four enemy ships were displayed with all known vulnerabilities highlighted. Glancing up quickly from her own Command console, she was gratified to see that two of the four cruisers were of the same type they had encountered previously — each suffering from the same field of fire limitations *Ingenuity* had used to great advantage in the battle at Gliese 667. Thus far, no such vulnerability had been noted for Charlie 3 and 4, but since all four warships had similar hull configurations, she had confidence that something similar would apply to them as well. Completing an exhaustive analysis of the cruisers' engine configurations, the AI added the now-familiar gap between each ship's sublight engine nozzles and their aft shields.

"Same lobing pattern as before near the engine nozzles on all four targets, Captain," she reported, nodding in the direction of the tactical assessment. "Charlie 1 and 2 also have the same limited firing envelope on their main weapons we saw before. The other two cruisers are something different — defensive platforms maybe, based on their long-range energy weapons."

"Excellent. That might come in handy, but I'm still hopeful it won't come to that. I'm not all that concerned about this incoming fire just yet. We're well out of their effective beam weapon range based on what we know about their cruisers so far. What we're seeing right now actually seems like some kind of automated defensive response. For the moment, I think we just need to sit tight and see what they do. We have to give them time to receive our message and decide how to handle it before we take any definitive action ourselves."

"Do you intend to close with them?"

"Unless they stop shooting at us, hell no!" Prescott laughed. "If we're going to have a conversation, however, it would be helpful to get a *little* closer. If they agree to talk to us, I'd say we can move in to three hundred thousand kilometers or so. That will give us a manageable, one-second comm delay, but still provide us enough room to maneuver if they do something unexpected."

"I have their surveillance drone, sir," Schmidt reported, excitement creeping into his voice. "Firing …"

Outside, a single, gimbaled beam emitter mounted amidships on *Theseus'* starboard side swiveled in the direction of its target and discharged, vaporizing the drone within a fraction of a second as if it were barely worthy of the destroyer's attention.

"Target destroyed," Schmidt reported.

"Nice job. That should at least make us a little harder to hit. We must have transitioned right on top of that thing, and I'm guessing that's how they got our two *Hunters* as well. Make a note that we need to tweak our passive scans to pick those up, if possible. They have to be giving off some kind of emissions we can detect."

"Aye, sir."

Just prior to the surveillance drone being destroyed, *Hadeon's* fire-control AI had finally perfected an extreme-range firing solution for its target, sent the necessary corrections to its starboard beam emitters, and fired. Ten seconds later, the salvo began arriving at its target. In response, *Theseus'* AI detected, then localized the infinitesimal interactions occurring between the incoming energy and its own gravitic fields, performed the immensely complex calculations required to deflect the energy, and then dramatically increased power to create an intense gravitic distortion at the chosen location. The first set of shield intercept events occurred above the destroyer's bow, each one creating a brief flash of light in the visible spectrum.

"Whoa … I'm pretty sure that was a hit on the forward shields," Lieutenant Lau reported. "Yes, several confirmed hits. The AI is reporting successful intercepts. Zero hull impacts so far."

"That's the best news I've heard all day," Prescott replied, exhaling with relief. "Tactical, let's add your hull impact counter to the tactical plot. Helm, they will probably lose their firing solution now that we have destroyed their drone, but go ahead and perform some evasive maneuvers to further complicate their targeting. Maintain roughly the same range and bearing to the Resistance ships for now, but keep them guessing. I'd prefer they not have the opportunity to start gauging the effectiveness of our shields just yet."

"Aye, sir," Lau and Fisher replied.

"Commander Logan, bridge."

"Logan here. Go ahead, Captain."

"We've had some shield impacts. Anything we need to know?"

"As long as you know someone is shooting at us, I think we're good for now," Logan replied. "Those hits wouldn't have done much damage at this range anyway, but it looks like the system is performing as advertised so far."

"That's outstanding news, Commander. Let us know if you see a problem. Prescott out."

"Sir, they appear to have ceased fire," Schmidt reported.

"And they are hailing us," Dubashi added from the Communications console. "Textual only. It reads: 'Parley request granted. Power down all weapons and approach to within four hundred thousand kilometers. Do not exceed .01 c. Any acts of aggression will result in your vessel's immediate destruction. *Hadeon* out.'"

"Not exactly rolling out the red carpet, but good enough, I suppose. Fisher, how long will that take us at one percent light?" Prescott asked.

"Including acceleration and deceleration time, just under twenty minutes, sir," he replied immediately.

"Thank you. Make it happen, please. Dubashi, go ahead and reply with a simple acknowledgment and an ETA. Also, please have a message sent to the medical bay requesting an update on Admiral Naftur and urgently requesting Ambassador Turlaka's presence on the bridge as soon as she is available."

"Aye, sir," she replied.

"I don't guess I need to point out that they may have stopped firing because they lost their drone and recognize this as an opportunity to have us willingly fly right into their optimal kill range?" Reynolds asked.

"That's a little cynical, don't you think, Commander?" Prescott said with a grin. "Fine. Let me tell you what I have in mind, just in case that happens …"

F-373 "Gamble 22," Near the Original Pelaran Resistance Rally Point
(In hyperspace - 3.3 light years from Earth)

"Admiral Patterson wants us to what?" the pilot asked, incredulous.

"Now that *Theseus* has arrived and the supporting flights of additional fighters are standing by to assist, he has asked us to attempt to follow the trail of particle emissions left by the departing Resistance ships," the fighter's AI replied in a matter-of-fact tone.

"*What* trail? You never said anything about any trail. Why are you just now mentioning this?"

"I didn't detect it at first, but once we established data links back to the *Navajo*, I was able to get some help processing all of the data we've been collecting. Admiral Patterson had already requested that the *Navajo's* AI try to determine the destination of the departing ships, so we've been working on the problem together while you and I have been stuck out here waiting for further orders."

"I'm happy for you both. What did you find?"

"It turns out that there is a faint trail of what you might refer to as exotic particles, but it decays over time. We actually just came to the conclusion that it should be possible for us to follow the trail only a short time ago. The *Navajo's* AI then brought it to Admiral Patterson's attention and … Hey, look at it this way, at least now we have something interesting to do again."

"Hold on a second, there. What, specifically, are we being asked to do?"

"Now that we know there are four Resistance capital ships guarding their original rally point, and we have seen two additional ships depart since we got here, Admiral Patterson believes the bulk of their forces are no more than one light year away — perhaps much closer. We're simply going to follow their trail until we find them."

"Oh sure, that sounds simple enough. Seriously, how are we supposed to do that?"

"The quickest way is a series of consecutive C-Jumps. We jump, look for the trail, jump again … lather, rinse, repeat. Assuming the particle emissions lead all the way to their destination, it shouldn't take us very long."

"Okay, so if and when we find where they left hyperspace, are we expected to transition out and take a peek?"

"No. The last thing we want to do is spook them into moving again. So we'll most likely need to C-Jump back here to transmit a real-time report. It's a pretty big deal, actually. If Fleet knows where all the Resistance forces are located, it becomes much more straightforward to orchestrate a decisive attack, if necessary."

“Alright, alright. I’ll grant you that it’s better than sitting out here with nothing to look at. By the way, did you just say ‘lather, rinse, repeat?’”

“You say it all the time. Are you interested in hearing a playback of the five most recent occasions?”

“I say a lot of stuff I wouldn’t want you to repeat, but I have never in my life, not one time, said *that*,” he replied, knowing that this argument was well and truly lost. “I assume you have a series of C-Jumps plotted?”

“You should be able to see a waypoint indicator for the first one now. All systems in the green. C-Jump range 48.5 light years and stable. We are prepared for transition.”

“Execute,” the pilot ordered, resuming his businesslike and deadly serious tone.

Chapter 20

TFS Theseus, Location Dagger

"Four minutes to our waypoint, Captain," Dubashi reported.

"Understood," Prescott said. "Still no update from Medical?"

"Nothing yet, sir," she replied, just as the aft bridge entrance door opened to admit an exhausted-looking Nenir Turlaka, still wearing her surgical scrubs.

All activity on the bridge ceased momentarily as the entire bridge crew stared expectantly at the Wek ambassador-turned-surgeon.

"He'll be fine," she finally said with a broad smile, after which the room immediately erupted in applause and relieved expressions of gratitude and congratulations for the two surgeons who had narrowly managed to save the Wek admiral's life.

"You could not have brought more welcome news, *Doctor* Turlaka," Prescott beamed, shaking her hand gratefully as he ushered her towards one of the vacant command chairs at the rear of the bridge.

"I've actually been sitting with him in recovery for some time. I apologize for not letting you know sooner, but I was afraid the news might distract you at a critical time."

"He's awake already?" Reynolds asked.

"In a manner of speaking, yes, but he's still pretty groggy at this point. If it were up to him, I'm sure he would be up here on the bridge anyway. That was probably an error in judgment on my part … I should have anticipated that would be a problem and just left him sedated," she replied, shaking her head. "In any event, when I received your message I threatened to knock him out for the remainder of the mission and came up here straight away. How can I help?"

"I wish I knew," Prescott replied, shaking his head. "Honestly, without Admiral Naftur, we're pretty much making this up as we go. We could definitely use your advice and assistance during the negotiations, though. At the moment, we are approaching a group of four Resistance ships who have agreed to an official parley just a few minutes from now. From what we can tell, they are here guarding their task force's original rally point while they await the arrival of additional warships. It was always my understanding that Admiral Naftur believed he might somehow be able to convince their senior officers to stand down — that Humanity was not a threat to the Sajeth Collective, and that an attack on Earth was unnecessary."

Turlaka breathed in deeply and released a long sigh accompanied by a low, mournful sound from the center of her chest. "My dear Captain, there is, of course, much that you do not understand about our world, our culture, and Rugali Naftur. The truth is that he may well be capable of such a feat by sheer force of will. I will say no more on this subject, for it is simply not my place to do so. I will, of course, do everything I can to help you in this … negotiation, but I must tell you that I am not optimistic about our chances for success."

"Surely they realize that things have not gone as they originally planned. Don't you think they might be looking for an alternative strategy at this point?"

“Some of them might be. The vast majority of those serving in the Sajeth Collective military are Wek, as you know. On the whole, we are an honorable race with a proud history of bravery in battle, public service, and, when necessary, sacrifice for the ideals in which we believe. Unfortunately, those same qualities have sometimes allowed our people to be manipulated by those who are … shall we say … unburdened by the influence of guiding principles. I believe this ‘Pelaran Resistance’ movement is the ultimate expression of just such a manipulation.”

“Are you telling me they are unlikely to negotiate in good faith?”

“I’m telling you that you are unlikely to be negotiating with a Wek officer. Ironically, the movement is led primarily by the Damarans. Do not misunderstand me, for I do not mean to condemn their entire civilization. Like any other, their people have both positive and negative qualities, but in the Sajeth Collective, their traditional role has been tending to the machinery of our alliance’s enormous bureaucracy. While it is exceedingly rare for a Damaran to serve in the military, it is all too common for a member of their race to be the root cause of military conflict. We will almost certainly be negotiating with a Damaran today. Be on your guard, and know that they are keenly attuned to what they believe to be the current balance of power. If they perceive weakness, they will not hesitate to resort to violence — even in a situation where they have given their word to the contrary.”

“Thank you, Ambassador. We are, of course, very grateful for your help. We’ll just have to do the best we can under the circumstances and hope for the best." Prescott paused to take in the situation on the bridge before addressing the crew in a strong voice. "Everyone listen up for a moment. If this negotiation does not go as we hope it will, much will depend on how quickly and effectively each of us is able to respond. I need you to listen closely for orders that concern you, but I'm also relying on you to execute the plan we have discussed without input from Commander Reynolds and me. Does anyone *not* understand what is expected of you or have any questions about what we're doing?"

Prescott's question was met with shaking heads and concerned but confident expressions around the room.

"Alright, let's get this over with," he said calmly. "Dubashi, did Captain Zhukov and Commander Waffer understand their role in the plan?"

"Yes, sir. They can, of course, see everything that's going on with only a short comm delay and are standing by for our signal. Our data will allow them to transition in very close proximity to the Resistance ships, if necessary."

"Good. Tactical, any change in those cruisers?"

"No sir," Schmidt replied. "All four have kept their shields and weapon systems powered up since we first arrived."

"Sir," Ensign Fisher interrupted, "we have arrived at our waypoint."

"And we are being hailed by the *Hadeon* again," Dubashi added.

"At least they're prompt," Prescott said, coming to his feet and smiling at Ambassador Turlaka as he worked to quickly focus his mind. "On-screen, please."

A window immediately opened on the view screen to reveal an alien species never before encountered by Human beings. Although expecting to see something other than a Wek, Prescott still felt the same strange, almost involuntary sense of shock as when he had first laid eyes on Nenir Turlaka, now standing to his immediate left. With so much at stake, he forced his personal observations to the back of his mind for later, but knew immediately that he was speaking to a Damaran. Based solely on appearance, it didn't take much imagination to better understand some of the comments he had heard from both Naftur and Turlaka over the past month.

"I am Captain Tom Prescott of the starship TFS *Theseus*. You may already know Nenir Turlaka," he said, nodding to his left, "the Sajeth Collective Ambassador to Terra. Thank you for agreeing to speak with us."

"I am Captain Woorin Miah, and I can assure you that I represent the true will of the Sajeth Collective much more than your so-called Wek *'ambassador*.' I do know of you though, Miss Turlaka, and it is gratifying to see that you were not slaughtered by the Humans with the rest of our ships sent to extend them the hand of friendship. For your own safety, perhaps the first thing we should do is get you transferred to one of our ships."

"If I may," Turlaka began, "I have no idea where you received your information, Captain Miah, but our squadron was destroyed by the Pelaran Guardian, not the Humans. Captain Prescott and his crew saved my life in the aftermath of the attack. I have been treated with the utmost respect and hospitality during my stay on Terra and believe we have nothing to fear from the Humans. In fact, it will be my strong recommendation to the Governing Council that we work to form closer ties with them in hopes of solving our mutual problem of Pelaran aggression."

Miah looked around his bridge momentarily as if trying to determine if Turlaka's words were being heard by any members of his crew. "Do not despair, Miss Turlaka, it is clear both from your words and from your appearance that you are under duress. Captain Prescott, using one of our citizens in this shameful manner is a clear violation of the rules governing an official parley. Unless you agree to transfer her to us immediately, there is little point in further discussion," he said, as if looking for any excuse to resume open hostilities.

"I'm sorry to keep interrupting, Captain Prescott, but if I may be allowed to address Captain Miah's points," Turlaka began again, her voice now more forceful and commanding than he had ever heard previously. "I am in no way under duress of any kind. I am here of my own free will and continue to act in my capacity as an ambassador on behalf of the Sajeth Collective. Duress, indeed! I do not believe either of us can name a single instance in recorded history when a Wek has been compelled to say or do anything that would put so many others at risk in such a cowardly manner. As to my appearance, I have just come from assisting a very skilled Terran surgeon in saving the life of Admiral Rugali Naftur onboard this very vessel."

"Lies!" Miah hissed. "Captain, you and this Wek impostor have failed to negotiate in good faith and have hereby lost the status afforded you under the rules of parley. If you will heave to and peacefully surrender your vessel, you and your crew will not be harmed. Otherwise, you are hopelessly outgunned and will surely be destroyed."

"Captain Miah," Prescott said. "Please allow me to assure you once again that we Humans mean you no harm. We came here today seeking to avoid hostilities between our peoples and in the hopes that we can …" Prescott stopped himself mid-sentence as the window previously displaying the Damaran abruptly closed.

"Transmission terminated at the source, sir," Dubashi confirmed.

"Humph, that went well," Prescott grumbled. "Will he attack?" he asked Turlaka.

"Almost certainly, unless his crew refuses to follow his orders, which would be an exceedingly rare occurrence."

"All hands, this is the XO," Reynolds announced as Prescott and Turlaka took their seats and allowed the AI to secure them firmly in place. "Combat operations imminent. All personnel should be restrained at this time. Reynolds out."

"Helm, back away slowly. Let's give them the opportunity to allow us to leave peacefully, but keep our bow towards them for now," Prescott ordered.

"Aye, sir," Fisher said as the distant, rumbling sound of *Theseus'* sublight engines increased slightly as she began to slowly accelerate stern-first away from the Sajeth Collective cruisers.

"I'm seeing a power spike on three of the four vessels, sir," Schmidt announced from Tactical 1. "They're firing!"

“Everyone execute now!” Prescott bellowed. “Comm, get those fighters in here. Tactical, designate Charlie 4 as a noncombatant until she proves otherwise. Charlie 1 is our first target.”

At the Helm console, Fisher first applied maximum forward thrust, allowing *Theseus* to arrest her slow, stern-first retreat in mere seconds. As the destroyer began to surge forward in the direction of the Sajeth Collective ships, he immediately C-jumped to a location above and directly in front of the BD cruiser *Hadeon,* now designated as Charlie 3.

“Straight at ‘em from here, Ensign Fisher,” Prescott ordered.

“Aye, sir!”

Directly ahead, *Hadeon* had opened up once again with her starboard energy weapons banks, and had expected to be joined by the two older, but still incredibly powerful heavy cruisers, Charlie 1 and 2 — both of which had prepositioned themselves to allow for overlapping fields of fire at the outset of the engagement. After Fisher’s short C-Jump, however, *Theseus* was no longer conveniently located within their planned “kill box.” With the Terran destroyer now suddenly bearing down on the *Hadeon’s* position, Charlie 1 and 2 found that their beam weapons no longer had a firing solution at all and they dared not engage with missiles for fear of hitting their own BD cruiser.

“All weapons ready, Captain,” Lau reported.

“As we pass over Charlie 3 dead ahead, you should have a clear shot at Charlie 1’s stern. Hit her with all five forward plasma torpedoes. Helm, as soon as the torps are away, turn to bring the aft tubes to bear.”

"Aye, sir," both officers answered.

"Lau, fire at will with all beam weapons and railguns. Concentrate your fire on their stern just like last time. Lieutenant Lee, are the shields holding?"

"Yes, sir, but they're taking a hell of a beating at the moment. Zero hull impacts so far," he responded from the Science and Engineering console.

At hundreds of locations surrounding *Theseus'* massive hull, an unbroken series of flashes burst forth to light the immediate area as her AI worked to intercept the relentless hail of incoming fire from the enemy BD cruiser. The awesome spectacle playing out on the bridge view screen reminded Prescott of a time-lapsed video he had once seen condensing several hours' worth of lightning from an intense thunderstorm into only a few seconds. As the bolts of energy streamed in from Charlie 3, *Theseus'* AI deflected as many as possible in the direction of Charlie 1, adding to the barrage of beam and kinetic energy weapons fire already hammering the cruiser's aft shields.

"Fisher, as soon as the second torpedo salvo is away, C-Jump one light minute straight ahead."

"Looking forward to it, sir," he replied.

For a brief moment while *Theseus* passed directly over the *Hadeon*, both of the BD cruiser's energy weapons banks had the opportunity to target the destroyer's underside simultaneously. The firing was so intense and from such close range that some of the bolts managed to impact the ship's ventral hull. The destroyer shook with several impacts as sections of her outermost armor were ablated by the incoming fire. A few anxious seconds later, as the sound of the impacts finally ceased, each member of the crew stole a quick look at the hull impacts counter on the tactical plot, which now stood at seven.

"Lieutenant Lee, damage report."

"No apparent damage so far, Captain," he answered without looking up from the Science and Engineering console. "The shields apparently start to lose some effectiveness when we have multiple hits with low angles of incidence, though."

"Thank you, Lieutenant. Hear that, Fisher, let's not try that again."

"Got it, sir," his young helmsman replied enthusiastically as the first salvo of five plasma torpedoes issued forth from the ship's forward tubes. Traveling at nearly thirty percent the speed of light, the compressed bolts of plasma reached the stern of Charlie 1 in less than three one-thousandths of a second, delivering over seven times as much energy to the cruiser's aft shields as *Ingenuity's* had during the previous battle.

"Forward torps away," Lau said, after the fact.

"Direct hits," Schmidt reported. "Their aft shields are still up, but fluctuating."

"Aft torps, as quickly as possible," Prescott replied.

On cue, Fisher pulled the destroyer into an aggressive climbing turn to port that shortly thereafter allowed her aft torpedo tubes to acquire their target.

"Aft torpedoes away," Lau reported again as *Theseus'* railguns continued to pound Charlie 1's stern with a steady stream of kinetic energy penetration rounds.

"Tactical C-Jumping," Fisher reported.

As relative calm returned to the bridge, Prescott suddenly felt uncomfortable with the idea that Turlaka might be about to witness the deaths of thousands of her people at the hands of a civilization she had only recently met. "Madame Ambassador, you have our deepest gratitude for your assistance, but please allow me to have you escorted somewhere more comfortable for the remainder of our encounter with the Resistance forces."

"By that, you obviously mean that you intend to wipe them out completely," she replied calmly. "No, Captain, you and I have both acted appropriately. The Pelaran Resistance is an illegal, rogue regime that is putting all seven worlds of the Sajeth Collective at risk with their cowardly, dishonorable conduct. I do not relish the idea of anyone, Wek or otherwise, losing their life, but today, I believe we are doing what is necessary to protect both your home and mine."

Prescott stared at her briefly, wondering if she was truly prepared for what she might be about to see. "I am very sorry it has come to this. You have my word that I will continue to do everything I can to avoid any unnecessary loss of life."

"Sir," Fisher reported, "I've plotted a return transition point that should keep us well clear of our fighters as well as Charlie 2's field of fire. We will still be close enough to reengage, if necessary."

"Execute your C-Jump," Prescott replied.

With the ship no longer in immediate danger, the AI took a few extra seconds to both warn the crew of the impending transition and complete a more exhaustive set of diagnostics than during what Fisher now referred to as a "Tactical C-Jump." "Capacitive hyperdrive engaged," the AI's synthetic voice announced ship-wide, "transition in 3 … 2 … 1 …"

In the center of the bridge view screen, the three Resistance cruisers reappeared and smoothly expanded to fill the bottom center of the display as *Theseus* covered the seventeen-million-kilometer distance back to Location Dagger in the blink of an eye.

"I have the fighters," Schmidt reported. "They are staying well clear of the cruisers, sir. The two flights are designated Badger 1 and Badger 2 on the tactical plot. Charlie 1's shields are still up, but they're intermittent at this point."

"That's good," Prescott replied. "I'm pretty sure one of those hits we took would have been more than enough to take out one of our fighters. Besides, they don't need to get close. All they need is good data to execute their attack, and we've given them plenty of that. How about Charlie 4? Any change?"

"No, sir. She is continuing to move downrange — steady course and speed."

"Hopefully, that's one less to worry about," Prescott said. "Something tells me they weren't happy with the way Captain Miah handled things."

"Nor should they be," Turlaka interjected. "If he were a Wek officer, he would most certainly be court-martialed for gross misconduct and cowardice in the line of duty. Breaking the terms of a truce or parley is a capital offense on Graca."

"Sir, Charlie 3 looks like she's trying to line up for a shot at us again. She's ignoring the fighters for now," Lau said.

"Thank you, Lieutenant. Helm, just work on complicating their firing solution for a little longer. The fighters will have their undivided attention shortly," Prescott ordered.

"Missile launch!" Schmidt announced. "Multiple missile launches from Charlie 1 and 2. Badger 1 flight just launched a salvo of missiles as well. Stand by."

Near the stern of each heavy cruiser flanking the *Hadeon*, bright plumes of fire could be seen as a number of missiles rose from their vertical launch cells.

"Helm, be ready with another Tactical C-Jump. Let's not rely on the shields unless we have to."

"Aye, sir," Fisher replied.

"Sixteen missiles inbound," Schmidt updated. "Time to impact, two five seconds."

"Not this time, I think," Reynolds muttered under her breath as she placed a zoomed-in view of Charlie 1 on one side of the view screen just in time to witness the ship's stern flare brightly with a rapid series of explosions. The impacts occurred only seconds after two C-Drive-equipped missiles had been fired from each of Captain Zhukov's flight of twelve F-373 fighters. Once the cruiser's stern was partially visible once again, it was immediately clear that she was out of the fight. While her hull remained largely intact, the drive section was a mangled mess. Raging fires and secondary explosions could be seen in a number of locations where what must have been oxidizer and propellant were being rapidly vented into space.

"The AI counted twenty-four missile impacts in the area around Charlie 1's stern," Lau reported. "They appear to be without power … engines, shields, weapons

… all offline." Lau paused as *Theseus'* AI continued to update its battle damage assessment, then continued. "Confirmed, Captain, she is adrift with multiple hull breaches."

"That's exactly what we were hoping to see. Dubashi, hail the *Hadeon* — text only. Instruct her and her consort to lower their shields and power down their weapons immediately, or we will have no choice but to destroy both of their vessels. Keep repeating the message until they reply."

"Aye, sir."

Not for the first time, Prescott wondered at the Sajeth Collective warships' lack of point defense weapons. Was there some technical reason — perhaps related to their shields — that rendered such systems less effective, or had their shields proven so reliable in the past that there had simply been no need for additional defenses until now? Admiral Naftur tended to become rather close-lipped when it came to discussing such things, but Prescott nevertheless made a mental note to ask the question at some point. He also wondered how many ships they would allow themselves to lose to C-Drive-equipped missiles before they found some way to make themselves less vulnerable — particularly at the stern.

"Helm, go ahead and C-Jump us over in the vicinity of our fighters. I doubt those incoming missiles will reacquire us, but keep an eye on them."

"Aye, sir. Tactical C-Jumping."

This time, *Theseus'* AI depicted the transition from one side of the battlespace to the other as a "flyby" of the Resistance ships, the final result of which was their arrival at a point halfway between the drifting hulk of Charlie 1 and the original Location Dagger.

Suddenly finding themselves with no target, but still in relatively close proximity to friendly vessels, all sixteen missiles fired by Charlie 1 and 2 self-destructed.

"No remaining missiles in flight at this time," Lau reported after allowing a few seconds for light to arrive from their previous location. "Charlie 2 and 3 have ceased fire."

"Thank you, Lieutenant. Green deck, XO. Let's try to make it as clear as we can that they really only have one option at this point."

"Aye, sir," Reynolds replied, entering a series of commands at her touchscreen to provide the necessary clearances to *Theseus'* Flight Deck.

Seconds later, twelve of the destroyer's twenty-four *Hunter* RPSVs lifted off from her aft flight apron, split into two groups, and headed for defensive flanking positions to port and starboard.

"Twelve *Hunters* are away, sir," Schmidt reported. "Twelve more launching in zero two minutes."

"Keep them on anti-missile duty for the moment. If we need to attack again, I'd prefer to allow the *Reapers* to do what they do best."

"Aye, sir," Schmidt replied. "Charlie 2 and 3 just lowered their shields and powered down their weapons."

"*Hadeon* is hailing again," Dubashi announced.

"Let them wait a moment," Prescott replied. "Ambassador, assuming we are dealing primarily with Wek crews, how can we expect them to respond to an order to surrender?"

"Generally speaking, you can expect a Wek officer to do exactly what he says he's going to do," Turlaka replied. "If he surrenders, or is ordered to surrender by a superior officer, he is honor-bound from that moment forward to conduct himself and his vessel as a noncombatant. Under normal circumstances, however, Wek captains do not surrender their vessels unless they have no hope of either victory or escape. I suspect what we are witnessing today is a confused, perhaps even mutinous situation created as a direct result of Captain Miah being imposed upon these crews … particularly given that he holds the rank of commander and is a captain only by virtue of his current assignment."

"Well, if they do surrender to us, it creates a bit of a problem. We really don't have sufficient personnel to put together a single prize crew, let alone two or three."

"We also can't wait here for reinforcements from Earth, sir," Reynolds interjected. "By the time they arrive, it's a safe bet that the rest of the Resistance task force will have had enough time to reestablish communications with these ships from their new rally point …"

"And enough time to send help," Prescott said, finishing her sentence. "Alright, we may be solving a problem that doesn't even exist, so let's see how this conversation goes and we'll figure it out from there. Dubashi, put Captain Miah from the *Hadeon* on-screen again, please."

Seconds later, a vidcon window opened once again in the center of the bridge view screen. This time, Captain Miah's face had been replaced by that of a powerful-looking male Wek officer.

“My compliments, Captain Prescott,” he began formally. “I am Commander Yuli Takkar. I have relieved Commander Miah of command and placed him under arrest for violating the rules of war when communicating with your ship earlier. My apologies for taking so long to do so, but we do not take such actions lightly. Given the circumstances, would you be willing to continue a dialog with me under the terms of the original parley?”

“I appreciate your offer, Commander, but I think you will agree that the situation has changed significantly since then,” Prescott said, smiling pleasantly. “It was not our original intent to engage in combat with your vessels, but we were fired upon, defended ourselves, and now hold an overwhelming tactical advantage. Would you agree to a parley at this point if you were in my position?”

“I’m sorry, Captain, but Commander Miah used a communications terminal for his conversation with you, so there was quite a bit that I was unable to hear. What was your original intent?” Takkar asked, sidestepping Prescott’s question.

Prescott shook his head, chuckling to himself at the thinly veiled attempt to redirect their conversation back to something approaching the terms of the original parley. “Alright, Commander, you seem like a reasonable officer, so I will agree to have a brief conversation with you. Let me be absolutely clear, however, that this is your final opportunity. Any further aggression …”

“You have my word, Captain,” Takkar replied earnestly.

“Very well. And you have my word that we will not interfere with rescue operations.”

“Thank you, Captain. We will begin launching shuttles immediately,” he replied, turning to nod at his second-in-command. “When you were speaking to Commander Miah, I did hear something mentioned about Rugali Naftur. If you have recovered his body, we would appreciate your allowing us to return him to Graca so that we may render the final respects appropriate for someone of his stature.”

“His body? No, Commander, Admiral Naftur was seriously injured earlier today, but came through emergency surgery just fine, thanks to Ambassador Turlaka here,” Prescott replied.

“That’s simply not possible, Captain. We know that his squadron was destroyed by Human forces, no doubt with the help of the Pelaran Guardian, over a month ago,” Takkar growled, his eyes flashing into barely contained fury. “The opportunity to avenge his death is, in fact, the reason most of us are here.”

“Contact!” Lieutenant Lau announced from Tactical 1. “It’s not one we’ve seen before. She’s *big*, sir — thirteen hundred meters.”

“That would be the *Baldev*,” Commander Takkar said with a fierce smile. “Captain Prescott, I will, of course, honor my word not to fire on your vessel, but I cannot speak for Captain Yagani. He is a senior captain, so I expect he will assume command of all Pelaran Resistance forces in the area. Once again, if you would turn over Naftur’s body …”

At that moment, the aft bridge door opened and Doctor Jiao Chen walked onto *Theseus’* bridge pushing a grav chair bearing a tired, but surprisingly alert Admiral Rugali Naftur.

On the view screen, Commander Takkar's eyes went wide with immediate recognition. "Your Highness!" he gasped, dropping immediately to one knee with his right fist clasped over his heart. Aboard *Hadeon*, the ship's AI recognized the acting captain's gesture and widened the field of view to encompass the entire bridge. Within seconds, every visible member of her crew had knelt and was saluting in similar fashion.

TFC Pine Gap Shipyard Facility
(Northern Territory, Australia - 35 km southwest of Alice Springs)

It had taken "Gamble 22" less than an hour to pinpoint the end of the particle trails marking the location where twenty-six Resistance task force warships had transitioned back to normal space. Possibly chosen to allow their slowest warships to remain within one hour's flight time of the original rally point, the newly christened "Location Crossbow" was still a respectable 22.9 light days (five hundred and ninety-three billion kilometers) distant. After a final C-Jump back to the Location Dagger comm beacon, the solo F-373 had transmitted its valuable reconnaissance data via NRD net to TFS *Navajo*, where it immediately received Admiral Patterson's undivided attention.

Seeing an opportunity to gain the initiative for the first time since the Resistance forces began assembling for their attack on Earth, the admiral had quickly made the decision to position all of the C-Jump-capable forces he currently had at his disposal for a surprise attack. Although not nearly as formidable a force as he would have preferred to send, the number of ships indicating a "mission effective" status had increased significantly over the past forty-eight hours …

***

It was already early morning of the following day in the Australian Outback. Shattering the serenity for which the surrounding bronze-colored deserts and rugged canyons are often known, a low frequency rumble echoed through the predawn darkness as the Pine Gap Shipyard's massive blast doors slowly opened. As the gap between the doors reached two hundred seventy-five meters, a sleek, brownish-grey bow emerged from the dimly lit entrance cavern. Once clear of the shipyard, the *Theseus*-class destroyer *Karna* climbed silently into the sky, shortly thereafter breaking into full sunlight as Earth's terminator approached from the east.

Less than three minutes later, the *Karna* was joined in line-abreast formation by her five sister ships from the Pine Gap Shipyard Facility. After a brief pause to allow their AIs to execute a series of systems checks, the ships synchronized their departure vectors with two similar flights rising from the Yucca and Yamantau Mountain Shipyards, then disappeared in six simultaneous flashes of grayish-white light.

THANK YOU!

I'd like to express my sincerest thanks for reading *TFS Theseus*. If you enjoyed the book, I would greatly appreciate a quick review at Amazon.com, or wherever you made your purchase. It need not be long or detailed, just a quick note that you enjoyed the story and would recommend it to other readers.

I hope you will be interested in the next installment of The Terran Fleet Command Saga. I don't have a release date, or even the full title as yet, but rest assured that writing is underway, so please stay tuned!

***

For updates on new releases and upcoming special offers, please visit my web site and subscribe to the newsletter at:

AuthorToriHarris.com

Have story ideas, suggestions, corrections, or just want to connect? Feel free to e-mail me at Tori@AuthorToriHarris.com. You can also find me on Twitter and Facebook at:

https://twitter.com/TheToriHarris

https://www.facebook.com/AuthorToriHarris

Finally, you can find links to all of my books on my Amazon author page:

http://amazon.com/author/thetoriharris

ABOUT THE AUTHOR

Born in 1969, four months before the first Apollo moon landing, Tori Harris grew up during the era of the original Star Wars movies and is a lifelong science fiction fan. During his early professional career, he was fortunate enough to briefly have the opportunity to fly jets in the U.S. Air Force, and is still a private pilot who loves to fly. Tori has always loved to read and now combines his love of classic naval fiction with military Sci-Fi when writing his own books. His favorite authors include Patrick O'Brian and Tom Clancy as well as more recent self-published authors like Michael Hicks, Ryk Brown, and Joshua Dalzelle. Tori lives in Tennessee with his beautiful wife, two beautiful daughters, and Bizkit, the best dog ever.

Made in the USA
Lexington, KY
23 May 2016